The Lord Came at Twilight

By Daniel Mills

CONTENTS

TWILIGHT'S TRUE LORD
an introduction

I discovered Daniel Mills.

I mean that, selfishly, in the traditional sense of discovering talent. I like to believe I was the first to read Daniel's fiction, and it was due to my championing of it that he has managed to stack up the accolades he has thus far. Of course, in reality, my discovery of Daniel's work was in the more pedestrian sense, where I simply stumbled blindly onto something that was already becoming established on its own. After all, one of Daniel's first published pieces of fiction was alongside one of mine in the third volume of Tartarus Press's fantastic *Strange Tales* series, and by the time I read it and was suitably impressed, Daniel had already sold his first novel, *Revenants*, to Chômu Press. In other words, Daniel never needed any help from me. He was doing quite fine earning all those accolades on his own.

But from where should such a talent emerge? One of the blessed aspects of the last decade has been the rise of technology, which has allowed small operations to more easily publish and distribute high quality books than ever before. It was only natural then that some of these publishers would start with the public domain, and bring back into the light some of the unjustly forgotten books and writers of the ghostly and weird. True, we already had writers like Poe, M. R. James, and Henry James in our bookstores, but now they were joined by some of the sometimes lesser known writers like Machen, LeFanu, Chambers, Burrage, Wharton, Marsh, de la Mare, and so forth. Writers who built and added to the foundations of the genre, writers to whose work all the Horror writers that followed owe a huge debt whether they were aware of it or not. These reprints provided striking counter-programming to what was happening in mass-market horror — namely, a continuous dissolve into non-relevance. In some way, the last great revolution in horror was its rediscovery of its past.

I can't say for certain when Daniel Mills discovered these old masters, but it's clear he has learned their lessons well. He is not the first author whose work recalls an earlier time — there are plenty of Jamesian pastiches available nowadays — but unlike that aping style that finds itself confined almost exclusively to an ever-dwindling group of readers interested solely in what James called "a pleasant terror", Daniel has discovered the true power of the past — as a tool to describe and illuminate the present. It's here he joins the ranks of an increasing number of contemporary horror writers like John Langan, Richard Gavin, Joseph Pulver, and Reggie Oliver, all of whom are able to re-contextualize what's come before in new and exciting ways. Where Daniel differs from these writers is his investment in the milieu of the past, of New England, yet even using these historical settings he has somehow managed to meld them with the present to produce a unique kind of old school hybrid, done with a startling amount of sophistication and skill. Take for example the horrific images deep beneath the meeting house burying ground in "Dust from a Dark Flower". Or the existential angst our protagonist in "MS Found in a Chicago Hotel Room" suffers due to his trip to New York. Or the implications of the title story's dark finale and what it says about us all. These are Campbellian ideas, Ligottian ideas, infused into tales that owe their machinery to the Bensons or Wakefield. Or, and most especially, to the old man himself, Howard Phillips Lovecraft.

Yes, I said it. Lovecraft. The name that unleashes more trouble than one hundred Necronomicons. I think the old man would have loved Daniel's work because Daniel manages to utilize the setting of historical New England, and yet unlike Lovecraft, does so to reflect and describe the emotional turmoils of his characters. And that may be the most striking of Daniel's talents (alongside his expert and subtle use of language to evoke both mood and setting) — Daniel's characters feel unique, distinct, lived-in. They feel *alive*, which makes the horrors they face all the worse. Even temporal distance offers us no protection.

There are plenty of horrors waiting for you in the pages of this book. But along with the horrors you'll notice how carefully Daniel crafts his atmosphere, how delicately he weaves his narratives together. Daniel's characters are not always the bravest or the strongest, and he often foregoes the presumption that good Horror fiction ought to end with some sort of victory or closure. Instead, Daniel's denouements are often clear only in hindsight, his themes revealing themselves upon reflection. Like all great works of literary fiction, his stories hand you everything you need to decode them, but it's up to you to do the actual work.

So here we are, finally, at twilight. Look up from this book and at your smudged sitting room window. See the dust of years accumulated on the sill. Look closer at that dusty blanket and notice the four thin lines dragging toward the glass, as though someone had very recently reached in and used that dusty sill as leverage, as a hold to pull its tremendous weight in from beyond. That thing which is past, which is the horror of New England, the threat both misty and ancient. There's a man outside watching you, isn't there? A tall bearded man, thin, smiling as you slowly step away from your window, hoping — praying — he hasn't seen you. But he has. Daniel Mills has. And now he's moving toward you, that horrible lord of twilight. I would suggest locking your doors if it weren't already too late. You already hold his incursion in your trembling hands. Best look back to this book and read his missives while you are still able. After all, it is only a matter of time until he steps inside.

Simon Strantzas
August 15th, 2013
Toronto, Canada

THE HOLLOW

I know them, these hills. Their shadowed slopes.
Their ridgelines toothed with broken stone.
When I was a boy, the logging camps stretched
for miles, separated from each other by swathes
of thorn and bramble. Villages grew up from the
scrub: transient places, often nameless. I spent
my childhood in such a hamlet. I live there still.
The camps are abandoned, the townsfolk long
gone, but the land has not forgotten.

Two miles to the north, the ridgeline curls
back against itself, forming a hollow. The edges
are close and shaded, dark with hemlock, while
the basin is flat and circular, strewn with dead
leaves. An oak tree stands at the center, ancient
as the oceans, spreading from bud and branch to
fill the natural amphitheater.

I was a boy of eight when Father told me
of the hollow. We sat together in his library, as
we called it, though it was only a narrow space
beneath the eaves in which his books were
shelved. The hollow, he said, marked the very
footprint of God, a remnant of those early days
when He walked with man in Eden.

I have often thought, he continued, *that we
are even now in the Garden, and that the oak tree
bears upon its branches the very Fruit of Life. Un-
tasted once, it begs us now to eat of it, to know the
Life Eternal.*

This was shortly before he deserted us,

slipping from the house while we were abed. He did not take his books, not even the battered volume of Milton's poetry which he prized above all, so that we thought for a time that he intended to return to us.

In his absence, Mother changed. The beatings became more frequent, their causes more obscure: a broken glass, a sullen look. Mornings, she wept and paced the house, cursing, praying. In the afternoon, she took down her cloak and went to the camps, while I shirked my chores to prowl the barren scrublands, those manmade fields of deadfall and brush.

In July, I found the hollow for myself. I had struck north from the village, as I often did, and walked until I reached the camp road, down which I turned and made my way. After half-a-mile, I heard voices from the path ahead and concealed myself among the brambles. I watched them pass: two men with my mother in-between, the three linked arm-in-arm and laughing.

I fled. I scrabbled up rock ledges and pelted down hare paths, unable to outrun the resentment that raged inside of me. I ran until my breath failed me and I came to the hollow.

At first, I took the oak tree for a vision, a mirage, for it seemed to me a thing woven from pure heat. I wiped the sweat from my face, but the tree remained. It was larger than any I had encountered, its trunk malformed, bark mottled, amber and ash.

I walked until I reached the oak. There were shapes in the bark — eyes, suggestions of eyes — half-shapes layered one on top of the other until they blurred into abstraction like words on a palimpsest. I placed my palm against the bark. With eyes closed, I imagined the sap running like blood beneath the surface, blossoming into knots of brown-gray flesh which curled together like unclothed bodies. My mother's breasts. The men twined round her.

A wind came from the south. The oak tree rustled and flared out in answer, its foliage erupting into the momentary kaleidoscope of green on white, leaf-top and leaf-bottom. An open mouth: the lips puffed and dark and grossly swollen. I heard a voice, tinny and pleading.

Pull me out, a man said. *Pull me out.*

Mother came home at dusk. She found me in the library, where I cowered amidst my father's books, quivering. Seeing my fright, she took me in her arms and pressed me to her chest. I smelled the sweat on her, moonshine and musk. She stroked my hair.

I told her of the oak tree and the hollow. I did not want to upset her and so I did not mention the voice I had heard. Nonetheless it was clear to me that my words pained her, somehow, and she was quiet for some time before she spoke.

Your father knew that place.

My father?

He went there the day he left us.

She said nothing more, but in her silence, I glimpsed the gulfs of her sorrow — the escape for which she likewise yearned — and understood that she would leave me, too, as Father had done.

The weeks drifted past. Summertime stretched and cooled, evaporating with the first frost. The camps moved east, and Mother went with them, taking only her cash-purse and cloak.

Alone, I lived on crabapples and tubers and berries gathered by the creek. I took to thieving, raiding the houses of the other villagers and returning home with canned meats or jars of fruit, which I cached beneath the boards in the common room.

It could not last. The townsfolk grew suspicious. The minister came to the door, but I hid from him and would not withdraw the bolt. He returned the next day with the sheriff. They forced their way inside, but I was already gone.

Years passed — years in which I avoided town and hollow alike and roamed these hills like an animal. I slept in caves, or in clearings, where I covered myself with rushes and watched the stars appear: dim as the lights of distant towns and equally remote. They were like fragments of memory, the past I had abandoned — scattered like so many leaves beneath the oak tree.

For ten summers or more, I haunted the eastern camps and the roads between, subsisting on theft and forage. One night in autumn, I remember, I drew too near the light of a campfire, and a man fired a pistol in my direction. The shot went wide. A woman screamed — out of fear, I thought — but then she was laughing and singing and I recognized her voice.

Mother. She stood, swaying, and circled the fire with dancing steps, thin as the shadow which followed after her, which remained even after she had passed from view.

The last of the camps closed in the spring. The men departed with a grave and uncharacteristic dignity, proceeding like mourners with axes hefted over their shoulders. My mother must have already moved on, for she was not among them, and I found no evidence of her amidst the ruins they left. Axe-handles. Saw-pits. A still with its barrels smashed. Strangest of all was the large steam engine that had powered a band-saw. By summer's end, it came to resemble a marooned locomotive, tossed by storms and washed up miles from the nearest track.

Winter came — the worst I have experienced in my seventy years. It snowed for weeks, months. I removed the blades from the steam engine and used it for shelter, huddling inside on nights the winds blew frigid and drove the drifting powder. When I could, I trapped small game: squirrels, rabbits. Otherwise I fished in the creek, smashing the ice with my axe to afford myself an opening.

Day after day, I held the fishing lines between my chapped hands and watched the skin on my fingers turn red, then black. During the course of that winter, I lost two toes to frostbite and hacked off a third when it showed signs of rot.

In spring, the snow melted into puddles and streams, forming rivers of muck that swept clear the hillsides and buried the rabbits in the ground. Toadstools grew up from their submerged warrens: blood-red, glistening. There was nothing else to eat and so I gorged myself on grubs and fungi until sickness overcame me and I tumbled over the rim of fever.

Half-starved, desperately weak, I descended the hill, crawling hand over elbow through squelching mud until I came to the old road. Eventually, I reached the town, the village in which I was born. Only three buildings were standing: the grange and the schoolroom, the house my father built. All deserted.

My past took shape before me. Names returned, and faces, disgorged by the recent floodwaters, so that I thought of bones, laid to rest in graves digged too shallow. In the same

way, my past had fixed itself in the ground—
bound to these hills, alive within them—and I
shook with dread and awe for the hold they held
upon me, and upon all the dead.

I entered my father's house. My gaze lit
on shattered glass, furniture speckled with
decay. The snows had drifted against the eastern
wall, causing it to buckle, but the western wall
held fast. His library remained intact, books
preserved upon the shelves.

In the common room, I pulled up the old
floorboard and thrust my hand inside. From the
hole, I withdrew two tins of salt-pork, which I
broke open with my axe.

I was ravenous. I sucked the juices from
inside each tin and cut my tongue when I licked
out the bottom. Nauseated, I crawled beneath
the library eaves. Stars floated out of the
darkness, filling my vision like the final descent
of the Angel.

When I woke, the fever had passed. Too
weak to brave the hills, I slept in the bed I had
shared with my mother and banked high the fire
with wood from the schoolhouse—the desk at
which I had sat, into which I had scratched my
name.

I regained my strength. At night, I read by
the light of the hearth, poring over my father's
books, his copies of Milton and Blake. By day I
foraged for food and firewood, occasionally
venturing into the northern woods. It was on

one such trip that I found the hollow once more.

Time had left it unaltered. The massive oak still dominated the rocky basin, shading out all but the hardiest shrubs and grasses. Yellow weeds crept like snakes along the ground. High above, the leaves sparkled and sighed and seemed to whisper, while the gray bark teemed with faces, naked bodies in the thrall of lust, or ecstasy.

I forced myself to approach, threading the basin's perimeter until I reached the far side of the tree, where the ground bore the marks of some long ago disturbance. The soil, dry and barren, had subsided into a rectangular depression, eight feet by three. An old grave.

Damp soil. Molded leaves.

Your father knew that place.

The oak stirred. Leaf upon leaf, it produced a scratching murmur, a voice so soft I could not discern any words — if there were, in fact, words to make out — for surely there were none for the emptiness my father now inhabited.

I did not disturb the grave. I returned home to an empty house, an abandoned village. I grew old. From time to time, the breeze carried smoke from house-fires to the south, and I was grateful for my isolation and the shame it spared me, the guilt none but myself could understand.

And then this morning I heard the ravens and saw them circling. Carrion birds: black as storms though the sky was clear. I went to find their prey. Taking my axe, I climbed uphill along the old logging road, traversing the grade from west to east until a murder of crows materialized, flapping and squawking overhead. They scented blood, decay, the rot on which they fed themselves. I followed. Their cries led me from the road and across the wildwood until I reached the place wherein their echoes began—and ended.

The hollow. The tree was even larger than I remembered, its leaves long and barbed and autumn-red, layered so densely as to blot out the light and kill the weeds that had thrived beneath it, exposing the cratered earth.

An object hung from a low branch. The body of a young woman. She swayed, gently, her bare feet downturned. She must have scaled the trunk and shimmied out onto the low-hanging limb before securing the rope and leaping to her death.

She had not been there long. The birds had eaten her eyes, but the remainder of her body was intact. The ruined face: blackened skin, swollen lips. Her dress was plain but cut from fine cloth, so that I knew her to be of good stock. Almost certainly she was a refugee from the towns to the south, though I could not but wonder why she had taken flight.

The oak hissed and spat and shook down its crimson leaves. I severed the rope. The girl fell against me, stiff with the cold. She weighed little more than a child — and she was young, scarcely older than I was when first my mother left me. A sadness stole over me then, the knowledge of lives unlived: her life, mine.

I stooped and lowered her to the ground. Her eye-sockets bored into me, dark with congealed blood. I covered her face with my shirt and took my axe to the ground. The soil yielded with every blow, loosening. I carried no shovel but contrived a spade from a split timber and applied myself to the task of digging.

The daylight dwindled. Ravens and crows floated about the oak, trapped within its orbit, buoyed by the wind and rising. By dusk, my labors were at an end. The grave was prepared, deep enough that the birds would not disturb it. I lifted the girl and walked with her to the hole that waited. There I laid her down and buried her with the past at the foot of that bloodied tree.

Full on night. I made my way home and supped by the hearth as was my habit. The windows rattled. Beyond the house, the night lay open — cloudless, cold for autumn — and I retired to bed with the shutters drawn, the crisp air whistling through.

I slept. I dreamt.

From dreams I woke, roused by a voice from the north.

I rose, sweating, and went to the window. The shutters fell open on a tranquil scene. White pines in rows and trembling. Lights flickering in the looming void.

Pull me out.

The words were delivered without emotion, a prayer repeated so many times it had lost the power to comfort. The voice belonged to the girl I had buried—somehow I was certain of this—and I imagined her soul, beating like a pulse in the ruins of her body, chained to this world where she had wanted only to be free of it, to be forgotten.

In this, my father too had failed. *Pull me out*, he had pleaded with me, all those years ago. He had been dead for months—a suicide, buried by my mother while the ravens swooped and circled—but death alone could not release him from the burden he carried. Even decades later, he survived in memory, the curse to which each man is heir. Life Eternal.

The wind shifted. The stars dimmed.

Pull me out, my mother said, and I knew that she had died in these hills, rolled into an unmarked grave when madness overtook her at last. Other voices swam out of the south, joining hers in the chorus of indifferent anguish: the rough accents of the men who had cleared the forests, who died of drink or disease in the wastelands they had created.

Pull me out.

And I thought of the oak tree. There were faces in the bark, bodies writhing, brown on gray — and mine among them. For we are all ghosts, even the living. We live, we die, and still the land remembers. These hills offer no rest, no escape. In that lonely hollow, the oak tree broods as it has done since days of Eden, feasting on the dreaming dead, alight with autumn's fire.

It must be felled.

The sky is clear tonight. There is a moon.

I will take my axe and climb to the hollow. I do not know what awaits me there, but I am not frightened. If I die, I die. It matters not, so long as there is no one to remember me.

MS FOUND IN A CHICAGO HOTEL ROOM

The establishment had no name. The night clerk made this clear to me.

It may have had once, he explained. Probably it did. But the signboard outside had long since faded, weathered by years of rain and winter. Any lettering had been erased completely, while the remaining paint was cracked and peeling, yellow with age.

A pale, sickly kind of color, he added. *Like a wound gone bad.*

Wounds were one subject of which the hotel clerk possessed an intimate knowledge. His left arm terminated in a stump at the elbow, the sleeve cut short to reveal a mass of scar tissue. The man was in his fifties, old enough to have fought in the war against the Confederacy.

I was, I admit, skeptical. While my work had taken me to New York on many occasions previously, I had never before heard of this strange establishment, unnamed and outwardly unremarkable save for the color of its signboard.

And you're sure I'll find… I trailed off meaningfully.

You trust old Everett, he said, winking. He chuckled, a horrible, scraping sound, wet stones on cobble. *Ask for Camilla.*

He went on to give directions. I was to

leave the hotel and continue down Mulberry toward the old Five Points slum. *But don't go no farther than Canal Street*, he warned. Instead, I was to take Canal over to the Bowery.

You'll find the place a few blocks down, he said. *Can't miss it.*

I can find my way, I'm sure.

I never doubted it, he said, grinning. *And if you find yourself lost, you can always ask about that old yellow sign. Someone's sure to know what you're talking about.*

I reached into my coat and plucked a dollar from my purse. I placed the coin face up on the counter. Columbia's face glinted, gray and dull.

The clerk's hand shot out to cover it.

There's also the matter of the key. He eyed me expectantly, mouth drooping like a bloodhound's, the lips vivid and red.

Key?

I'll need your room key from you. Before you go.

But I may be late. Shouldn't I take it with me?

Oh, I'll be here. Don't worry yourself about that. You just hurry on back.

*

It was a miserable night, sweltering, and the damp lay like a pall over that stinking corpse of a city. Within minutes, it had seeped through my shirt and coat, soaking me to my under-things. Sweat stood like fever on the faces of the men who hurried past, attired in brown coats and bowlers, their hands in their pockets.

Women watched from second-floor windows, little more than silhouettes, while children roamed the street below: knobby limbs, tattered garments. They traveled in packs, mostly, keeping to the dark between streetlamps, visible only in moments, like moths glimpsed beyond the circle of firelight.

Several blocks down Mulberry, I entered an unfamiliar quarter. Here refinery furnaces burned through the night, painting the stars into obscurity. The air was fetid: I breathed in smoke and breathed out ash, forming clouds on my lips like fragments of the need that lived inside of me, which drove me into the night as surely as the winds that swept down to the East River.

I followed the clerk's directions to the letter. At Canal Street, I turned east toward the Bowery. Once there, I traveled south for several blocks, doubling back when I realized I had gone too far. The yellow sign proved elusive. *Can't miss it*, the clerk had said, but I wandered the same stretch of the Bowery for the better part of an hour until at last the heat pressed hard upon me and I had to sit down.

In the distance, I heard the moan of the ferry, the layered din from the music halls. Songs overlapped, merging one with another, while voices issued from the tenement behind me, a babble of conversations carried on in Irish, Spanish, Italian. I closed my eyes and lowered my face into my hands.

Good evening, a voice said. *Are you alright?*

I lifted my head, surprised to find myself confronted by a young man of twenty or twenty-one. He was handsome, in apparent good health, and his clothes were well-made. Under one arm, he carried a slim valise, three feet by two but little thicker than a cigar case. He smiled broadly, his lips curling to meet his moustache.

Thank you, I said. *I'm – quite well.*

Rising, I offered my hand, giving a false name as I did so. He introduced himself as Robert and folded his hand around mine. He squeezed, strong but gentle, his skin cool and dry despite the heat of the evening.

And now, my good fellow, you look rather the lost sheep. Might I be of some assistance?

I looked him over again, taking in the fine clothes, the thin case. For a moment, I half-fancied him for the religious sort, one of those well-meaning young men who would carry bibles into the depths of Tartarus itself as long as he could return home to his wife and townhouse with everything in its place. But his ready smile and obvious amiability put me at my ease.

There is a – place – nearby. It has no name, I'm given to understand, but the sign outside is a most peculiar shade of –

Yellow?

His eyes glittered.

Well — yes.

He laughed, a roar of surprise and delight. *And here I thought you meant to ask me the way to the nearest music hall.*

You know of it?

He nodded. *As it happens, I'm going there myself. Perhaps you might care to accompany me?*

I fell into step beside him.

It's good of you, I said. *Truly.*

Not at all. We're not far off now. You'll see.

We continued to the end of the block, where my companion turned sharply to the right. He plunged down a sunken roadway — long abandoned, half-flooded by a cracked water main — and I followed him through puddles that were ankle-deep and warm as bathwater.

Eventually, we reached another street even more decrepit, where the air reeked of piss and spoiled milk. Laundry-lines flapped like sails overhead, festooned with colorful rags. After two blocks, my guide ducked down another side street before completing the circle by turning right once more.

This should have brought us back to the Bowery, but the street we entered bore little resemblance to the noisome squalor we had left behind. The crumbling tenements were gone, replaced by elaborate structures of concrete and steel. There were no street children, no milling crowds. Instead, an orderly procession of impeccably-attired men and women walked arm-in-arm down the sidewalk, talking and laughing, engaged in an animated discussion of an opera or play they had all just attended. In the lane, carriages were pulled up, black and gleaming, drawn by fine specimens of horseflesh. Even the street signs were unfamiliar: Genevieve Street, Castaigne Court.

Is this the Bowery? I asked, confused.

Of course. Don't you recognize it?

I offered no reply.

We walked on in silence. My companion maintained a brisk, nearly martial pace, swinging his arms with such vigor that I worried he would lose his valise. Clearly, he was no young missionary equipped with bibles and the armor of self-righteousness. And yet I did not think to ask what he carried inside the case.

He halted. *Here we are,* he said. He pointed up at the splintered sign board, a faceless plank of weather-worn timber caked in faded paint. The color may have once been gray or brown but now appeared yellow in the glow cast by a streetlamp opposite.

The establishment itself occupied a three story building in the Queen Anne style, the walls fashioned from red brick. The windows were numerous and brightly-lit, though masked with damask drapes that hid the rooms beyond.

Come along, Robert said.

He led me inside into an elaborately-furnished sitting room, characterized by paintings in expensive frames and couches upholstered in dark velvet. Most prominent among the room's many ornaments was a gilded clock, which stood over six feet in height. Its face was divided into several dials of various sizes, the largest of which gave the time as a quarter past two—but surely that couldn't be right, I reflected, as it wasn't yet ten-thirty when I left the hotel. Other dials appeared to tell the month and the year, though these, too, were incorrect. A final gauge noted the phase of the moon. Waning.

A woman received us at the counter. She was tall and emaciated, the skin stretched tight over her skull. In color, she was so pale as to be transparent. Her veins showed like scrimshaw under the skin, darkening to violet where they gathered at her temples. She addressed my companion.

Back again, are you? Here to see Cassie, I take it.

Robert grinned. *You know me too well! Would the lovely lady be available?*

For you, young man, I dare say she'd make *herself available. Of course, it probably wouldn't matter to you, even if she wasn't. Maybe you'd prefer it that way.*

Maybe I would, he said, flashing the same winning smile. *Indeed, fair lady, I think you may be right.*

Fair lady? she scoffed. *Ah, go on, up with you. He won't be back for another hour at least. I'll let him know you're in there.*

You have my thanks. He turned and offered me his hand. *Do you think you can find your own way from here?*

I nodded.

Good man, said he, and clapped me on the shoulder. He transferred the valise from under his arm, and then, carrying it at his side, stepped round the counter and passed through the curtained doorway beyond.

The pale woman turned her attention on me. *And you, sir?* she said, speaking more formally than before. *I believe you're joining us tonight for the first time?*

Yes, that's right.

One moment.

She stooped beneath the counter, disappearing from view. I heard the click of a key in a lock, the groan of oiled hinges. Then she straightened, holding a ledger in both arms. The binding was good, the pages crisp and new. She placed it on the counter — gently, the way a mother carries a child — and opened to the marked page.

She looked up at me. With one hand, she held a fountain pen. The other rested on the counter, placed with apparent casualness, though the barrel of a Derringer was just visible where it poked between her fingers.

And which name should I use?

I told her, employing the same pseudonym I had used when meeting Robert. She nodded and noted this down. *And do you know who you're here to see?*

Camilla.

Camilla? You sure of that?

I am. Is there a problem?

No, sir. None at all.

She continued to write for the better part of a minute, the nib scratching and scratching. A glance into the corner of the room confirmed what I had initially suspected: the clock's hands had not changed position. In this unnamed establishment, it was always a quarter past two.

The woman pressed the ledger shut and secreted it away beneath the counter. The gun, I noticed, had disappeared as well. *I'll need payment from you upfront*, she said. *Not many men can afford to see Camilla.* She named a price. It was expensive, but not exorbitant, and ultimately less than I had expected, given the general opulence of the establishment.

I paid it gladly.

She motioned to the curtained entrance behind her. *Go on up to the third floor. Camilla's is the fourth door on the right.*

The curtains parted, ushering me into a narrow corridor marked at either end by a twisting stair. The hall was lined with closed doors carved with scenes from mythology: images of Io and Leda, women sprawled under gods. The smell of smoke was especially pronounced, the cloying odor of cigars. From behind one door came a man's voice, muffled and gravelly, followed by a woman's laughter.

I proceeded to the end of the hall and climbed to the third floor, emerging in a new corridor identical to the first in all respects save the wallpaper, which was painted with a pastoral scene: rolling hills, castles, olive groves. A mass-produced print, I decided, though an artist had made certain embellishments, adding a courting couple to the riverbank and again to the castle's battlements.

The woman stood with her back against the tower-wall. She was arrayed in silks and ruffles, a woman of means. Her golden hair streamed with the wind, hiding her face. The man kneeled before her, as though requesting her hand, but his bare back was turned to the audience, and I wondered why he should be naked.

They were not alone. Another figure could be seen at the far end of the battlements, a man watching. His face was lightly sketched, presented in profile, but there was something vaguely familiar about him, a likeness I couldn't place.

I reached Camilla's door. I knocked — gently at first but louder when I received no reply. The handle gave way at a touch. The door swung inward, admitting me to a dimly-lit chamber. The hearth was cold, the lone window shaded with purple damask. The only light emanated from a candelabrum on the mantelpiece, casting layered shadows over the elaborate wallpaper, the four-poster hung with scarlet drapes.

Camilla stood by the window, robed in silk. Her hair was black and curly, gathered atop her head in a series of nested spirals, while her gown was in the Chinese style: crimson, clean lines, the back stitched with a sunburst in gold.

Hearing my step, she turned, and I was surprised to discover that she wore a mask. It was made from porcelain: bone-white and perfectly smooth, a cold facsimile of feminine beauty with elliptical holes left for eyes and mouth. She held her robe closed across her chest, alluringly modest, a triangle of pale skin visible at her throat, merging with the shadows where it plunged to hidden curves below.

She did not speak. Gliding to the night stand, she withdrew a glass pipe from her robe. It was long and slim, a delicate stem that sloped to a shallow bowl. At the night stand, she pushed back the lid of an ornate snuff box. Inside, I could see a coarse black powder, gritty like coal-dust. She withdrew a pinch and placed it in the bowl.

With the pipe in one hand, she

approached the hearth and took down the candelabrum. Her robe fell open, revealing her breasts, the thatch of hair between her legs. She made no attempt to cover herself but merely held the candelabrum at her chest and gazed at me through the twitching flame-tips. Her eyes bored into me: black and deep and bracingly still. I returned her stare, unable to look away.

She exhaled, extinguishing two of the candles so that only one remained lit. Tilting the candelabrum, she held the flame to the side of the pipe-bowl and slipped the stem into her mouth. The powder glowed, orange then black. Her inhalation lasted several seconds.

She replaced the pipe and candle on the mantelpiece and turned her gaze on me once more. Extending her hand, she beckoned me closer, one finger curling back, drawing me in. Only then did I realize that she had not exhaled, that she was in fact holding the pipe-smoke in her lungs.

I stepped forward.

For a moment, she regarded me closely, silently. Then, with queer violence, she grabbed hold of my hair and tugged down my head, crushing my face against the mask. Her mouth found mine through the gap in the porcelain. Her lips were as dry and coarse as parchment.

Smoke filled my mouth, my lungs. Darkness bloomed inside my skull, the acrid stench of blood-iron, slow decay. My vision blurred. I coughed and staggered back, losing my balance and tumbling backward. I landed on the bed. The blankets yielded — gave way — and closed over me. The bedroom vanished, and I sank into oblivion.

*

Stars. A billion pupils — constricting, expanding — like holes cut through the dome of the sky. Every star provided me a glimpse of a greater illumination beyond, of the light that was always there, though sometimes hidden, cloaked in darkness in the same way Camilla wore a mask, and for the same reason: to hide the face of God.

Years passed like ghosts at broad noon, unremembered, unseen. The Earth groaned and shifted underfoot, releasing a cry of agony that stretched over eons and millennia, dulled by time to a gentle hum. It gave little warning of what came next.

The sun exploded, bursting like a fever-mark. Heat poured out to cover all things. The stones liquefied, the air evaporated. The sky fell away, and I hurtled into the stars.

Surrounded now, I observed that they were not pupils as I had first imagined but flaming suns, ringed with planets like half-lit moons. These new suns arranged themselves in strange patterns around me, forming bands of color, spirals that recalled the coils of Camilla's hair.

But even these were left behind when I passed beyond the farthest star and entered a darkness more alien—and yet more fundamental—than the womb that gave me birth. I was right to have thought that Creation wore a mask, but it was one of light, not dark. The stars served only to conceal the silent tempest that lay beyond, the storm in which I now found myself, shivering and cold. But I was no longer among the heavens. Instead, I had descended inward, to the very center of my being, and discovered there the same boiling chaos where my soul should have been.

Despairing, I crawled forward, unable to rise, while the cosmos cracked and fell to pieces around me. This was the storm that lived inside of me, inside of all men: a thousand cities scorched and shattered, reduced to spinning fragments. Providence. New York. Chicago. Black snow on ceaseless wind.

Footsteps. From somewhere far off, I heard a child's steps: stumbling, uncertain. The night parted and re-formed, the storm taking shape as the wind snapped back against itself, smashing those broken cities together, until they coalesced into the silhouette of a young boy, no more than three years old. He tottered toward me with his mouth open—screaming, I thought, though I heard nothing.

How can I describe this?

It was you. *You*, my boy. The reason I'm writing this. Years before I met your mother, before you were born, I knew that we would share this place, would always. There was comfort in that thought, and there was sadness, the latter cutting deep when you offered me your hand. You were frail and sickly, exactly like the child I would watch you become, but still you took my hand, and raised me to my feet, and lifted me out of that silent storm.

*

In Camilla's bedroom, the candle had burned down. It guttered into insignificance, spreading a shadow over the stained bed sheets, the cracked and peeling wallpaper. Around me, the room had fallen into disrepair, all elegance stripped away. The air was dank with the stench of mildew and perfume, a sweetness like high fever.

Camilla stood at the window. She was dressed in imitation silks, her face turned to the slit in the drapes. She had removed the mask, which now sat on the nightstand, but the darkness hid her features, and for this, I was glad. She sighed, faintly, and it occurred to me that she was waiting for something, or someone. I gathered my things and slipped from the room.

In the hallway, I encountered my young

companion, his valise tucked under one arm. Evidently, he had just let himself out from another bedroom.

His eyes widened upon seeing me. His face went pale.

But – that's Camilla's room!

Yes. I was told to ask for her –

Who told you that?

The night clerk. At my hotel.

My God! You must get out of here. If he finds you...

He? What are you talking about?

She's King's girl. Camilla. Cassie is too, though he doesn't mind me sketching her.

Sketching?

Realization dawned at last. The man from the wallpaper — the figure who stood watching — was none other than my young companion. Though drawn with the vaguest of lines, the face was unquestionably Robert's. Moreover, I realized that it must be a self-portrait. The valise, no doubt, contained his pencils and sketchbooks.

He took me firmly by the arm.

We have to go, he said. *He'll be back soon, but we can take the fire escape. With luck, we might manage to avoid him.*

My mouth fell open, but I could not find the words to protest. Robert didn't wait for me to speak. He spirited me down the corridor, which I now saw to be every bit as dilapidated as Camilla's bedroom, and through a doorway at the end of the hall that led out to the fire escape.

I don't understand, I managed at last. *Who is this King?*

Silas King. A former ship captain and smuggler. Originally from England, I understand, though he now styles himself The King of the Bowery.

A gang leader, then?

Yes. You might say that. Camilla has been his since she was a little girl. Don't you see? She belongs *to him. All of the Bowery knows better than to ask for her.*

All at once, I understood the night clerk's deception, the thin woman's surprise when I mentioned Camilla. With a thrill of fear, I followed Robert down the fire escape, moving slowly so as to mute my clattering steps. By now, it was nearly midnight, but the air had not cooled. The breeze from the East River brought only heat and soot, the mingled smells of smoke and sewage.

Careful, Robert warned as we reached the ground. The alley before us teemed with faint movement, the scurrying of hundreds of rats. They parted before us like a sparkling sea, fleeing into rubbish bins, piles of twisted metal.

Moments later, I saw what had brought them into the alley to feed. Opposite the fire escape were buckets of slop and grease, which half-concealed two sheeted forms that may have once been human. Children, I thought, dead on the street. Or the bodies of King's victims.

The alley led back to the Bowery, but there was no sign of the wealthy theater-goers or their gleaming carriages. Outside a barroom, two foreigners fought with knives while a crowd looked on. A young family huddled together in a doorway. The mother called to us, begging for coin. *For the babe*, she said, but we paid her no heed.

Halfway down the block, we passed beneath the yellow sign once more. Formerly grand and imposing, the establishment now bore the marks of neglect: bricks crumbling, windows cracked or broken. I glanced up to the third floor, where Camilla was still visible: a faceless shadow, an outline glimpsed through tattered curtains.

We hurried past.

*

Robert froze. Cursing, he took me roughly by the arm and shoved me into the mouth of an alley. I cried out in surprise, prompting him to drop his case and grab me by the collar.

That's him, he hissed. *King.*

Whatever I had expected, I was unprepared for the size of the man who came into view. King was tall, nearly seven-foot, and grossly corpulent. The flesh of his neck was soft, doughy. It gathered in folds above his collar and swung free like a turkey-wattle, rippling with every labored footfall, his entire body vibrating, a drawn string. His hair was black and thickly-greased. His complexion was sallow, shockingly pale, and his face was pitted with disease. An open sore marred his upper lip, red and glistening beneath the thin mustache.

And yet, for all this, his clothing was exceedingly fine. His top hat and frock were of the best workmanship, and a gold chain stretched across his quivering gut. He had lost his left ear but wore a porcelain substitute in its place, and he walked with the aid of a cane, a wrist-thick shaft terminating in a shard of yellow quartz: uncut, its jagged edges showing between his flabby fingers.

King glanced down the alley as he passed. His eyes met mine, briefly, and I saw that they were black: the same non-color as the shadow inside me or the places beyond the stars. He must not have seen me, though, for he kept walking, his cane striking the pavement like a pistol's report. The sound dwindled and disappeared.

Robert released a breath. He turned to me, brow shining with perspiration.

We have a few minutes. Where will you go?

Back to my hotel, I suppose.

He shook his head. *I wouldn't do that. The clerk thought he was sending you to your death. He will be ill-pleased to see you again.*

The police, then.

And you think they would listen? They might turn you over to King themselves if they heard he was looking.

Then what?

Make for Grand Central. I'll pay for a hansom — it's the fastest way. From there you can catch the first train home.

And then…?

He shrugged. *Stay away from New York. And if you have to come back, then for God's sake, don't come near the Bowery. He really is a king there — and not the forgiving kind. However, you should be safe outside of the city.*

Should be, I repeated.

He's pursued some men as far as San Francisco and for less cause. You gave a pseudonym? Good. Then he doesn't know your name or what you look like. He might never find you. Nevertheless he won't stop searching. You can be sure of that.

I recalled the moment in which our eyes had met — black on black, mirrors turned to reflect one another — and realized that it didn't matter what he knew, or what I looked like, for we carried the same tempest inside us.

My companion collected his valise from the ground and proceeded to the end of the alley. He hailed a cab, which drew to a shuddering halt, its lanterns casting us into sharp relief. The horses snorted, slick and steaming in that heat.

Robert helped me into the carriage.

Remember what I said. Avoid the Bowery.

And you?

You needn't worry about me. King and I have an understanding. In any case, it hardly matters. I'm leaving soon, maybe for good.

Where are you going?

Paris. The School of Fine Arts. He hefted his valise. *I'm going to be a proper artist.*

With that, he grinned broadly and wished me goodnight. The driver cracked his whip, snapping the horses into motion. I glanced back over my shoulder, hoping for a final glimpse of my friend, but he was already gone, lost somewhere in that hell of smoke and night.

I never saw him again.

*

For years, there were nightmares. In sleep, I plunged once more into seething chaos and surfaced in a place of solitude, cast up in the midst of the silent storm Camilla had showed me. Again, I forced myself forward, crawling hand over elbow, unable to stand, and again, the darkness whirled and took shape ahead of me.

Silas King. He towered over me like the looming specter of ultimate horror, and though I tried to crawl away, I was never fast enough. He found me, always, and I woke up gasping, panting after breath that would not come.

Around this time, I met your mother.

When I proposed, she squealed with delight and threw her arms around me. She kissed my neck and whispered love-words in my ear. In those days, you see, she was not yet your mother, the woman you would know. That came later.

But the nightmares persisted, worse than before. Every night, I came awake screaming, choking on sweetness and fever. In the morning, the taste of King's breath lingered in my mouth, recalling the stench of dried blood or the dust Camilla had burned, the smoke with which she had filled me.

Then you were born, as slight and sickly as I had dreamed you. The nightmares ceased soon after, another miracle. At night, I descended into darkness, our darkness, and there found you waiting, not King. Only then did I begin to understand the nature of the blessing and the curse that Camilla had bestowed on me.

It couldn't last, of course. In late '92, I traveled to New York on business. I stayed far from the Bowery. I was careful. All the same, King must have learned of my visit, for I soon became aware of someone following me.

One afternoon, in Boston, on a crowded street, I happened to look behind me and spotted him twenty yards back. He was attired in his customary hat and frock, the gold chain glittering on his belly. He smiled, perhaps in recognition, and hastened toward me, as though advancing to meet an old friend. He moved quickly for his size, loping like an animal, and I took to my heels, thinking only of escape.

I ran. My flight brought me here: to this city, this hotel. Ten after two. There isn't much time. I can hear him in the hallway, pacing beyond the door. His cane taps and taps on the boards, doubling the sound of my heartbeat. Soon he'll knock. He'll rap on the door with that shard of quartz. He'll say my name, my real name, and then I'll have to let him in.

WS Lovecraft, 1893

DUST FROM A DARK FLOWER

*Being a true account of the recent happenings
at the burying ground in Falmouth Village
as related by the murderer Hosea Edwards
on the night before his death*

I

I am Hosea Edwards, physician to the Village of
Falmouth in the New Hampshire Grants and
Deacon to the congregation thereof. Sentenced to
hang for the murders of the Verger Samuel
Crabb and the Reverend Judah Stone, and the
subsequent destruction, by fire, of the Falmouth
meetinghouse, I leave behind these pages, that
they might be found by my jailers after my
death.

Tomorrow evening, I will be ashes, my
body burned on my instructions; and though I
die a criminal, my conscience is clear. At my
trial, I offered no plea or protest of innocence, for
I hoped yet to spare you the knowledge of these
events. But the time is short: The White child is
dead and buried these two days, and the long
night nearly spent.

There can be no more hesitation. A full
accounting must be made.

II

Last winter, the Reverend Ambrose Cooper, who first ordained me to the Deaconate, and with whom I had traveled from the town of Marshfield in Massachusetts to Falmouth on the west bank of the Connecticut River in the year 1767, returned to the Lord at the age of one-and-sixty. The ground being well-frozen, his body was transferred to the vault following the funeral to be buried in the spring.

The season soon passed; the grave was prepared; and, on the second of April, we lowered him into the ground. Our church's request for a minister had not yet been fulfilled and, so, the Reverend Crane from neighbouring Putney presided over the burial and erection of the slate headstone, upon which Samuel Crabb, the Church Verger, had laboured all winter.

'Twas a thing of singular elegance and beauty: fully four feet high and so heavy it required the village's five stoutest men to lower it into the sod. The stone was further distinguished by some of Crabb's finest work, including an inset likeness of the minister in his vestments, followed by some words of tribute that I had myself prepared. At the base of the stone was an epitaph that the minister had chosen when he sensed his time was upon him:

And he carried me away in the spirit to a great and a high mountain, and he shewed me the great city, Holy Jerusalem, descending out of heaven from God (Rev. 21:10).

They were sanguine words, perfectly befitting a man of his character, but on that dim April morning, with a soft rain falling and the wet earth yielding before us, I found I could not share in their hope; and afterward, when I returned home to my cottage, I fell to my knees before the fire and wept.

While the Reverend Cooper was in all respects irreplaceable, the Church soon dispatched a new minister to Falmouth. The Reverend Judah Stone, formerly of Norfolk in the British Isles, arrived in town on the 22nd of April and immediately assumed residence in the parsonage, which was sited outside the village proper at the base of Meetinghouse Hill.

A man of thirty, Reverend Stone seemed possessed of an imperturbable mildness and good humour. Many was the morning I saw him pass before the windows of my cottage with his hat tugged down to his brow, waving to all he encountered and greeting them with his usual cheer. His fondness of children was well-known, as was the patience he exercised in all aspects of his ministry, from the pulpit to the sickbed.

That is not to say that he was without eccentricity: His abhorrence of human contact quickly became apparent to us (and to me, personally, when he refused to take my hand on the occasion of our first meeting) and he was regularly attended by the aroma of the rose-water in which he washed. Furthermore, he was said to suffer from some obscure ailment of the joints, which pained him constantly, though he never consented to be examined.

But these were minor matters and inconsequential to us, given the depth of his knowledge and the strength of his faith; indeed, there were times that he seemed to us more spirit than flesh. In short, we soon came to believe that the Reverend Stone had been delivered unto us in answer to our oft-repeated prayers — but that was before the strange events at Meetinghouse Hill.

III

The Verger Crabb was the first to take notice. He raised the matter with the Reverend Stone, who dismissed the Verger's concerns with his customary solicitude and urged him to think no more of it. But Crabb could not push the matter from his mind and passed an uneasy night in his one-room cottage by the burying ground. The next morning, he yoked his ox, and readied his cart, and traveled to the village to seek my advice. When I learned of his discovery, I wasted no time in insisting that I accompany him to the churchyard that very day.

The sun was nearing the meridian when we arrived at the hill. We chained the ox at the base of the drumlin and completed the climb on foot. Crabb led me to one corner of the graveyard, northwest of the meetinghouse, to the grave of the Mead child, a girl stillborn three years before. The low slate had sunk halfway into the ground and now listed to one side at a sharp angle, as though to indicate the nearby grave of her unmarried mother, who had followed the infant in death, despite the Reverend Cooper's tender ministrations.

"You must watch me," quoth Crabb, "and closely."

Kneeling beside the infant's grave, he ran his index finger along the stone. 'Twas a gentle gesture, of exceeding delicateness, and yet, the slate itself seemed to crumble upon contact with his skin. The stone flaked away in a cloud of black dust, finer in consistency than gunpowder, but of much the same colour. The Verger shewed me his finger, the tip of which was beaded with granules of the strange material. I noticed then, for the first time, that the man himself appeared pallid and gaunt, as in the throes of illness.

"For how long has it been like this?" I inquired of him, thinking, perhaps, that the stone's position on the outskirts of the churchyard had left it vulnerable to the influence of weather; but Crabb's answer made this impossible:

"Since yesterday morning."

I waved the Verger away and placed my satchel on the ground beside the headstone.

Extracting a scalpel from my bag, I moved the sharp edge along the top of the slate and observed, once more, the curious manner in which it yielded to the faintest contact; first, in brittle shavings like a hardened cheese, and again, as a black powder. The latter form clung to the blade, but was wiped away with ease, leaving behind a stain. In this, I was reminded of nothing so much as the dust from a dark flower.

Next, I applied myself to an inspection of the marker's face, which I found to be in a similarly delicate condition. My scalpel stripped away the stone with ease, exposing a layer of black, ash-like sediment below the surface. Of this I collected a sample and secreted it away in my bag for further study. My initial observations had already led me to suspect that the substance was organic in nature; I hoped subsequent tests might lend further credence to this theory.

Afterward, Crabb and I descended the hill together and rode back into the village, where he left me off with a solemn promise to inform me of any further developments. Then he turned round the cart and clomped back toward the meetinghouse.

IV

Though I am not a man of science, my years at Philadelphia College bestowed on me a robust appreciation for, and passable knowledge of,

Descartes' Method. Upon returning home, I set about preparing an appropriate framework by which to analyse the chemical properties of the black powder.

Having first divided my sample into three parts, I sifted the first third into a pewter bowl, which I left exposed to the air, while adding the second third into a glass dish containing water, retaining the final third for additional tests, as necessary.

On the following morning, the first sample appeared no different. However, the second sample, which had steeped in water, had undergone a singular transformation. By some obscure agency, the powder had congealed overnight and extruded itself into a series of black hairs, fibrous and delicate, all of which were fastened by unknown means to the bottom of the dish, as though seeking for purchase there.

The stench was indescribable; I can only say that it reminded me of the fluid from a lanced boil. Dark specks leapt into my vision and I turned swiftly away, lest I succumb to a spell of fainting.

That evening, I lighted a tallow candle and subjected the substance to one final test. With the aid of my steel forceps, often employed by me during so-called "breach" birthings, I gathered a small quantity of the remaining powder and held it to the flame. To my surprise, the sample ignited with startling swiftness and burned down to the forceps in the span of a heartbeat, releasing a plume of acrid smoke that caught like bile in my throat.

Afterward, when I went to wipe the instrument clean, I was surprised to find it devoid of char or ash. Whatever its nature, the substance in question had evidently burned through completely, leaving no trace of itself behind.

V

The following day, a Wednesday, I received a second visit from Crabb. He sought me out at the White farm four miles from the village, whereunto I had been called to perform an amputation on the eldest White child, Ethan, whose right leg had begun to exhibit signs of gangrene.

The procedure was performed with assistance from the boy's mother, who provided rum and a leather strap while the younger boys, Martin and John, watched from the doorway. The dressings in place, I made my farewells and exited the house.

Crabb waited for me outside with the ox and cart. As before, the Verger appeared sickly, his eyes hooded as if he had not slept in days. "The matter has become serious," intoned he with his typical solemnity. "I came for you at once."

We arrived at Meetinghouse Hill early in the afternoon and scaled the steep hillside. Our steps brought us to within ten paces of the parsonage windows, behind which the Reverend Stone was just visible to us, his sharp edges softened by the distortive effects of Crown Glass.

I inquired of the Verger whether Stone knew of these new developments, but Crabb shook his head. "It seemed of little use," he said. "His pain has been worse, of late, and he does not wish for me to disturb him."

The northwest corner of the burying ground had, it seemed, been subject to some queer manner of flooding or subsidence. The infant Mead's stone was now completely black and featureless, with shards of broken slate littering the ground before it.

Each of the stones around it, including that of the child's mother, was likewise speckled with the same black dust, which loosed in whirling clouds whenever the wind swept down from the meetinghouse and shook the *arbor vitae*. A faint odour hung over that dreary scene, not dissimilar to the pus-smell produced by my earlier experiments.

A cursory inspection of the child's stone confirmed that it was no longer slate at all; instead, it seemed wholly composed of a porous organic material. I turned my attention to the base of the stone and cleared away the wet earth with one hand, only to learn that the growth reached deep into the ground, rooted somewhere below our feet.

The conclusion to which I came was, admittedly, fanciful, but also undeniable, for surely this black thing had come out of the ground and then, penetrating upward, proceeded to replace the slate from *inside*. Eventually, the outermost layer of stone cracked open like an acorn, leaving a faceless duplicate in its place.

Our course of action seemed clear. If this were some manner of sickness particular to the earth—a "gangrene of the soil," as I described it to Crabb—then we had no choice but to seek out the source of the infection and cut it away.

"But first, we must put the matter to the Reverend," said I, "and let him be the judge. Though I am not desirous of disturbing this consecrated ground, it may yet prove necessary."

VI

Sometime later, we rapped upon the door of the parsonage and were received into the parlour by the Reverend Stone, who invited us to sit by the hearth. The minister was attired in his usual austere robes, with a high collar that reached to the throat, and the scent of rose-water was, as ever, evident. He offered us ale, which we refused, and settled himself in a chair opposite us, wincing as he did so for the pain of his ailment. "'Tis a distinct pleasure," said he, with a forced smile, "but I sense you have not come merely to visit."

We admitted this was so and Crabb proceeded to summarise the strange happenings of the last three days. He made rather a neat account of it, pausing, from time to time, only to cough into his kerchief. When he had finished, I offered my own conclusions and advised in favour of delving beneath the graveyard so as to find the source of the infestation. At this suggestion, Stone raised his hand, and addressed us in tones of tired admonishment.

"We must not be overly hasty," said he. "Your findings are strange and, undoubtedly, they are suggestive. However, they are, as yet, little more than that."

He stood and shewed us out of the parlour. "And now I fear you must excuse me, for young Martin White will be here shortly. Please be assured that I shall pray upon the matter, as you have described it, and that you shall soon have my decision."

Outside the parsonage, the Verger and I bade each other farewell, but the other man lingered purposefully beside his cart, so that I knew he had more to tell me.

"There is something else," said he, after a moment's consideration. "I did not like to say, at first, for I know the esteem in which you hold his memory, but the rot has spread to the new section of the burying ground, southeast of the meetinghouse, where the Reverend Cooper lies."

"Show me," said I, attempting an air of authority, though my words came out strangled and faint. And so it was that we climbed the hill to the churchyard once more and made our way to the Reverend Cooper's stone. Dread beset me as we entered the new section, followed in turn by a surge of terror at my first glimpse of the Reverend's monument. Although every grave-marker bore a dusting of black powder, Reverend Cooper's stone appeared most sorely affected.

The rot had pushed out from behind his carved likeness and rendered him faceless: as grim and terrible as the specter of Death. My words of tribute had been erased entirely, blotted out by the spreading stain, so that only the final words of his epitaph were visible:

Out of heaven from God.

'Twas a dire omen, suggesting, as it did, that this strange infestation was visited upon us as a judgment from the Almighty; yet, I knew this could not be the case, for there was no man alive or dead more saintly than the departed minister. Our town deserved no such punishment, I was sure, but I was likewise certain this was no deed of man or nature. That left only Lucifer, the Father of Lies. But is it not true that even the work of the Devil glorifies His Holy Name?

Much shaken, I returned to my horse, mounted, and kicked the beast toward home. After forty paces, I encountered Martin White, a boy of twelve, who was evidently en route to his appointment with the new minister. He walked with slate and hornbook beneath one arm, and with face downcast, as though immersed in a reverie. He did not lift his head, nor display recognition of any kind, but merely passed by me without speaking and, thusly, into the shadow of Meetinghouse Hill.

VII

For the next two days, I strove to push the matter from my mind and see to my duties about the village. But when Friday came with yet no word from the Verger, I decided, myself, to call on him at once. I readied my bag, and the instruments of my profession, and rode to the meetinghouse, where I found the man at work on the edge of the churchyard.

His illness had worsened and he was plainly quite weak — too weak, I thought, to manage the ox and cart on his own, thereby explaining his prolonged absence. Nonetheless, he refused an examination. "It is not yet so bad as that," said he, "nor is it physick I require."

I did not understand his meaning, for the

man's illness was clearly of a deteriorative nature: His collar was soaked through with sweat, while his breast was flecked with bits of black spittle. Crabb shook his head. "You must not think me a fool, Doctor. I am unwell, aye, but such sickness as I may have lies not only here" (He pointed to his breast with his thumb) "but all round us. In the graveyard. In the earth itself."

He coughed noisily into one cupped hand, then turned over the palm to shew me. There was spittle there, and blood, but also present in suspension were fine strands of a black material identical to those produced by my experiment.

Crabb smiled horribly, baring his teeth. "The rot is far-progressed," said he. "The Mead girl's stone is crumbling, shedding itself like the skin of a leper, while the Reverend Cooper's grave is blackening more each day. To-morrow, 'twill be naught but dust and ashes."

"We must tell the Reverend Stone. Has he rendered his decision?"

"He has not. Nor will he welcome the interruption."

"Perhaps not, but I see no other recourse."

"Aye," the Verger agreed. "I have kept the folk of the village away, but they shall learn of it in time—by the Sabbath morn, if not before. What then?"

He was right, of course; I could well

imagine the ensuing panic, the fear that takes hold in small towns like Falmouth and soon breeds itself into hysteria, as in Salem Village or in the days of the last war. We needed to act, and quickly.

The door to the parsonage was opened by the Reverend Stone, who wore his customary robes and perfume. By the grimness of his bearing, 'twas plain that he was ill-pleased by our presence there, while his features were pale and contorted as in pain.

He did not invite us inside, but heard us out from the doorway, careful to maintain a courteous manner throughout our relation, despite his clear displeasure. After we had finished, he remained silent for a long time before addressing us with a voice like spring's last ice.

"Yesterday, you sought my counsel and today, you tell me what must be done? In all likelihood, this 'rot' you speak of is merely another natural phenomenon that Men of Science," (and here, he looked directly at me) "for of all their claims to erudition, are helpless to explain. Under no circumstances will the Lord permit us delvings in this graveyard. I would implore you both, as your pastor and as shepherd to this community, to trouble yourselves no more. Good day."

With that, he shut the door on us. The sound echoed from the hill with the finality of a musket's shot. Crabb turned to look at me. His canines appeared startlingly white against the black depths of his throat and his breath, too, was foetid.

By instinct or intuition, I knew he would not live to see another Sabbath, but we were not, as yet, helpless to save him. What is more, I could not countenance his death, any more than I could allow for the final profanation of the Reverend Cooper, a man unblemished in all things, who had gone to his grave with humble dignity to await the Day of Resurrection.

The time was short. I detailed my plan to the Verger, who gave his assent, and arranged for me to meet him in the dark of the midnight. Then I mounted and returned home.

VIII

Four hours after twilight, I readied my saddlebags with spade and mattock, set a fresh candle within my lanthorn, and stole behind the house to the stable, where the horse stood sleeping. I woke him with a gentle pat and laid my saddlebags across him. Then I climbed into the saddle and nudged him to a walk.

Soon, we were outside the village and amidst the woods, where the trees were budding, though not yet in blossom. Black and cancerous, their branches rattled with the wind, bending themselves to the cries of the owls and the calls of wolves from the north, so that they formed a kind of music, an eerie cacophony that followed me from the village and trailed me like the moonlight to the base of Meetinghouse Hill.

Fifty paces from the parsonage, I dismounted and ascended the hill on foot, with the saddlebags over my arm. There were no lights visible inside, not even the faint glow of a fire, but I waited until summiting the drumlin before lighting my lanthorn.

Crabb lingered near the gate of the churchyard. He was attired in heavy furs and woollens, with cold sweat shining on his face. With both hands, he held an unlit torch, the end of which trembled visibly, though with fright or fever I could not tell.

We did not speak, nor had we need of it. Crabb ignited his torch and, lifting high the light, shuffled toward the northwest corner of the burying ground. He was unsteady on his feet, dangerously so, and I made certain to walk beside him, so that I might catch him if he fell.

As Crabb had indicated, a profound change had taken place in the days since my last visit to the graveyard. All of the stones in the northwest corner had succumbed to the rot, including that of the Mead girl's mother. Around her marker lay strewn innumerable shards of slate, which had cracked and fallen away, leaving behind a stone-shaped duplicate composed of that queer material: dark and spongy, not unlike the inside of a bone.

I handed to Crabb the mattock and took the spade in hand. Together, we began our diggings, confining our efforts to the vicinity of the infant's grave. We soon learned that what had formerly been her stone—and was now a monstrous outgrowth—reached all the way down to the small coffin. Indeed, upon closer inspection, this black column seemed to grow *from* the box itself, narrowing to a rough circle, no wider than a man's closed fist, where it breached the lid.

"More light," I urged Crabb, who leant forward to direct his torch's glow into the grave itself. In that flickering illumination, I observed clearly that the black thing had, in fact, grown up from *inside* the coffin. In appearance, it resembled a kind of hideous, ropy cord that had been braided and twisted several times over. As I watched, it quivered faintly along its muscled length, pulsing rhythmically, as with the beating of a heart.

My stomach turned; the fever-stench was overwhelming.

With a prayer for courage, I raised the spade and brought its edge down hard upon the unnatural growth. I directed the blow toward the narrowest point of the rope, only to find that its essential substance was as dense as granite: The spade cut no deeper than half-an-inch before being repulsed. I employed my bone-saw but to no better result, for the teeth, despite their sharpness, failed to find their grip. Crabb offered his assistance, but was likewise unable to sever the ropy fibers with the mattock. We had little choice, then, but to prise open the already-ruptured coffin, though we were both affrighted of what might lie within.

Crabb removed the nails with the blade of the mattock, but could not lift the lid on account of the obtruding growth. We dared not risk breaking open the box, as the resulting din would surely lead to our being discovered in our ghastly work, but I contrived a solution with the use of the bone-saw and successfully removed the bottom two-thirds of the lid, thus allowing us to shine a light inside.

After three years in the ground, the child's flesh had been eaten away, leaving a rough jumble of bones and joints. I glimpsed her feet first of all, then discerned the shape of the ribs and pelvis. What I saw next chilled the very breath in my lungs.

The babe's skull was shattered, burst open like a bird's egg. The black growth sprouted up from the remnants of her jaw, eruptive, in the manner of a seed that has nourished itself on the earth before exploding into flower. Reeling, I staggered back and dropped to my knees, as in weary supplication to whatever dread power had loosed itself upon the village.

The child was dead these three years. Naught remained save bones; on what, then, had the black rot fed itself? I thought of Paul's first letter to the Corinthians: *There is a natural body and there is a spiritual body.* In the absence of the former, had this creature, whether of God or the Devil, found sustenance on the latter; and then, finding it to its taste, proceeded to *feast*?

I trembled to think of the departed minister, who had gone to the grave with the promise of resurrection, only to find waiting his own annihilation: a patient, noisome darkness like the fires of Gehenna.

Crabb stooped down beside me, breathing hard through lungs half-choked with dust or fluid. "We have uncovered the root," said he and pointed down into the coffin, indicating a position immediately below the broken skull. "Do you see?"

A thin cable, one inch round and similar to an umbilical cord, had entered the infant's skull via the trachea, having first penetrated the box from below. Arising, I stooped to shift the weight of the coffin, moving it just enough to expose the tail of the umbilical underneath.

From the coffin, the cord led southeast toward the meetinghouse. I dared not touch it, and could scarcely breathe for weight of the realisation, but Crabb hesitated not at all. He hefted the mattock behind his head, and then, with one deft stroke, split the root in two.

We breathed easier, then, and the moon shone bright upon us as we filled the grave with wet sod. I suggested we conceal the disturbed ground with weeds and brown grasses, to which task the Verger attended ably, but our labours that night were not yet at an end. Crabb sensed this as well as I did, and I motioned to him to collect our tools and follow me to the new section, hiding our lights when we passed within view of the parsonage.

IX

We arrived at the Reverend Cooper's stone, which the lanthorn revealed to be completely featureless, the last of the chiselled epitaph having been erased by the creeping rot. I nodded to Crabb and took from him the spade; and though it pained me worse than grief, I knew we had no choice but to disturb my dear friend's grave.

After the Gale of Sixty-Eight, in which the aspens came down, we had uprooted the stumps out of the earth, where, to our surprise, we found the trees were not in themselves separate, but grew from a single root. Much in the same way, I thought that if we were to trace the roots from every fibrous branch, every dark and crumbling flower, then we might yet pinpoint the source of the infestation and cut it away.

Crabb broke the earth with his mattock,

the blade biting deep. From out of the ground steamed that familiar odour that was at once sweet and bitter, like that of moulding apples. Together, we worked at unburying the minister's coffin. The labour wore hard upon the Verger, I could tell, for he rested often, and coughed and shook, but always returned to the task with the listless focus of a somnambulant, or of a man long dead.

At last, the outline of the minister's box revealed itself, whereupon I turned away, aghast, and could not stir myself to continue. I covered my face with my hands, but could not tamp my ears, which heard first the shriek of the dislodged nails as they were removed, followed by the distinctive squeal-and-bite of the saw-blade and the groan of the shifted lid.

The Verger inhaled sharply. Silence ensued, stretching for a minute or more before the spade descended and struck the inside of the coffin with a hollow *thunk*. I heard the coffin lid replaced, the mournful sound of sod on coffin-wood, and then — nothing.

I opened my eyes. Crabb had perched himself upon the edge of the grave with the spade-handle resting betwixt his legs. On his face he wore an expression of utter shock and bewilderment. I lowered myself beside him. His head swiveled. He looked at me directly, but his expression was curiously placid, almost vacant.

"'Twas horrible," said he. "He looked the

same as on the day we laid him down, no different save for the rot. It had grown out of his throat, the black thing, wide enough for to crack the jawbone. His mouth was open, as if he were crying out in agony, and the expression on his face—I have never seen such despair."

"It is done?" I asked, not wishing to consider the implications of his discovery. "The root, it has been severed?"

"Aye," he affirmed. "It is done. Though I fear we may have tarried too long."

"Where did it lead?"

"Northwest."

"Toward the meetinghouse?"

He turned his eyes upon me again, the moon glimmering like foxfire upon his pale visage. "Not toward it," said he, shaking his head. "Not 'toward' it at all. But *to* it. There can be no question but that it began there."

X

Scarcely an hour of darkness remained by the time I reached the village. Exhausted and unsettled, I resolved myself on sleep, only to be roused from slumber after no more than a quarter of an hour by a frantic pounding at the door.

'Twas John White, the youngest member of his family. The sun hung low in the eastern sky, violet at this early hour, and I realised upon seeing him that John must have left his home, on foot and unaccompanied, in the darkest hour of the night.

I wasted no time in extracting the tale from him. Earlier that evening, his younger brother Martin, who had been ill these last three days, had taken a turn for the worse and slipped into unconsciousness. With Ethan unrecovered, and his mother occupied in tending to Martin, she had sent her youngest child to fetch help. And so, he had come to me.

I dressed myself and readied the horse. Then, taking John behind me in the saddle, I rode hard for the White farm. The road was empty before us, the maples green and flowering, and I knew, by the warmth of the light on my back, that the day would be humid in the extreme.

At the White Farm, we dismounted in the yard. I handed John the lead and bade him stable the horse while I flew into the house and climbed the narrow staircase to the loft space, adjacent the chimney, wherein the family customarily slept.

But upon that morning, not one member of that household lay slumbering: Ethan, aged 16, tossed restlessly on one side of the bed and cried out piteously, pained by the itch of his missing limb, while Martin lay quietly beside him with his face upturned, soaked through with fever, his underclothes hanging from him like wet rags. Their mother occupied a chair by the bedside, one hand resting on Martin's brow, holding in place a scrap of white cloth. She acknowledged me with the slightest of nods, but I knew she did not intend for rudeness. In widowhood, she had grown strong, but these latest trials had nearly defeated her.

Immediately, I made haste to examine the unconscious lad. By inclining my ear to his chest, I ascertained that the heart was still beating, though its rhythm was uneven. His breathing was likewise staggered and shallow, so that I suspected the presence of some obstruction in the lungs. I rolled back the fabric of his shirt, exposing his chest to the light of my candle. At this, his mother gasped. I fear that I, too, may have recoiled in shock.

For the boy's chest was obscured by a mass of tumourous black growths, domed in the manner of warts and sprouting from the flesh to either side of the sternum. They must have seeded in his lungs and thenceforth expanded until breaching the skin like mushrooms after a rain. I touched my finger to the top of one such growth and observed its porous consistency; the tumour depressed at contact before springing back to resume its earlier shape. This recalled to my mind certain facts: not only the infestation in the churchyard, but the Verger's sickness and the visit that Martin himself had made but recently to Meetinghouse Hill.

I rolled the lad onto his right side, so that I might better view the pale flesh of his back. Here, my candle picked out the same dark growths, presented in rough alignment with the position of his lungs in his breast. 'Twas a miracle, surely, that Martin yet lived, but I knew his chances of recovery to be slim. Nonetheless, I could not allow this illness to claim him uncontested.

I opened my bag, removing first the cups, then the curettes. By this time, John had joined us in the loft and I asked him to heat the glass cups in the fire downstairs. He returned shortly, at which time I took the cups from him and applied them directly to Martin's back.

The skin swelled and blistered, and his mother winced at the sizzle of charred flesh. Incredible though it appeared, the sickness itself seemed to retreat from the outer edges of the cups, and even flamed up under the dome of the glass, where the heat was most intense. Slowly, boils took shape beneath the cups, drawing the ill-humours out of the body and concentrating them in a single place, so that they might be easily lanced and drawn away.

Removing the cups, I placed each of them twice more, so that a total of six boils had formed, three to either side of the spinal column. Selecting the slimmest and sharpest of the curettes, I lanced the fluid from each of these boils in turn, collecting the bloody runoff in a pewter dish, which I directed John to empty into the fire downstairs.

This being speedily accomplished, I bandaged the open wounds. Calling next for water, I scrubbed clean the cups of char and pus. Then I uttered a quick prayer for the boy's recovery and wished his family farewell.

I was halfway home when the cough overtook me. My chest heaved with every painful hack, as though attempting to expel, by force, some foreign body that had lodged itself inside of me. I reined in the horse and gasped for air, lest I collapse, unconscious. At length, the fit passed, and when I wiped clean my mouth, my hand came away smeared and flecked with dark matter.

XI

The remainder of the day was spent in prayer and fevered meditation. I had already correlated the illness of the White child with that of the Verger Crabb; the onset of my own cough with my recent proximity to the aforementioned persons; the location of the infested graves with the site of the meetinghouse; and, perhaps most alarmingly, the onset of the rotting sickness with the arrival in Falmouth of the Reverend Stone. Confronted with such evidence, I knew not in which way I should proceed, but knew only that I could not stand idle.

And so, I rode for Meetinghouse Hill. Arriving at dusk, I climbed the hill to the Verger's cottage, careful to avoid the windows of the parsonage, and rapped peremptorily at his door. No answering cry came within, no din of footsteps. I waited; knocked again. Receiving no response, I admitted myself to the common room.

Crabb lay sprawled, face-up, on the dirt floor. His mouth was wide, his cheeks so blue and swollen that I scarcely recognised him. 'Twas likely he had died of suffocation, which was, I believe, a small mercy, as it spared him the sight with which I found myself confronted.

From his throat there protruded an erect black coil, three inches across and hooked at its end, terminating more than a yard above his mouth. Knotted, rope-like, it rippled and twitched in place, moving like a leech, clawing upward, as though to seek the light.

I turned and fled. I dared not halt until the door was shut behind me and I was well clear of the cottage. I thought of the Verger's soul, on which the thing had fed itself, and forced myself to leave him, making for the graveyard, certain, as I was, that I could do nothing further for him.

By this time, the sun was all but gone, leaving behind a fragrant darkness, scented with the musk of spring shoots and the aroma of contagion. In less than a week, the sickness had germinated, rooted and given flower. The Reverend Cooper's stone was crumbling into powder, as were the graves all around, and there was not a single stone in that churchyard that did not carry the signs of infestation and decay. Only one place remained for me to explore.

I crossed the graveyard to the meetinghouse and unfastened the door to the sanctuary. The air inside was at once stale and damp and nauseating. The sweet stench of putrescence lay upon that place, as strong here as in the minister's opened grave, but, even in the gloom, the interior appeared to me unaltered.

Lighting my lanthorn, I stepped through the doorway. The windows were dark and the shadows, layered thickly, unravelled in the lanthorn's beam to reveal the same unpainted trusses, the familiar pews. I proceeded midway down the aisle and turned to scrutinise the balcony overhead. All was as it should have been and yet, the churchyard infestation had begun here; of that, there could be no doubt.

Then to my ears came the rustle of fabric, like a broom being dragged over the floor. I spun round, terrified, and directed my light toward the pulpit, beneath which stood the Reverend Stone.

His bearing was stiff, as from hours knelt in prayer, and he stood before me shirtless with a Cat O' Nine Tails in hand. The barbed rope-ends shewed crimson in the lanthorn's glow, beaded with blood where they had scourged his back. Worse still was the sight of his chest, which was covered with dark tumours in such thick profusion that I nearly mistook them for hair.

But it was his expression which froze me with horror, at the same time that I was moved, somehow, to pity. For never before had I seen such anguish in a human face, nor would I have dreamed it possible to bear such agony and live — if he were truly living.

The whip dropped from his hands. His eyes bulged, the whites shining, and he stumbled toward me with arms outstretched, as though to catch me in an embrace.

Sickened and fearful, I forced myself to step backward, nearly tripping over the aisle's skirting as I did so, but unable to turn around, unwilling to show my back, even for a moment, to this man — this thing — that continued to advance on me, not with menace but with pathetic desperation, murmuring his prayers all the while.

"O God, as You are my judge, You know I never meant for it to happen. You alone know what it is like to bear this burden, to be cursed with this affliction for the greater glory of Your Name. I ask only that You help me, for I cannot help myself."

He lunged toward me. His bare arms, like

his chest, were covered in black growths, and I understood at once the reasons for his habitual manner of dress. I threw myself backward, but caught my foot on the skirting so that I dropped heavily onto my back. The lanthorn went sailing through the dark, striking the low balcony overhead, where it shattered.

The wooden beams ignited. Fire raced up the tresses to the ceiling, traversing the sanctuary with shocking speed, as though the building were not merely infested with the black rot, but verily *made of it*, formulated entirely of the selfsame sickness as the minister possessed, the same corruptive influence of which Martin, Crabb, and I, too, had been made a victim.

Stone paid the flames no heed, but fell upon me like a crying child, moaning as he fastened his arms round me. "Hold me," said he. "Hold me."

I smelled the sickness on him for the first time, the odour that lurked beneath the rose-water in which he regularly washed. I gagged, lost my breath, and nearly fainted, but, by some supreme effort born out of terror, succeeded in dislodging the diseased minister and throwing him wide so that he landed in the aisle.

The ceiling dripped overhead. Coals fell, burning, from the balcony, igniting where they landed amidst the pews. The windows exploded outward, causing an in-rush of cool air that fanned the blaze ever-higher, sweeping toward us like a rolling wave. The heat was unbearable, the stench even more so, but I forced open the door and threw myself beneath the flames, which erupted at this new incursion of air, and rolled until I reached what I judged to be a safe distance.

I looked back toward the meetinghouse. Through the doorway, I glimpsed the minister, who continued to gaze at me through the flames, his face a mask of the uttermost anguish, watching me even as the fires broke over him and consumed him from the inside-out.

Shortly thereafter, the roof fell with a splitting crash, causing sparks to fly loose in great clouds. I lurched to my feet once more, ignoring the pain of my many burns, and staggered down the slope of the drumlin, turning round one final time to watch the Reverend Cooper's grave go up like a torch, followed by the whole of the northwest corner and the Verger's cottage. I fell to the ground before the parsonage and there lay insensible until the villagers found me.

XII

I awoke in the custody of the law, accused of lighting the fire and of the two deaths that resulted. On the following morning, I was taken in chains to the courthouse in Westminster and detained until my trial. There, it emerged that the Falmouth meetinghouse had burned through in mere minutes. My lanthorn was recovered, though no traces of the man of whose murder I stand convicted, while Crabb's cottage was likewise consumed with his body inside, leaving me as the final witness to the strange events on Meetinghouse Hill — or so, for a time, I allowed myself to believe.

This evening, I learned of the fate of Martin White, who died three nights past of a "sickness like the pox," and was buried quickly, for fear of spreading contagion. I hesitate to write this, for I am acquainted, intimately, with the hardships his family has endured, but the lad's body *must* be exhumed, and speedily, and burned as I am to be. He shall have neither corpus nor stone, but the Lord will not forget him, even as He has not forsaken me throughout these latest trials.

My illness has worsened in the days since the fire. The black tumours, now present in abundance, grow from my chest and back so that I scarcely sleep at night, and even then, I dream. In the mornings, I wake to this filthy cell, my shirtfront dirtied with blood and spittle, but I remain untroubled, knowing myself fortunate, for these sufferings will end — and soon.

Only with the most acute grief do I think of the Verger Crabb, who died in agony on the floor of his cottage, and of my dear friend the Reverend Cooper, the greatest man I have known, and of the black thing that fed upon them both, denying them, in this way, the promise to which Election made them heir. For them, there is only darkness, as there was for the Reverend Stone, and I can but mourn them as the unbeliever mourns all life, all loss, and the final passing of this world into a night unending.

Thus concludes my account.

May the peace of Our Lord Jesus Christ be upon your spirit—

H. Edwards
Westminster, 1773

THE PHOTOGRAPHER'S TALE

I heard this story from a passing acquaintance, a fellow photographer whom I shall call Lowell. I met Lowell in June of last year at a mountaintop resort in New Hampshire. I had traveled there for my health and was surprised to meet another who shared my profession.

The two of us struck up a conversation one evening after supper as we took cigars on the veranda — two old men alone with the wild hills before us. Photographic technique was the object of our discussion, and as I recall, we argued back and forth for some time regarding the utility of the new flash lamp.

"I'm not denying that it might be useful," Lowell conceded. His haggard features were visible only by the pale orange tip of his cigar. "But only up to a point. There are places — interiors, I mean — corners so dark they cannot be lighted."

I shook my head. "I'm afraid I don't follow you."

He exhaled, releasing a cloud of smoke. His mood was unreadable. Turning from me, he looked out toward the distant mountains, black beneath the hidden moon. A long minute elapsed, a silence spun from the murmur of crickets, the moan of an owl.

He sighed. "Perhaps I had better explain."

*

The morning of December 1st dawned cold and gray, promising an early snowfall. After breakfasting in his apartment, Lowell descended the back stair to his studio, where he was surprised to find that a shipping crate had been left for him with the first post. There was no return address, but he recognized the handwriting on the label and knew it to be from Patrick.

Lowell had first encountered the boy on the streets of Providence some twelve years before. Patrick was no more than eight or nine at the time, one among hundreds of beggar children who had resorted to thievery and worse in order to survive. One night in October, Lowell returned to his studio to find the boy curled up in the doorway: soaked and shivering, delirious with fever. Lowell brought him inside and allowed him to spend the night.

Days went by—Patrick's health improved—but Lowell did not turn him out. The boy served as his apprentice for the next seven years, assisting in the darkroom in exchange for room and board. Their relationship was a close one, and in time, the unmarried Lowell came to regard the lad as something like a son, only for Patrick to leave him—as sons will do—at the age of sixteen.

Whatever its cause, their final parting, when it came, was not amicable. Lowell blamed himself for it. He sought shelter first in alcoholism and later in the Roman Church. Five years passed. Throughout this time, Lowell's letters to Patrick went unanswered but from time to time he received word of his former apprentice from colleagues in New York.

At the time, Patrick was just twenty-one years old but already esteemed an expert in the field of portrait photography. He was said to possess an eye for hidden beauty and feeling that allowed him to reveal, with considerable skill, "the very soul" of his subject. Lowell admitted to a twinge of jealousy in this. Certainly, his own work had never inspired such hyperbole.

Now he knelt before the shipping crate. He lifted the lid, peeling back layers of straw and brown paper to reveal a studio camera. It was a newer model, equipped with a built-in viewfinder and only slightly used by its appearance. A length of ribbon had been fastened around the front standard, the ends tied up in an elaborate bow.

Lowell plucked the camera from the crate and tested the action of the shutter. *Click*. His anxiety departed, evaporating like shadows at sundown. He must write to Patrick. No, he thought—a telegram. He hurried to the doorway and took down his hat and coat. His first client was not due for another hour, which gave him ample time to walk downtown to the Post Office and dispatch a message of thanks to New York.

Outside, the weather was dismal, but the avenue bustled with carriages and pedestrians. Clerks and scriveners scurried past Lowell en route to their respective offices while paper boys shouted the day's headlines, their voices shrill above the rattle of wheels on cobble.

A pair of young women proceeded down the pavement in his direction. They were sisters, evidently, their good humor unaffected by the wind and imminent snow. The two walked arm-in-arm, laughing, even as their guardian gasped and panted behind them, burdened by a picnic basket and a pair of canvas shopping bags.

One of the sisters smiled at Lowell. The other tittered and tightened her grip on her sister's elbow. Their treatment of their guardian showed them to be callous, even cruel, but Lowell grinned back at them. He could hardly do otherwise: they were simply too young, too beautiful, too alive.

He crossed the street and passed by Saint Andrew's church, where he had taken to attending mass. Every Sunday morning, he knelt before the altar and prayed, rocked by yearning though he dared not take the Host. That morning, walking past, he let his fingers trail along the rough stones and sighed to hear the bell strike the half-hour.

At the post office, he composed a brief message to be wired to Patrick's studio in New York. RECD CAMERA, the wire read. DEEPEST THANKS. PLEASE WRITE.

He asked the clerk to contact him in the event of any delays and hurried home to keep his first appointment, smiling first at the sisters, whom he passed once more, and then at the paper boy, unable to contain his elation, even in that late season, even as the first flakes of snow drifted down and settled in his hair.

*

Mrs. Lavinia Perkins was Lowell's most reliable client, a middle-aged teetotaler of extraordinary vanity and peculiar habit—to wit, her insistence on having a new photograph of herself taken on the first of every month. These she used these to chart the course and extent of her aging, regularly searching the resulting photographs for signs of graying hair. This was, of course, an impossible task, but perhaps this was why she preferred the photographer's lens to that more ordinary (and less expensive) instrument: the mirror.

That morning, she breezed into the room with the haughty assurance of a beloved monarch. She did not wish Lowell good morning but instead assumed her usual standing pose against a canvas backdrop painted with ruined columns, dancing satyrs.

Lowell had already positioned Patrick's camera on the tripod. The plate was loaded, the flash box readied, and he wasted no time in going beneath the hood.

"Are you ready?" he asked.

Her pose spoke for itself. She stood perfectly erect, one arm draped over the Brady stand, and turned her face from the camera so that she appeared in profile.

He lifted the flash box with one hand and sighted the widow through the viewfinder. He steadied his fingers over the triggers for flash and shutter and began to count down, whispering the numbers to himself in the blackness of the hood.

The widow's features warped and changed. Her curls turned wiry and grey even as her cheekbones sloped inward to breach the mottled skin. From beneath the sallow flesh emerged the outline of a skull, the jaw-bone bursting from the sinews of her face. Even her teeth, usually white, were now brown and stained by the corruptions of the grave. A worm's tail thrust from behind her ear, puncturing the skin. A shower of corpse dust drifted to the ground.

"Well?" the widow inquired. Her voice, at least, was unaltered, but the coolness of her tone did nothing to dispel the image in the viewfinder. "Is something wrong?"

Lowell could not reply.

"Mr. Lowell?" she repeated, irritably.

She turned to face him, but her eyes were gone: the sockets empty, rimmed with pitted bone. A mass of white worms writhed within the hollow of her skull.

Lowell released the trigger on the flash box. The magnesium ignited, and a wave of cleansing light flooded the room. Somehow he possessed the presence of mind to open and close the shutter, capturing the widow with a blast of white lightning.

He wrenched his head from the hood and dashed to the side cabinet. There he found the brandy bottle, scarcely touched in the days since his conversion.

He poured himself a glass. He gulped it down.

"Whatever is the matter?" Mrs. Perkins asked. "You're acting *most* peculiarly."

The room shimmered, retreating from Lowell as the alcohol took hold. He clenched his eyes shut. He shook his head but could not speak.

"Open your eyes," she snapped. "Look at me."

Lowell lifted his head.

The widow's appearance had returned, mercifully, to normal. She peered at him through the lenses of her silver lorgnette, her magnified eyes more hawk-like than ever.

"I'm—quite well," Lowell gasped. "It's the—weather. My arthritis…"

She nodded. "I am glad it's nothing serious," she said. "Did you get the picture?"

He shivered. He poured another glass and drained it. Tears leapt to his eyes as the familiar ache spread through his chest. Mrs. Perkins sniffed in disapproval, but at that moment, he hardly cared. Even the thought of that photograph chilled him to the marrow.

"Well?" she demanded. "Shall we take another?"

"No," he said, quickly. "There's—no need."

"Good." She cast a scornful glance at the glass in his hand. "I shall come by later this week to collect it. Good day."

She proceeded to the door and let herself out.

Lowell gulped down another drink. The alcohol steadied his hands somewhat but could not drive out the images that crowded about him. When he shut his eyes, he saw the widow as she had appeared in the view-finder: gaping eye-sockets, the skull that lurked beneath her thinning skin. Other images too. Blue eyes, bruises. A palm-print on white skin.

He poured a fourth glass and contemplated the liquid for a time before returning it to the bottle. Already he regretted this return to his old habits. Guilt rose like a tumor in his throat, a gorge he could not spit out or swallow.

He mopped the sweat from his brow. Turning his attention to more material concerns, he replaced the bottle in the side cabinet and went into the darkroom to ready the developer.

*

In the years since his conversion, Lowell had come to see the development process as a kind of miracle. While he was, of course, familiar with the various chemical principles at work, he could not but marvel at the thing itself, which he understood as a singular indicator of God's grace. To watch a human face form on albumen paper, to see it slowly assume shape, its fine lines betraying either hope, or grief, or pain…

Today, he found no such joy in developing the plate. His hands shook with fright, nails kneading the flesh of his palms as the positive image emerged on the albumen. His fears proved baseless. The widow Perkins looked much as she always did. While her pose was slightly different—for here she looked directly into the camera, confusion playing across her features—the photograph closely resembled the three-dozen he had already taken of the widow. In no way did it hint at the horror he had witnessed through the viewfinder.

He made a second print of the

photograph and left the darkroom, feeling neither terror nor relief, but persistent unease. He settled himself down in a chair beside the window and allowed his gaze to stray into the street.

The snow continued. Nearly an inch had accumulated in the last hour, covering over muck and dirtied straw. The clustered roofs and gambrels of the block opposite bore a fine dusting, as iridescent and fine as a poplar's cotton. Even the soot-black stacks of the distant metal-works appeared white and pure, standing like twin ghosts against the horizon, holding back the early dark. Soon the city would be covered, first by snow and then by night—all beauty and squalor erased by the whispered sough of white on black.

*

His sleep proved shallow and troubled, haunted by visions of blazing cities and crumbling churches, the worm-filled skull of the widow Perkins. To his relief, he was roused by the sound of the bell. He wiped the sleep from his eyes and went to answer.

He opened the door to reveal a clerk from the post office. The young man was clearly possessed of a nervous disposition. His eyes darted furtively from side to side and seemed to settle on Lowell only by chance.

"Your wire, sir. It came back."

"I'm sorry?"

"It could not be delivered."

"Has he moved?" wondered Lowell to himself.

"I don't know, sir."

"Then find out! Wire New York and see what you can learn from them. Then try sending the message through again. It's—well, it's important."

"Yes, sir. Of course."

"Good."

The clerk looked down at his own feet.

Lowell sighed, regretting his outburst. "Go on then," he said, as gently as he could manage. "I'll try and drop by later. That should save you the trip."

"Yes, sir. Thank you."

The clerk donned his hat and shuffled from the stoop. Lowell watched him disappear down the alleyway and then looked up, finding the sky in a crack between two buildings. The blizzard had intensified since morning, leaving the heavens snow-filled and sunless, iron-grey but for a varicose network of dark veins and fractures.

He turned from the doorway. A quick consultation of his watch showed the time to be a quarter to three. He pushed shut the door and returned to the studio to ready it for his next appointment. Less than an hour remained before

Arthur Whateley and his young wife, married this past November, were due to arrive.

He unrolled the pastoral background on which they had agreed, arranged two chairs before it, and fell to the task of readying the camera—Patrick's camera. The results of the development process had not entirely put his earlier terror to flight, but they had at least given courage, and he resolved to confront his fears. To this end, he positioned Patrick's camera at the appropriate distance from the canvas and drew a breath before lifting the flaps over his head.

He peered through the viewfinder at the wall of his studio. His palms were slick, his breathing rapid, but no dreadful apparition materialized to confront him. Instead, he saw only the painted trees of a familiar country scene. Their leaves wavered, delicate and still, as though waiting for the first breath of wind, a summer storm sure to come.

*

Arthur Whateley was one of those rare men upon whom Fortune has never ceased to smile. Wealthy, well-groomed, and recently wed, his generosity was matched only by the honeyed warmth of his voice and by the kindness of his demeanor. He was handsome, notably so, but his dusky good looks were more than equaled by the beauty of his wife Gertrude, a noted heiress. She was, like him, dark of hair and eye, but blessed with a delicate complexion, with cheeks that flushed from white to rose and would not tolerate the sun.

Whateley himself was in all respects the consummate gentleman. Lowell had met him for the first time two weeks before when the young tycoon came to the studio to make arrangements for his formal portrait. Lowell had found him as charming and personable as any man he had ever met, well-versed in an array of subjects ranging from architecture to the theater and indeed most topics one could name.

The young man was also exceedingly punctual. At half past three, the bell sounded, and Lowell hurried to the door to admit the happy couple. Arthur grinned broadly and offered his hand. Mrs. Whateley blushed to meet Lowell's gaze and wished him a soft "how do you do." She wore an unusual amount of powder on her cheeks and brow.

"Please," said Lowell. "Do come in. Everything is ready."

"Excellent," Arthur said. "But I'm afraid we cannot stay long. We are expected for dinner in half-an-hour's time."

"I understand," said Lowell. "This will but take a minute." He gestured in the direction of the prepared background. "I believe we agreed on a seated portrait?"

"Indeed we did," said Arthur.

He steered his wife across the room and helped her settle into a chair before taking the seat beside her with one hand thrust into his jacket, the other resting lightly on her knee.

"Ready when you are," said Arthur.

Lowell approached the tripod. "And you, Mrs. Whateley?"

Her husband answered. "Oh, you needn't worry about Gertie," he said, cheerfully. "Isn't that right, darling?"

Mrs. Whateley nodded.

"Shall we proceed?" asked Arthur.

"Of course," said Lowell, nodding. He had already prepared the collodion mixture and adjusted the lens. All that remained was to open the shutter. Taking up the flash box, he slipped his head under the cover and placed his eye against the viewfinder.

The powder vanished from Mrs. Whateley's brow. In its place he noted the swelling of an under-skin bruise. As Lowell watched, horrified, the colors deepened and spread, leaching through flesh and tissue to collect in a series of purple bruises down the woman's neck, creating the imprint of a man's hand around her throat.

Lowell's stomach clenched. The air left his lungs, and he gasped for breath that would not come. She looked up at him then—perhaps only to wonder what was taking so long—and in her eyes he saw a silent suffering, such as he had once glimpsed in the eyes of another, and all at once, he understood everything.

Whateley had come to him seeking concealment. Like many clients, he wanted an image of false happiness, another mask for the violence and cruelty they both strove to hide—he with his airs and false benevolence and she with her daubs and powders. Mrs. Whateley gazed back at Lowell through the viewfinder, her eyes bloodshot, sightless.

He swallowed. "I'm—sorry," he said and withdrew from the hood. He stepped backward from the camera. "But I cannot go through with it."

"Whatever do you mean?" asked Whateley. "Is there some kind of problem with the camera? Surely you must have another you can use instead."

Lowell shook his head. "It isn't that."

"What, then?"

"As I've said, I cannot take the picture. You will have to go elsewhere."

Whateley's expression hardened. "You owe me an explanation."

Lowell looked from the camera to the seated couple.

"Yes," he conceded. "Perhaps you're right."

"Well?"

He pointed to the area above his own right eye and nodded toward Mrs. Whateley.

"It's her makeup, I'm afraid. It's playing havoc with this light. Could we try one without?"

Whateley's face turned crimson. He sprang up from the chair and grabbed hold of his wife's arm. Without a word, he dragged her to her feet and spirited her toward the doorway.

In the entryway, he retrieved his cane and spun on his heel to address Lowell.

"You have wasted my afternoon, sir," he declared coldly. "And you will not see me again. Nor will you see my friends again, either. I will certainly warn them to stay far away from a fraud and a charlatan such as yourself."

He stepped through the doorway, pulling his wife after him. She tripped on the stoop and looked back at Lowell, her expression at once pleading and resigned, as though craving a deliverance she no longer expected. Her despair bit deep, instilling in Lowell a terrible, inescapable guilt.

He ran after them into the alleyway.

Dusk was descending. A heavy snow filled the air.

"You swine!" he shouted after Whateley. "I will tell the world what you are!"

Whateley halted and turned around. He released his grip on his wife's arm and advanced on Lowell with a menacing sneer, brandishing his cane like a common thug.

"Run!" Lowell shouted to Mrs. Whateley. "He will kill you. Don't you see that?"

She did not move but looked on without expression, watching as her husband approached her would-be rescuer. Whateley lifted the cane high above his head and brought it down across his chest, a pendulum descending.

Lowell dodged to his right and managed to evade the blow. The cane impacted the frozen ground with a hollow report. Whateley cursed but did not drop the cane. Seeing an opening, Lowell took the offensive and dashed toward Whateley with fists raised.

The other man was ready for him. He stepped to one side and caught Lowell with his outstretched boot, scooping the legs out from under him. Lowell struck the ground, hard, his weight landing on his elbow. His arm went numb.

Lowell attempted to regain his feet, but the younger man was too quick for him. Whateley kicked him in the side then stomped down on his exposed gut. Lowell screamed. He attempted to crawl away, dragging himself through the snow, but Whateley followed him.

He wielded the cane like a riding crop, delivering a series of blows across Lowell's back and dropping the photographer onto his stomach. Lowell tried to speak — to apologize, perhaps, to plead for mercy — but found he had not the breath for it.

From the corner of his eye, he saw

Whateley raise the cane and take aim at his left
temple. The blow connected with a startling
crack. The world flashed white before him and
the vision in his left eye flickered and dimmed.
A warm trickle poured from the torn scalp,
staining his shirt and collar. He closed his eyes.

Snow settled above his brow and melted.
Cold fluid streamed down his forehead and into
his damaged eye. Patrick's face returned to him
in that moment, surfacing from the crimson
cloud that obscured his vision.

"Forgive me," he murmured. "Please."

Whateley wiped his stick on Lowell's
shirt and spit on him as he would a beggar or
criminal. Then he turned away. His footsteps
retreated, muffled by fresh snow.

"Come," Lowell heard him say. "We
mustn't be late for dinner."

*

Lowell opened his eyes. Night had fallen. Hours
might have passed or mere minutes — he could
not be sure — but the agony he experienced on
waking was indescribable. His chest ached. His
temples pounded, and he had lost the sight in
his left eye. Nauseous, he rotated his head and
threw up into the fresh snow. His vomit was
yellow and dark, the color of old bruises.

He crawled to the nearest wall and
propped himself against it. Slowly he counted

down from five, whispering the words to himself as he did before a picture. When he reached the end, he vaulted himself into a standing position. He wobbled dangerously, nearly fell, but caught himself against the wall. He cast his gaze back in the direction of his studio. The door was open, but he could not bring himself to return there.

Breathing heavily, he hauled himself down the alleyway, emerging into the gas-lit sheen of the street. Only this morning he had walked this same block, but tonight, everything had changed. Providence itself swam in the lens of Patrick's camera. Even the newest buildings bore signs of decay, marked by smoke stains and fallen roofs, brown curls of dying ivy on every wall.

It was late, but the city hummed with activity. An endless stream of carriages banged and clattered past. Lowell stumbled into the path of a police officer, but the man ignored him, turning up his collar to hurry past.

No one took notice of him. He passed among the midnight crowds — anonymous, unseen — cursed by solitude as in the year that Patrick left him. A dogcart flew past him, missing him by less than a yard. He took two steps backward, lost his footing, and tumbled into the gutter.

He lay there for a time, quite collapsed, while men and women passed him by. At one point he spotted the two sisters from the morning and observed that their faces had grown heavy with the accumulation of years, all vestiges of their former beauty spoiled. On a chain between them, they carried a purse that bulged with miserly excess.

Behind them, shackled to the purse by a pair of manacles, walked a young woman of waxy countenance who wore nothing but a cotton shift. Lowell could see that she alone understood his plight, but she only lifted her shackled wrists, as though to indicate her own helplessness, and then shuffled past, dragged on like a dog by the women she served.

Nobody would help him — that much was clear — and he called on reserves of strength he did not know he possessed in order to regain his feet. Once he had steadied himself, he began to walk, continuing down the pavement toward Saint Andrew's. He shivered in his shirt sleeves, occasionally spitting blood into the slush at his feet.

He thought he must be dying.

On the corner, he passed the paper boy. The lad grinned wickedly through his front teeth and shoved the evening circular into his face.

"No," Lowell said. "I don't need it."

"Yessir," the boy drawled. "But ye do *want* it, don't ye?"

Lowell tore the paper from the boy's grasp and threw it into the street. He pressed past him to the church of Saint Andrew's, where he mounted the stone stairs. He took them slowly, his legs weakening with each step. At last he reached the high doors. He rattled the handles but to no effect. Locked fast. Even the Church had closed its doors to him.

In despair he cast his gaze heavenward, seeking out that point in space where the cross-topped spire disappeared into endless snowfall. Then he saw it: the cross had become a crucifix. A living figure writhed in agony on that bronze tree, naked and abandoned with only the dark for comfort. Lowell recognized him at once, even at that great distance.

He fell to his knees, trembling as before the altar. He heard a cry — a boy's voice, he fancied, though he could not make out the words. The world was falling from him, a garment shed. His head tipped back and he tumbled into nothingness.

*

He woke up swathed in snow. His clothes had frozen to his body, and the blood had thickened in his beard. He wiped the snowmelt from his face, relieved to find that he could see through his left eye, and levered himself into a crouch. The pain was excruciating, but perhaps not as intolerable as before.

He was in the alleyway behind his studio.

His nightmare, then, had been a nightmare in truth, a vision brought on by the blow to his skull. It made no difference. He was a man haunted, damned beyond atonement. Years might pass, but nothing could erase from his mind the image of that crucified figure.

He limped back into the studio.

A fire smoldered in the grate and the room was still warm. From this he concluded that his unconsciousness could not have lasted more than an hour. He went to the side cabinet and extracted the brandy bottle. He took three quick slugs before replacing it.

He crossed the room to the corner where the shipping crate lay discarded, left behind in his excitement over Patrick's camera. He turned it upside down. A brown envelope slipped free and drifted to the floor. No name was indicated, but he knew it was meant for him.

Inside was a photograph. Lowell recognized it as one that he himself had taken many years before. In the picture, a young child regarded the camera without smiling. Patrick. The child's features were fair, his nose turned slightly to the right where it had once been broken. His eyes were blue: wide with terror, blank with suffering.

Lowell blinked. His vision blurred. The room swam before him and the blood rushed to his ears. He thrust the photograph into the fire. He watched it light—the child's face blackening, falling through—and then lunged for Patrick's camera.

He toppled the tripod, dashing the instrument onto the floor. He ripped free the hood and shattered the slide loader, punching through the mahogany frame, his knuckles splitting where they connected with brass. He plucked out the lens from the viewfinder and carried it into the darkroom, the glass slipping between his injured fingers. In the darkroom, he held up the lens to the mirror and glimpsed himself in its depths.

What did he hope to see there?

He could not say. Some hidden truth, perhaps—some veiled hope of which he was only half-aware. But his appearance had not altered. In the lens, he saw only the same broken man as in the mirror, a bloodied beast stalked by the same demons, the same ghosts. With a roar of agony, more animal than human, he hurled the lens against the far wall and heard it shatter.

He returned to the studio and shot the deadbolt, the better to escape down the neck of a brandy bottle. And so the night passed. He drank—he did not pray—and the darkness drew near as with the rustle of fabric, a starless hood that stretched to cover the city, to gather all creation in its sweep. At dawn, the wind turned southerly. The snow became a bitter rain that drummed like pebbles on the walls of the studio.

*

He was awakened by the doorbell. It was midday, the sun's glare doubled by slush and snowmelt. He went to the door and cracked it open, withdrawing the chain when he recognized the clerk from the Post Office.

"Yes?" he croaked. "What do you want?"

The clerk started, shocked by the change in Lowell's appearance.

"You didn't stop by, sir. Yesterday. Before we locked up."

"No," he said. "I was—delayed."

"I have this for you," said the clerk. "I am sorry, sir."

The tersely-worded missive contained the news of Patrick's death.

On November 29th, the young photographer had sold off his apartment and settled his debts before returning to the studio. After he failed to emerge, his friends had summoned the officers, who found him in the darkroom, a suicide.

It was later reported that Patrick had boxed up all of his possessions prior to his death: his books, his papers, his prints. Only his camera was found to be missing.

*

Lowell's story ended there. For a time neither of

us spoke. Crickets sang in the nearby underbrush. The moon emerged from a bank of clouds, recasting the landscape from shades of silver. Lowell stubbed out his cigar and disappeared inside.

Five years have passed since our brief meeting, and yet I find his story has not left me. Lowell spoke eloquently of light and darkness — and of the dark that cannot be illumined — and within his tale itself there is another kind of darkness, a history hidden from the light of narrative: shadowed, secret, and thus ineradicable.

I woke the next morning to find that he had gone. He had departed the resort at first light and returned to Providence. I do not know what has become of him. Sometimes I like to think that he has found some measure of peace, whatever the nature of his past sins. In any event, I doubt that I will see him again.

WHISTLER'S GORE

The old churchyard
Two miles north of Plymouth, VT

ANNA BURDEN
Beloved Sister in Christ
Consort to the Revd Abijah Burden
Returned to the Lord
19th Jun 1798
Æ 24 years
Born in Ireland, County Sligo
She came late to the Faith
Being married to the Revd Burden
In her 22nd year of age
And received into the Fellowship of the Saints
Deporting herself with an abundance
Of kindness & womanly virtue
Before falling from the Post Bridge
Into the rapid waters beneath
Wherein she lies drowned
Untimely born and stolen away

Who is this that cometh from Idumea?
(Is 63:1)

PHINEAS OLMSTEAD
First son of the Col. Silas Olmstead
Felled by the Hand of God
Æ 16 years
Mon 30th Jun 1798
Heard to pass an unquiet night
Following upon the Revd's sermon
He journeyed to the far fields
West of the Gore
And did not take warning
When first the thunder
Rolled and clapped on high
And thus caught unawares
Did not return with the other ploughboys
And was not found until daybreak
By J Cuthbert, Smith

Am I born to die?
To lay this body down?
And must my trembling spirit fly
Into a world unknown?

IN MEMORY OF

EDWARD CARTWRIGHT
Taverner
Died
Jul 2nd 1798
Æ 31 years

And though I waken to the dream
And dwell no more upon the Vale
I leave behind the burning skies
The One who yearns to die but fails

PATIENCE CARTWRIGHT
Amiable Consort
Died
Jul 2nd 1798
Æ 23 years

Pray do not mourn the end that comes
But count it gladly, as a grace
For in this death the Spider stirs
To mask with silk the Savior's Face

ALL MUST SUBMIT TO THE KING OF
TERRORS

JOHN CUTHBERT
Blacksmith, Deacon
Honest & upright in all matters
Devoted himself with saintly zeal
To the memory of his wife
And to the welfare of his countrymen
Perished in the flames
Jul 2nd 1798
Æ 27 years

Every knee will bow to me
And all the tongues confess
(Is 45:23)

ASHBEL ALLEN OLMSTEAD
Second son of the Col. Olmstead
Brother to the departed Phineas
An Innocent & Child of God
He apprenticed to John Cuthbert
And died in the fires of July the 2nd
That destroyed the tavern and the smithy
Returning to the ground
Æ 14 years
Reposing there in darkness
Where the silent waters flow

A land of deeper shade
Unpierced by human thought
The dreary regions of the dead
Where all things are forgot

ZERAH CARTWRIGHT
Brother to Edward & Jerusha
Departed this Dark Valley
Upon the 5th of July 1798
Æ 34 years
Having left the church
In the final days of his life
Upon hearing the words of the Revd Burden
And being granted a vision of realms beyond
He submitted himself to the Angel's yoke
And was washed clean in the waters
Wherein he fished by morning
And in which his empty boat was found

For there shall arise false Christs and false prophets
And they shall show great signs and wonders
(Matt 24:24)

BLACKBRIDGE

GIDEON JOSEPH
Capt, Massachusetts 1st Militia
B. Apr 12th 1753
D. _____

JERUSHA MARGARET
Wife & Mother
B. Oct 27th 1770
D. Jul 8th 1798

PATIENCE
B. Jan 1st 1793
D. Jul 7th 1798
Æ 5 years

FAITH
B. Sep 5th 1794
D. Jul 7th 1798
Æ 3 years

(cont'd)

Born unto death
These babes await
The homecoming of their father
Capt. Gideon Blackbridge
A Hero of Bunker Hill
Who vanished into the wood
On the 5th of July
And could not save them
From their mother Jerusha
A midwife
Who christened them with pine pitch
And set the house alight
Before fleeing from the Gore
Found hanged at Adams' Point
8th Jul 1798

Now rest these babes in slumbers deep
The sleep that hath no dreaming
The sea o'er which their father waits
To join them in their weeping

SARAH OLMSTEAD LITTLE

Widow of Asher Little
Sister to Col. Silas Olmstead
Mother of Ephraim
Died the 10th of July 1798
Æ 52 years
Survived by her son
E Little, Stonecutter
These words he chooses
In anticipation of the coming day
When the holy fires dim
And all things cease to be

That day is a day of wrath
A day of trouble and heaviness
A day of destruction and desolation
A day of obscurity and darkness
(Zeph 1:15)

SILAS JAMES OLMSTEAD
Col., Massachusetts 5th
Born November the 12th in the year 1751
He acquitted himself with laudable valor
At the battles of Trenton and Princeton
Attaining for himself the rank of Colonel
Before the age of thirty
His was the first family to settle in Whistler's
Gore
Where he oversaw the erection of a
meetinghouse
And made provision for his fellow Christian
Through the winter of 88-89
A widower of long years
He raised two children from infancy
Only to lose them to lightning and to fire
Within a fortnight of one another
During these latter days
Died of grief
Jul 12th
May darkness show him mercy
Where the Lord has shown him none

Waked by the trumpet's sound
I from my grave shall rise
And see the Judge with Glory Crowned
And greet the Flaming Skies

^{Revd} **ABIJAH BURDEN**
A man of humility and moderation
Of benevolent aspect and amiable temperament
A teacher of the true faith, unsurpassed in
learning
Unerring in his efforts on behalf of the lost
Husband to the late Anna Burden
Who drowned beneath the Post Bridge
And whose body was not recovered
In her death he glimpsed the coming of the
Kingdom
And was moved to preach the Final Gospel
In this his church on the 29th of June
Speaking to no man afterward
And taking neither food nor drink
He succumbed to these privations on
On the 14th of July
Æ 26 years
And thenceforth joined our brothers
In the dark that knows no suffering
Whereunto I soon shall follow
And fall into the grave prepared me
E. Little, Stonecutter

Behold, I come quickly
(Rev 22:12)

From the sermons of the Revd. Abijah Burden.
Dated June 29th 1798.

*Upon that day of wrath they flayed the Son
with savage blows and drove the spikes through his
hands and feet. So, too, was he made to wear a crown
of thorns, and in his despair, he cried out to the
Father, beseeching the Godhead that dwells outside of
time, of Whom Christ was begotten and Who shared
His sufferings; aye, Who bears them still.*

*For though Christ died and rose, the Father
remains, trapped by His eternal nature in the moment
of His Son's uttermost agony. Therein He knows only
anguish and doubt and the terrible isolation of the
dying. So falls to us this awful choice: the elect He
preserves to join Him in the fire, while the damned
He snuffs like candle flames failing.*

*Where you will be, my brothers, when the
Final Trumpet sounds?*

*Where will you go, my sisters, when Death
descends on spider's silk?*

Who is this who comes from Idumea?

THE WAYSIDE VOICES

I. The Traveler

The tavern came out of the mist. Hearth-light
streamed through the shuttered windows,
slicing lines in the dusk. The signboard creaked.
The Wayside, it read. *Inn & Spirits.*

    I cannot say what possessed me to take
the Falmouth toll road. With the death of my
boy, I fell into the dream and could do naught
but walk the path my grief had blazed for me.
That morning, I left his graveside and allowed
my feet to carry me past the station and the
church. In time, I reached the old toll route,
disused since the arrival of the steam engine,
and so passed from one kind of emptiness to
another: the loneliness of fallen roofs, failing
villages.

    In such country I came upon the Wayside.
To either side stretched orchards and barren
farm-fields, the ground left to seed in this year of
war and rainfall. Even the locusts, leafless in
rows along the roadside, seemed half-feral,
imbued with kind of wildness. Their barbed
limbs dipped like hooks toward the roadway.

    I went inside. Smoke filled the barroom,
spreading outward from the fireplace around
which huddled a group of men in battered caps.
Two young soldiers stood at the counter and
jested with the innkeeper, a heavy man attired in

a leather apron. The boys roared with laughter, but the innkeeper's countenance was somber, and he did not join in their mirth.

A small girl lingered near the corner of the room. She was a sly and skulking scrap of a thing, no older than eleven or twelve, her fair hair in braids — the innkeeper's daughter, I presumed, though she looked nothing like him, being thin where he was portly and pallid where he was ruddy-cheeked, his whiskers sodden with crumbs and spittle.

The girl was the first to notice me. She darted a furtive glance behind her and scurried over to meet me in the doorway. She opened her mouth, as though she meant to speak, but the innkeeper caught sight of me then and waved me inside. He pointed to a table by a window. The damp steamed from me, forming puddles underfoot, but he did not seem to mind.

The men by the fireplace paid me no attention. At the bar, the soldiers heard the door and turned round. One of them smiled. In his uniform, he looked very much like my boy, though he could not have known what awaited him in the south, nor did he realize — as I did — that he would never again return to this desolate backwater which even the railroads had chosen to pass by.

I sat down at the table the innkeeper had indicated. *Let me pour you a drink*, he said, coming near, even as his daughter appeared at his shoulder bearing a mug of ale. For some reason this enraged him, though he strove to hide it, his hands twisted like claws in the apron. His daughter placed the drink before me and did not remain long enough for me to catch her eye or to ask what she had intended to tell me.

The wind moaned in the chimney.

Tree-limbs scraped and rattled at the shutters.

The innkeeper returned with a bowl of foul-smelling broth. Fish bones floated near the surface, and I caught the scent of something queer, a pungent aroma like barley gone to wild. The soup looked scarcely edible, and I lowered my spoon without tasting it. At this the innkeeper merely smiled — a little sadly, I thought — and did not trouble me further.

The soldiers excused themselves and made for the door. By the hearth, the men coughed and cursed the damp. I looked to the counter, but the innkeeper had vanished — then came the sound of heavy footsteps overhead, the shriek of a door thrown wide.

A young girl's scream. The sick slap of leather on flesh.

The others paid it no mind.

After some minutes, the innkeeper resumed his place behind the counter. As before, he looked grave and joyless, his eyes focused on nothing as he readjusted his belt.

The men greeted his arrival with a chorus

of slapped thighs and rattled cups. They whistled and stomped the floor and did not let up until the innkeeper brought out another tray of drinks. These new cups frothed and sloshed as he handed them out, retaining a single mug, which he placed upon the table in front of me.

For you, he said. *It will help.*

Help?

For the journey. We are late into autumn yet. Soon there will be a snow. His nostrils flared, ingrown with coarse hairs. *By God I swear it won't be long.*

There was no clock in the tavern, but an hour or more must have elapsed before the remaining patrons pulled down their caps and staggered to the door. They said nothing to me as they passed, ignoring me as they had done all evening, so that I half thought myself invisible, a living man among ghosts.

Once they were gone, the innkeeper circled the counter and banked high the fire, flooding the room with wood-smoke. My vision blurred, and I mopped at my face with the back of my hand. The innkeeper said, *You haven't touched a drop.*

His tone was gentle.

No.

You must be thirsty, he said, half-pleading.

No.

His face folded in upon itself. His lower lip thrust forward to suckle his moustache, and his expression softened noticeably, allowing me a glimpse of something inward, a queer and startling stillness. He shrugged and disappeared into the smoke.

I glanced down at the tabletop. The wood-grain was marred by scratches and scorch-marks, stains that could have been blood. From upstairs came a stifled sob, a wail of anguish.

Briefly, I was aware of movement behind me. The scrape of a boot on the floorboards. The whistle of air about my ears. And then the cold came over me, extinguishing all light, all memory, so that I found myself outside.

Again it was nightfall. The locusts rattled like surgeons' tools, like the bone-saw that had taken my boy's legs and stolen him away, binding us to the same dream, the same nothingness. I turned and found waiting the dark and the damp and the faint lights of the Wayside.

II. The Butchering Yard

There were so many. Men and women. Children with hair like lamb's fleece and skin like new-fallen snow. It was never easy. My every instinct rebelled against it, but it was necessary: a kindness, a mercy. For the God of Abraham breathes the life into His children and thenceforth casts them to the wilds, wherein they find no refuge, none save that which I offered them—a Love given freely to all who came, unloved, to the Wayside.

The end found them like a creeping mist, enveloping them where they sat or stood or lay. Many fought against it. Others begged for mercy, for time. Some prayed, it is true, but their despair was evident, even then, and I saw the marks His goad had left upon them, their flesh wrinkled and cracked like harrowed earth or the scars upon Old Abel's hands.

He was the first. I was a young man then and newly arrived in Falmouth. The town thrived in those days, the railroads some years away. With my inheritance I built up this tavern on the edge of Abel's Wood, as it was called, for it was the exclusive domain of an elderly recluse known only by his Christian name.

"Old Abel," the townsfolk called him, or "Queer Abel," as he was notoriously taciturn and liable to shun all company. Strangest to me was the manner in which he kept his hands and forearms hidden, whether by gloves in the cold season or bandages in summer.

Oftentimes he wandered in to the Wayside and stayed until I turned him out. Always he sat at the counter and drank in silence, unspeaking save to murmur his thanks after every drink. At midnight, I showed him to the door and there lingered a spell to watch him stumble home, singing to himself as he walked, songs without words or melody.

Around this time the Bennington coach was stranded here on account of the weather. It was a miserable night. The snows lay deep upon on the ground and hid the moon and the stars.

By rights, the tavern should have been empty, and Abel came in as he often did. He was wind-burned and wild-eyed, the snowmelt dribbling from his beard. He meant to stay a while, or so I thought, but he left without explanation upon seeing the Bennington coachman.

Later this same coachman approached the counter and inquired after the old recluse. As it transpired, he recognized Abel from long ago. He had grown up in a village some miles to the south, where Abel had kept a flock of two dozen ewes, who grazed and slept on the common within view of Abel's cottage: a square, thatch-roofed affair, wherein he resided with his wife.

His wife? I said, surprised.

Aye, said the coachman. *And he made of himself a devoted husband, loving the poor girl for ten year or more, though she bore him no children.*

What happened?

She died. There was a fire at the cottage, and the roof kindled and fell, catching his wife's clothes alight. Abel could not save her, though he nearly burned off his hands trying. The girl was pale and smallish and always in ill health. The smoke killed her.

After the fire, Abel dwelt a fortnight

amidst the ashes of his cottage. He made no effort to rebuild, nor to feed his flock, and it was only upon the fifteenth day that he roused himself from torpor. Thereupon he gathered his flock and led them across town to the butchering yard.

It was a kindness on his part, the coachman said. *For the life had gone out of him. Winter was nigh, and they would only have starved.*

Yes, I said. *I suppose so.*

The coach left late upon the following afternoon, departing for Bennington as soon as the road had been broken out. The horses were uneasy, frightened of the drifts, but the men were in high spirits. Seated within the coach, they smoked and laughed and played at cards, while the two women present—sisters—sat off to the side.

The younger sister eyed the men flirtatiously. She giggled behind her woolen gloves while the elder pressed her face to the window, as though to watch the countryside recede, a world stained and soiled by the snow. In that moment, I thought of Abel's flock—and of the butchering yard—and realized with the certainty of revelation what was required of me.

The deed was swiftly done. Abel was drunk, half-decrepit, and my hand was sure.

His absence went unremarked upon, as did the fate of various foreigners and deserters during the years of war. The other townsfolk must have known, or suspected, but said nothing. Even the minister made no move to intervene, crippled by doubt as he was, so that the work of rescue fell to me alone. This burden was heavy, yes, but it did not find me wanting, save on the lone occasion on which my resolve failed me.

The girl came in the night. I was nearly asleep when I heard her knock upon the door, her piteous cries for admittance. I opened the door to her. She was fat with child and woefully underdressed, wearing nothing but a threadbare shift.

Please, she said. *It is my husband. He will kill me.*

What choice did I have? I showed her inside and poured her a drink. Her husband, she said, had married her for money, having scant interest in the joys of the flesh and no desire for children. When she fell pregnant, he flew into a rage and sought to kill the babe inside her, beating her with a strap when the household was asleep. Somehow she had carried the child to term but now the labor was close upon her and she knew not where to turn.

He will send the child away, she said. *As soon as it is born.*

That night the pains came upon her, a punishing flood. I lit the oil lamps in the upper room and built up the fire in the hearth but could not drive out the cold.

A midwife, she mumbled. *A woman. The babe* —

There is no time.

No time, she said.

Drink, I said, proffering the bottle. *You must drink.*

She resisted at first. But when the pains worsened—and her voice grew hoarse from screaming—she grabbed for the bottle and took it about the lips and sucked from it greedily until she could drink no more. Then her eyes rolled back inside her skull and she slumped against the bedding, insensible with pain and exhaustion and the beginnings of drunkenness.

No time, she repeated, and the shadows moved over her face.

The child was born in the hour before dawn, a girl. Afterward the mother lay sprawled amidst the bedding, prostrate, with eyes like shuttered windows.

Gray light streamed into the room, and I clutched the babe to my chest, cradling her with my left hand, for my right still held the dripping maul. The blood made a sound like rain upon the boards as the little thing screamed and screamed.

I could not silence her. I could not offer her even this small mercy. By my weakness, I consigned her to the tortures of life, this dreamlike existence in the teeth of a raging God—and though she would twice betray me, she proved her Love in the end.

Sometimes I think I sense her presence—close to me now, though time and more divides us. I speak her name, the name I gave her. She does not answer me, of course—and cannot—though it will not be long before the Last Day breaks upon me, and upon us all, a creeping mist.

III. *Alive, Alive, Oh!*

Go to the Wayside, the men said, when they learned I was a virgin. *Out past Falmouth. You'll find a woman there, one you can buy. If you're lucky.* The weeks passed. I worked myself into exhaustion, manning the lathes until midnight or later, but it scarcely mattered: I was sixteen and the lust rode hard upon me, haunting my dreams, keeping me from sleep.

When payday came, I collected my wages and sneaked from the sawmill, taking the road where it plunged toward Falmouth. The village was empty, shutters drawn against the dusk. A freight train whistled in the distance, answered in turn by the call of a nightingale. Her song rose up from the brush, but I did not stop to listen.

I walked for the better part of an hour, traveling three miles or more along that narrow road. Brambles grew up from the roadside, flowering where they burst from hedgerows and weed-beds, stonewalls that had marked the boundaries of fields and orchards.

And then I was upon it. Twenty yards away, the Wayside sprouted from a row of swaying locust trees, discernible where it reared above the snarl of limb and leaf. Drawing near, I heard the rattle of cups, the roar of drunken men. A woman singing. *Alive, alive, oh!*

The door was ajar. Inside, the woman stood near the center of the barroom and sang, surrounded by low tables at which were seated a dozen men. She wore a dress the color of old wine with a scarf cut from yellow silk, which covered her hair like a gypsy's. Her age might have been forty, or older, and her painted lips cracked where the hearth-light fell upon them.

She finished her song. The men slapped the tables and shouted for another. I looked around me, but there were no other women present — none save the barmaid, a sullen girl of much my own age with hair like dry straw. She scuttled past me, saying nothing, and the gypsy woman launched into another ballad.

This new song was familiar to me. I recognized the story, though I had heard it sung with a different melody. In the ballad, a woman murders her two babies. Later in life, while walking in the woods, she is confronted by their spirits, who drag her down to hell. It was a long story, and tragic, and I knew it would be some time before I could approach her.

I went up to the counter and motioned to

the innkeeper. *A drink*, I said.

He regarded me curiously. His long
tongue, pointed like a cat's, swept back and forth
across his thin moustache. His cheeks were
sunken—his teeth gleamed, faintly luminous—
and he bore an atmosphere of sorrow about him
unrelated to the gypsy-woman's song.

He poured my drink. I took it from him
and crossed the room and settled myself on an
empty bench to watch the woman finish the
ballad. She had reached the final verses, when
the babes confront their mother and describe the
fate that God has prepared her.

Seven years a warning bell.
Seven years in the deeps of hell.

I drained my cup and did not notice when
the barmaid returned to top it off, as I was much
too absorbed in the scene laid before me. Those
faceless watchers in the fire's shadow. The light
on the woman's face as she sang in a childish
voice: at once innocent and alluringly despoiled,
garbed in crimson so that I knew I had to have
her.

The song was over. She turned away,
heedless of the hoots and jeers that followed
after her and disappeared beyond the firelight. I
leapt to my feet in pursuit and pushed my way
across the tavern until I cornered her in a narrow
staircase.

What do you want? she demanded,
spinning around. Her accent was rough, her

speech that of the western hills. *Why are you following me?*

My tongue went limp against my teeth. I fumbled at my pocket and produced a crumpled wad of dollar bills. *For the room,* I mumbled. *For the night.*

She looked down at the money and down at me. She inclined her head, tilted slightly to one side, and shook it slowly, her features downcast, the glimmerings of pity showing through.

Goodnight, she said, politely but firmly, and began to climb.

I lunged forward. *No,* I said, grabbing for her hand. *Please, they said —*

She slapped me. Her nails sliced through my cheek, drawing blood where they raked across my nose and mouth. Too late I attempted to throw up my hand in defense and almost lost my balance. The singer disappeared up the stairs, leaving me to collapse with my face in my hands, the tears stinging in my eyes.

But I wasn't alone. I uncovered my face and found her lurking nearby. The barmaid. She had seen it all, I was sure. She must have followed me from the barroom. I expected ridicule, a snort of laughter, but instead I glimpsed a hunger in her — a delirious thirst, as of some need unfulfilled — and she touched my shoulder and kissed my cheek and showed me upstairs to her room.

Here memory fails me. The rest of that night exists in fragments, glittering like the pieces of a broken mirror beyond which the world yawns blackly, blackening.

The dank heat inside her bedroom. The sensation of her tongue against mine. The taste of yellowed teeth, rotted gums. The salt of sweat upon her skin.

When it was over, we lay tangled together amidst the filthy bedding. She curled up against my armpit and fastened her arms around me.

Downstairs, the tavern was quiet. The hour was late — the others departed or retired — and in that hush, the girl said things to me, foolish things. *I saw it*, she said. *Your money. Marry me now and we'll go away together. We'll leave this place behind us.*

I could stand it no longer. I lurched to my feet and pulled on my shirt and trousers, ignoring her cries, conscious of nothing save my own sinfulness, the guilt that turned and kicked inside my chest. My hands shook. I buttoned my shirt and slipped away down the hall.

There was the landing. The sconces had been extinguished, but the moon shone brightly through the shutters, and I hurried down the narrow stair, desperate to be away from that place and out among the night. The window vanished. A shadow passed across it, swift and silent as a bird's wing, and I saw the gleam of bared teeth, the sparkle of bloodied metal —

IV. The Innkeeper's Daughter

I was seven, I remember, when first I heard the screams come down the hallway. Roused from sleep, I tiptoed to the door and cracked it open in time to watch a woman sprint past, weeping, leaving dark handprints down the length of the corridor.

My father pursued her, loping despite his girth, a cleaver in one hand. The woman reached the stairs, and hesitated, though my father did not. He barreled into her, sending her crashing down the wooden steps before descending after her with the cleaver raised.

Her screams ceased. I stood in the doorway, trembling.

Later, I tried to run. While my father was in the cellar, I donned my cloak and lowered myself from the bedroom window. The roof-line sloped beneath me, slanting to a low eave from which I dangled and dropped. Terrified, I fled north along the old road, passing flooded farm-fields, empty houses.

I was careful. Nonetheless I must have strayed — or so I thought — for I came upon the tavern once more. Morning had dawned, gray and lightless, and my father shouted my name from an upper window. I attempted to flee again that afternoon and again upon the following night, but it was all to no use, as every path returned me to the Wayside.

Then the traveler came. He was familiar to me, somehow, and in my childishness, I thought I could save him. I brought him a cup, hoping that he might take his ease and then depart, but by then, he was already ensnared. Drugged or not, my father meant to have him, and the punishment he administered to me that night was swift and severe.

If only I weren't alone, I thought, as I lay awake afterward. If only there were another beside me. For the Wayside thrived on the shame of the lonely, the sorrows of the damned. My loneliness was that of the traveler, just as his grief was my grief, and I kicked and thrashed in the trap that had been set for me.

At seventeen, I saw my chance for release and seized it, though the lad wanted nothing to do with me. Afterward, my father came into the bedroom. His rage was bottomless, terrifying, his apron dark with blood. He had exchanged the cleaver for the strap and fell upon me with the same cruelty he had shown to the others — but never before to me — thrashing me with his belt until my ears rang, and the world faded, and I lapsed into nothingness.

I heard them. An old man, his voice like worn glass. Two young girls, twins. A father stricken with grief. The slurred and mumbled speech of a madwoman. The last voice I heard belonged to the ballad singer, dead no more than hour. Her song hissed and gurgled through the slash in her throat. *Alive, alive, oh!*

When I woke, my bed was ruined, the sheets stained and soiled. The voices had faded, but my burden was lighter, for I now understood the nature of my isolation. This was why I could not leave the Wayside, its voices: even in life, I was no different from them.

That summer was dry. One morning, out cutting kindling, I ventured beyond the far stone wall and looked back at the tavern. The sun had climbed above the wild wood, illuminating the locust trees, the shuttered windows of the Wayside.

Smoke rose from the brick chimney like the last breaths of the dying. Months of drought had left the countryside as barren as its ghosts: the voices that haunted me in the night, the life that had taken root inside my belly.

A breeze parted the dry grass. The locusts blanched and crackled, shedding flakes of bark. *Good for nothing but firewood*, my father had said — and the same was true of the Wayside itself with its beds and linens and the spirits kept behind the counter. It would go up in minutes, I knew, given the right kind of spark.

Summer dwindled and still no rain. I made a dress from my bed-sheets and used it to cover my stomach. He would find out soon, I knew, but I bided my time before acting, siphoning rum from the bottles in the barroom.

And if my father realized the bottles were getting low, he said nothing of it, nor did he find the bottles stashed behind the headboard in my room.

The sawmill closed. Money was scarce, the travelers few. By night my father paced the length of his bedroom, pathetic in his despair, bewailing his lost purpose, the God whom he hated and against whom he raged in these late watches, though the darkness heard him not.

There was no one listening—no one but me. That night, I waited outside his door until I heard him fall to sleep. Then I padded downstairs to the kitchen and retrieved a knife from the block. I donned wool socks to muffle my tread and shuffled toward his bedside with exacting—excruciating—slowness. The floorboards groaned beneath me, warped in the years since he built this tavern, but he did not wake, not even when I paused and stood looming over him in the dark.

My hands were sweaty. I shifted my grip on the knife's handle and placed the tip against his throat. He murmured in his sleep. *So many,* he said. With one thrust, I drove in the knife and plunged it through a second time as he came awake sputtering. He burbled, choked, and dropped away into emptiness. I lowered my ear to his breast but heard nothing.

I retrieved the bottles from my bedroom and returned to douse the bed. Then I went for the lantern and cast its light upon a scene of horror. Dark stains on my hands and dress. The stench of alcohol and urine. His eyes glittered, dull within that dim light. The mangled throat yawned, slick and shining. He smiled.

I threw the lantern. It shattered, spilling paraffin down the bedclothes. The corpse ignited with a whoosh of air, the smiling face blackening, melting away.

The fire licked up the walls and crept along the floorboards. I turned and dashed down the hallway to the stairs. From behind me came a deafening crash, the roar of flames. I hurled myself into the night, sprinting with my dress held tight about me, the ends flapping like sails as the fire churned and belched and shook free the roof-slates, driving a column of smoke high into the air, where it would be visible for miles: a beacon, a warning bell.

Rain sheeted down. I pushed myself forward despite my exhaustion, heedless of the damp in my hair, the mud that spattered my dress, forcing myself to go on though I could not feel the child inside me. The downpour was cold, verging on freezing, and I passed a long night amidst the darkness and the sleet and the snow that fell in the hours before daybreak.

Dawn found the land well blanketed. Too weary to stand, I stumbled and crawled until I heard the snowfall cease and felt the warmth of the sun on my back.

There was the Wayside. Its savaged hulk was dusted with snow and wreathed in rising steam. The timbers were blackened, burned out, but the southern wall stood with the light in its empty windows, a whitish glow. The doorframe survived though the door had fallen and the building exuded a living silence like the hush that follows a storm.

I was alone. I could not hear them: their voices, mine.

I could not hear anything at all.

V. The Listener

His flashlight passes over broken walls and foundations, bending back upon itself where it strikes the bare snags beyond. Locust trees: bald and peeling, shining like white lines. He lowers the light and sweeps its beam across the cellar hole in front of him.

The ground has subsided from the northwest corner of the building. The stones have buckled and collapsed, spilling over into the cellar, but the brick chimney remains intact, a broken pillar. Dead leaves fill the whole of the structure, or what remains of it, and the darkness stirs within, immutable, alive with the whispers of night and stillness: present here in this late hour, in the glint of glass or bone amidst the rubble.

He turns and strikes back toward the

hiking trail, following the former toll route where it climbs toward the western mountains. After fifty yards he reaches his campsite. He unzips the tent and crawls inside, securing the flaps behind him.

He pulls the sleeping bag to his chest and lies with the flashlight against his collarbone, the beam tilted up. He hears crickets, the call of an owl, and imagines his shadow on the tent-wall behind him. It swims in place, flickering with every breath, every wind.

The wind in the locusts. The rattle of breath in the old chimney.

He switches off the light.

JOHN BLAKE

In the village of Eastbourne in New York there lived a lad of seventeen, a farrier's boy named John Blake.

His late father Edward was a printer by trade, a Patriot known for broadsheets in which he wrote of mankind's Natural Liberty and the tyranny of kings. He advocated protest, then warfare, and later he led the group that tarred and feathered a Royalist on Eastbourne Common. When fighting broke out, he shuttered his press to take up a musket and died at Long Island in August of '76.

In the autumn, Eastbourne's Loyalists raised a militia company and marched through town to the beating of drums, inciting reprisals against the town's Patriots. A mob assaulted Edward Blake's print-shop. They broke up the press and set fire to the building that housed it. Edward's widow Anne was said to have stood and watched from the cottage opposite, singing hymns over the roaring flames even as the child turned and kicked inside of her.

The boy John was born in October. He was a thoughtful child, halting of speech and given to long silences. In these characteristics, at least, he resembled his mother, who was thin and sickly and famously devout, a fanatical Calvinist who had suffered from convulsions since girlhood. She married late on account of this infirmity and soon came to worship the man she had wed. With Edward's death, she retreated into the low cottage wherein she raised the child on her own, safeguarding John against the world with all the jealousy of a god.

By the age of sixteen, John was already an imposing lad, well over six feet in height. Naturally, the town's farrier took notice. He approached Anne Blake and begged her leave to train the boy as his apprentice. To his surprise, she agreed. "John is a child no longer," she said. "He must learn to make his way." Perhaps she knew that she was dying.

So John was taught to smith and shoe and tend the furnaces, though he was melancholic by nature and showed little temperament for the farrier's trade. In the evenings, walking home, he would pause beside the stage road and watch the horses thunder past. Oftentimes he did not return to the cottage 'til after nightfall when he heard his mother calling.

In the spring of '94, Anne Blake passed through her final illness and was interred beneath the churchyard. The funeral proved well-attended, with some coming from as far away as Boston. For the most part, these were relatives of his mother, to whom she had written in her last days, but there were others there as well, with names and faces John did not recognize.

Among this latter group was the young

Margaret Carrier, his cousin's cousin, who lived with her father in a plantation across the river. She was pale and slender, as had been his mother, and likewise possessed the delicacy and grace of a frost-rimed blossom — and when they walked together, after the burial, she stopped and took his hand in hers and held it at her breast. In that moment, he heard the blood inside her, fluttering at his fingertips like the wings of a hummingbird. They did not speak, and John's shyness was such that he could not look at her, and several minutes passed before he realized she was weeping.

At home that evening, he opened his mother's jewelry box and took the ring from inside. With this ring, Edward Blake had won his mother's hand. The band was silver and finely-wrought, with an inset ruby that shimmered and slowed the light, opening depths in the stone. Tonight, in that whirling redness, John saw Margaret standing with her back to him, one hand outstretched and the ring upon her finger. She was fat with child, his child, and he watched as she turned to face him.

Sunday came, a day without work. He woke at dawn while the village slept and filled a sack with bread and cheese. He looped a cord through the ring and placed it round his neck, the band being too small for him to wear. He tucked the ruby inside his shirt and paused in the doorway, his head swimming with thoughts of his beloved: her dark eyes and sorrow, her heart's blood beating against his palm. He slipped from the house.

It was a distance of nearly three miles to the river, beyond which lay the Carrier plantation. The morning was cold. Trees rattled and shook with the wind streaming through, sifting down drifts of shriveled buds and leaves. The ford was running high with snowmelt, but he followed the river northward to the narrows, where a great tree had fallen, and there made his way across with shuffling, sidelong steps.

After another mile, he stopped to eat his breakfast. By then the morning frost had melted, though clouds remained to hide the sun. In the shelter of a hemlock grove, he seated himself on an uprooted trunk and wrapped his greatcoat round him. He listened for the songs of birds, the lowing of cattle, but heard only the wind, which was dry and constant and broke about his ears like the gnashing of teeth.

He did not hear the man approach. He would not have see him either but for his shadow, which stretched over the damp ground and covered John where he sat—and this despite the prevailing grayness, the absence of sun or other shadows.

John leapt up, startled. He spun round to confront his visitor.

The man was of normal height and build but plainly of great wealth. His breeches were silk and leafed with gold while over his shirt he wore a coat of rich blue wool. His face was hidden by his cloak, which was of a similarly fine fabric and dyed a pale and febrile shade of yellow. His boots gleamed.

The man spoke. "I trust you have not waited here long?"

His voice was refined in accent, possessed of a low timbre as smooth as the silks he wore.

"Forgive me, sir," said John, "but I fear you have mistaken me. I have not waited here for you—or for anyone. And I am certain we have not met before."

The other man was quiet. John imagined his eyes darting back and forth beneath the hood: assessing, probing.

"Perhaps not," the man conceded. "But I know you, John Blake."

He swept toward John with a single, fluid motion akin to the shimmer of light in water. John stepped back, stumbled, and dropped to his knees, even as the gloved hand came near him. The long fingers closed about the silver ring where it lay exposed upon John's breast. Evidently, it had slipped free of his shirt while he crossed the river.

For a time the man held the ring with exquisite delicacy, turning it back and forth as to catch the gray light through the hemlocks. Then he released it. The ring swung toward John upon its tether and thudded against his breastbone, striking once then twice, like the rapping of a visitor who stands upon the threshold and waits to be admitted.

"Yes," the man said. "I see that I am not mistaken."

John scuttled backward on his palms until he reached the fallen trunk. His pulse raced. He fumbled at his greatcoat and grasped hold of his knife, cutting himself as he did so. He gasped, felt the warm fluid spill from the wound.

"That ring," said John. "It belonged to my mother."

"So it did," the man replied. "But first it belonged to me."

John pulled the knife from his coat. The blade quivered in his hands and dripped to stain his shirt and breeches.

The other man spoke, softly. "You have done yourself some injury."

The blade shook wildly. The handle was slick, slipping.

"Who are you?" John demanded. "Your face. Why do you hide it from me?"

"I hide nothing. This cloak I wear for your sake rather than for mine."

And here he pushed back the hood, revealing the ashen remnants of a face. The lips were swollen, fat with weeping sores. The hair was thin, wispy, while the nose had caved in upon itself, exposing the sinuses where the flesh had flaked and rotted. He smiled. The lips curled up, causing the sores to burst at the corners of his mouth. Clear fluid dribbled down his chin, which he then licked away, the tongue long and red and snapping.

The knife dropped from John's hands. It landed, soundlessly, in the grass.

The man said, "You see me now, as I am, and still you do not recognize me. Am I truly so transformed?"

"Who are you?" John repeated. "Tell me your name."

"It is curious to me," he said, "that you do not know it already. For I was once accounted a hero in these parts, known in Kingston and beyond as a champion of Liberty. The King's Men spoke my name only with the utmost trembling, as did the redcoats themselves when in time we met upon the field of battle. Edward Blake. Some men took flight at the very sound."

"Edward Blake is dead. He was killed at Long Island."

"I was shot, it is true, but I was not killed of it, whatever I may have pretended. All my life, you see, I had meditated on freedom — my own and that of our new nation — but it was only there upon that smoky plain and with the fields of human wreckage strewn about me that I understood the true nature of Liberty — and the price that was commanded of me. When night fell, I stripped off my uniform and searching the field by moonlight stole the name and papers from a corpse. When New York fell to the King's armies, I sneaked into the City and with my stolen papers enlisted to fight alongside the Royalists."

"You were a traitor," John said. "You betrayed your own cause."

"I did no such thing. Always I served the cause of freedom, of Natural Liberty. I marched with Burgoyne from Quebec and served with St Leger at Fort Stanwix. Afterward, when the Indians deserted us, I chose to go with them. I lived a year among the Mohawk, and by God, it was good to run with such savages, hunting with them all through the heart of that wooded country. But for all their wildness, they weren't free — not truly. The Indians could not understand it, my betrayal, and would have wept like girls, I reckon, to see their scalps laid out like that on General Sullivan's table."

"So you betrayed them too."

"I changed only my name — that was all — and traded my red coat for blue. As a Patriot, I rode with Sullivan through the Indian Country in the summer of '79. I shot down braves and scalped them living and watched the crops and villages burn. I had my pick of the squaws, my choice of the boys for killing. I was free. And in this my Liberty, I slipped away once more and made my way to the southern colonies."

John could listen no longer. He placed his head into his hands and covered his eyes. He breathed through the blood on his fingers with the wind in his hair and his father's unnatural shadow in the trammeled grass, spanning the grayness that divided them.

"My mother," he said, hissing the words through his cupped hands. "She was devoted to you. She grieved for you. Why couldn't you write? Could you not tell her that you lived?"

"Your mother was devoted, yes," the other man said, "but hers was the devotion of a slave to his master. Doubtless she thought herself free, but she was chained to her God sure as any negro to his plow. Each night, as I recall, she would pray that He might end her suffering and always her God did nothing. But there was one prayer, at least, that He saw fit to answer. He gave her a boy, a child to suckle at her breast—but even this was intended for a chain."

"He gave her Salvation," John said, fiercely. "Life Everlasting."

John un-cupped his hands and forced himself to gaze upon that ruined face, the eyes like little lights enmeshed in folds of colorless skin.

"Life Everlasting," repeated his father. "Yes. That will indeed be her punishment: an eternity shackled and bound and serving on her knees. The Creator means for us to win our Liberty, each man for himself, just as we birthed this country from the blood of its old nations. There was King Philip then the Iroquois,

Parliament and the Crown. Liberty is ours, boy, or at least it can be. You must not forget that Lucifer, too, fought for his freedom — and that all of hell was his reward."

"That is the vilest blasphemy."

"It is the surest sense."

"You are mad. Diseased in mind and body."

"Diseased, yes. This affliction — it has rotted me, innards and loins alike, but I am ashamed of nothing. All goods carry a price, they say — and Liberty the priciest of all. I believe your mother sensed as much, though she was, of course, a simple woman. Lacking imagination, she yearned for death's dominion where she could see no greater freedom."

John stood, furious, and crushed his hands into fists. His nails settled in the long knife-wound, pain shooting through him. "Is this why you have come here?" he spat. "To scoff at her, your own wife? To jeer and mock her — and she not three days in the grave?"

"You think too little of me," his father said. The tongue darted out and licked again at his sores, lapping the liquid from his mouth and chin. "I am not a monster."

"Why have you returned to Eastbourne?"

"You cannot guess? Your mother is dead, and now you think to marry. I am Edward Blake, your father, and newly made a widower. Why should I not have the same fancy?"

John trembled. He shook with the rage that kindled in his nerves and spurred him to move. He walked forward, as does a man in a dream, approaching his father where he stood. He halted while yet within his shadow.

"That is why you have returned," he said. "Because you wish to marry."

His father's expression did not alter. "Perhaps."

"And who will have you? You are a traitor, a murderer. Worse."

"I believe that you know her," he replied, speaking with the utmost gentleness. Flecks of yellow spittle stood upon his lips. "Indeed I am certain of it. The maid is a cousin of yours— though you are but recently acquainted."

"You are lying."

"Not at all. I speak the baldest truth. She is promised to me, your beloved. Did you not think to wonder why she wept?"

"Her father, he would not—"

John's father became angry. His smile pressed itself into a sneer, and the saliva flew from his lips as he spoke. "Have you understood nothing, boy? All men are born slaves—to their bodies, their beliefs. It is no small effort to break free of such strictures, but all must make the attempt. With his daughter's marriage, Mr Carrier will be a wealthy man—fabulously wealthy, I have seen to it—and he will be at last unburdened, with no one left to love him. Surely there can be no greater freedom than that. Of what account to him then are her feelings? Of what possible profit to him, the ring with which you thought to woo her?"

John glanced down. His gaze strayed, unbidden, to the ring upon its cord, the stone reflecting nothing where the shadow lay upon it. In this light the ruby appeared lifeless, inert, betraying neither form nor depth. It was a trinket without value, a symbol of all that had bound him to his life. A hatred as red as the gemstone at its center. A love as cheap as the cord from which it hung. He tore the ring from his neck and threw it down at his father's feet.

"You are a devil," he whispered. "Corruption made flesh."

His father stooped and retrieved the ring. He held it before him with the band resting in his open palm. When he spoke again, it was without anger or any discernible emotion.

"Yes," he agreed, "I have been cruel. But you have learned this lesson, John—and you have learned it well. I trust you will not forget it."

John said nothing.

"And remember this, too: it was your saint of a mother who birthed you. I never wanted it, never wished for children. A body makes for a heavy chain, outweighed only by the soul. Some may carry it, perhaps, though all but the Elect must fall beneath its weight. This was one lesson your mother never learned. Now you are here while she is in the dirt."

His father stepped forward. He looped the ring around John's neck.

"What am I to do?" asked John. His voice was thin and cracked, notes from a broken reed.

"Forget the maiden," his father said. "Return to your mother's house."

"And then?"

His father held up his hands, the palms outward.

"Do what you will," he said and raised his hood to hide his face once more. "As for me, I mean to marry. Mr Carrier is eager to celebrate his good fortune. There will be ale and rum and the finest of French wines. And dancing. Boy, I promise that you have never seen such dancing. Then the bridal chamber, the wedding bed — I will teach her something of her chains."

He exhaled, heavily. The breath steamed from his hood.

"Farewell," he said, and departed, his shadow following.

The wind rustled amidst the hemlocks, and John was alone.

Sunlight intruded through the branches. Once more the ruby sparked and glittered, swimming with faces. Therein John spied Margaret Carrier, her hair gray, her complexion blighted, the fever-marks showing about her mouth and nose. His own father: the ashen flesh rippled with the breath through his exposed sinuses. Last of all he saw his mother, as she had appeared in the autumn of '76, when she was great with child — and imagined the clamor of distant drums, the crackle of flames from the his father's shop.

His fist closed round the ring. Holding it fast, he retraced his steps across the river and made his way toward Eastbourne while the sun rose to breach the cloud-line and the whole of the dew-wet world caught fire, blazing white then red like the glow inside a ruby.

Later that afternoon, around dusk, the residents of Eastbourne bore witness to a sad and curious spectacle. Young John Blake, the farrier's boy, had built up a blaze in the street before his late mother's house. Onto this he had laid her possessions: her gowns, shawls, and bonnets, those few books of sermons she had cherished above all. Now the boy struggled through the doorway with a mattress draped about his shoulders. It was clear what he intended, but he was a big lad, and strong, and the villagers did not interfere.

With a groan, John heaved the bed over his shoulder and onto the pyre. The stuffing inside was dry, tindery. It caught fire immediately, burning holes through the cover and whirling up, glowering, as the wind drove hard from the south — and all while John Blake stood before the fire, stone-faced, with his left hand balled and quivering, his right hand red with his own blood.

The blaze smoldered, went out. The villagers had seen enough: they retired to their houses to await the fall of evening. Only the farrier remained. He offered the lad a place to sleep, knowing he had no bed to call his own. John did not speak, but only nodded, and the farrier settled him on a pallet of straw and covered him with quilts against the chill. He waited 'til he knew the boy slept, then took up his lantern and hastened to join the others on the common—for tonight there was a feast across the river, and he did not wish to be late.

THE FALLING DARK

Virgil Lodge: sleepless, pacing, thirty-one.

His eyes are dry and painful, but he will not rest. Prone to night terrors, he avoids his dreams as carefully as he avoids his neighbors, their faces—all but that of the factory girl Katherine, who lives in the tenement across the street, from whom he cannot look away.

He has never spoken to her. He knows her name only because he heard it shouted once at dawn as she let herself out of her building. The shout came from an older woman leaning, half-dressed, from a third floor window. Katherine turned around. She said something, to which the woman (probably her mother) nodded in response and disappeared inside. Then the girl continued on her way, vanishing beyond the window frame—the same library window at which he pauses now to watch the streetlamps flicker and dim.

With his adoptive father's death six weeks ago, Virgil's isolation is complete. Every night he continues the late Professor's studies, working by candlelight because he can no longer afford oil for the lamps. When sleep threatens, he stands and forces himself to walk, pacing until daybreak when he watches Katherine leave for the factory and knows it is safe to sleep

Hours remain until dawn. He extends his hand and touches the tips of his fingers to the glass. The windowpane is cool, misted over by his breath, and the lamps beyond waver as a wind sweeps from the lake and shakes the flowering trees.

Elm, maple, basswood. Laden with blossom in this early season.

Sleep beckons, and with it, the promise of darkness: the emptiness of books unread, loss un-felt. His eyelids droop. He clenches them shut and rubs away his drowsiness. When he opens them again, the street is no longer deserted. There is someone standing outside of the tenement, a woman. Veiled in gray, she gazes up at his window and raises her hand in acknowledgment.

Katherine.

He fumbles with the window latch and pushes out the casement. Rain spatters his face. The streetlamp tilts with the wind, so strong it extinguishes the candles in the library, sinking the room into nothingness. The avenue is empty before him, all windows unlit. The woman is gone—if she was ever there at all.

He latches the casement and resumes his pacing, walking in the dark until the east begins to lighten. At half past six, Katherine leaves for work, attired in a plain brown dress. He watches her go then retreats to the bedroom, where he lies and waits for sleep to break across him.

*

The dreams, though bad, were worse in childhood. He cannot remember when they began any more than he can summon to mind an image of his mother's face, or his father's. Both perished in the infamous Canterbury Wreck. Virgil was present but remembers nothing of the event, being less than a year old at the time.

The collision occurred at dusk on a stretch of remote track miles from the nearest station. His parents' train had come to an emergency stop after the engineer sighted a warning light ahead. Behind them, the express train from Exeter had departed Canterbury Station ahead of schedule and failed to maintain the proper stopping distance.

At five minutes after seven, the express plowed into the rear of their train, resulting in the near-complete telescoping of the final carriage as well as the partial destruction of the penultimate car, where Virgil sat with his parents. The impact of the collision wrenched him out of his mother's arms. He flew across the carriage and landed unharmed near the front, thus avoiding the fate of his parents, seated in the fourth row, who were crushed to death when the rear carriage telescoped. His survival had been "miraculous" — or so the papers said.

Virgil was a teenager when he first learned of the accident. On his sixteenth birthday, the Professor presented him with a sealed parcel containing the details of his adoption along with a sheaf of press clippings from the time of the wreck. They never discussed the matter after that — neither his true parents, nor the manner in which they had died.

Thirty years later, he does not remember the screams or the breaking of timbers, the moans of the survivors. He can describe these things only so far as he has read about them. Nonetheless he has always had nightmares.

*

As a boy, Virgil willingly endured days at a time of sleeplessness if it meant a respite from the dreams. The Professor himself was an insomniac and thus proved all too happy to wait up with the frightened child through the latest watches of the night.

Of the many evenings they spent together, Virgil remembers one in particular. He was ten or eleven and the two of them were seated alone in the library. The oil lamps burned brightly between them, and the Professor told him a story, as he often did, to pass the hours.

The tale that night was Vidofsky's No. 27, "Of Silas and the Gray Woman," though Virgil did not learn this until much later. The Professor presented the story to him as a simple folk legend — as indeed it was, Virgil supposes, after a fashion.

"Long ago," the Professor began, "there lived a man named Silas. He was a good man, strong and upright, but his choice in friends was poor.

"It came to pass that he was accused of poaching deer from the Boyar's wood. He was innocent of this crime. The true culprit, Silas knew, was his friend Peter. But the penalty for poaching was death, and Silas was a good man, as I have said, and so said nothing.

"The Boyar took this silence for proof of guilt and ordered his execution. The deed was quickly done. After his beheading, Silas was drawn and quartered, the mangled corpse displayed in five pieces at the crossroads outside of town.

"For a day he lay there, dead as the snow, but it was later, in the cool of the night, that the gray woman came for him. She knew of his innocence, you see, and gave unto him the justice his righteousness had denied him.

"She gathered up the pieces of his body into her skirts and sewed them back together, patching over the seams with moss and silver lichen. Then she cradled his head and breathed the life back into him, taking flight when the church bells tolled for five.

"Silas awoke and found himself at the crossroads. His wounds were gone. In their place he felt the fur of moss under his fingers. He remembered the axe blow, his last view of the world as his head rolled free. Am I dead? he wondered. Am I alive? Is there any difference?

"He returned to town, where cries of terror greeted his arrival. Peter shouted an oath and fell to his knees, confessing his crime so all could hear.

"The two men were brought before the Boyar, who was so amazed by the miracle of Silas's return that he was moved to show mercy. He spared Peter from the axe and rewarded Silas's steadfastness with two gold coins. Peter turned to the Lord and entered a monastery, while Silas, resurrected, resumed his trade as a carpenter

"Years passed, but having died once, Silas did not age. The Boyar died and was replaced by his successor. In time his successor succumbed to the plague and the land passed into civil war. When Peter died at the age of one-hundred-and-eleven, Silas knew his time had come.

"One evening, around twilight, he left the town and went once more to the crossroads. There he lay himself down between the two forks, just as he had awoken so many years before. He placed the Boyar's gold coins upon his eyelids and waited there for nightfall. He waited in the stillness of the evening, his heart pounding, pounding—"

Here the Professor paused, as though lost in thought. He dragged on his pipe, blowing curls of smoke back against the lamplight. He sighed.

"In the morning, he was gone. Some say he walks the earth to this day, that God will not grant him rest. Others believe the earth swallowed him whole, while still others—"

"It was the gray woman," Virgil said. "She came back for him. She must have done."

The Professor shrugged and sucked the stem of his pipe, exhaling through his nose. "Perhaps she did," he said. "But no one knows—and no one *can* know."

"Why not?"

"Because of the crossroads. It is a between place, Virgil. A place of nothingness. And in that nothingness, all things are possible."

*

The story ended there—much to Virgil's frustration—but the mystery of it tantalized him somehow, so that he found himself returning to it again and again throughout the course of his childhood. Upon learning of his adoption, he became obsessed with the story, much as the Professor had always intended.

The late Professor T. Albert Lodge was a noted scholar of linguistics with an avowed interest in folklore and so-called "fairy stories," particularly those that had been compiled by the Russian scholar Alexandr Vidofsky in the mid-Nineteenth Century. Vidofsky himself was long dead, executed as an anarchist by the Tsarist government. Since then, his work had fallen into disinterest, if not outright disrepute.

This was hardly surprising. While Vidofsky was a gifted writer and artist, his scholarship could hardly be described as conventional. For seven years, he traveled on foot throughout the Ukraine and Byelorussia, recording in shorthand some four thousand variations on a set of eighty-one peasant stories.

But Vidofsky was not content merely to be a collector of Slavic folklore. After returning to St. Petersburg, he engaged upon the creation of his masterwork: a three volume sequence entitled *Ex Tenebris Tenebrae.* In this work, he refined and synthesized his four thousand variations to produce a sequence of eighty-one short tales of limitless implication and lingering strangeness. These eighty-one were further divided into three volumes of twenty-seven tales each—a nod to Vidofsky's interest in numerology.

Vol. III appeared when Vidofsky was fifty-one. He lived out the remaining twenty years of his life in seclusion. After his execution, a search was made of his belongings, but the original source materials—those four thousand stories he had collected as a young man—were missing. Later it emerged that Vidofsky had burned his papers himself, so that the "purified" texts (as he referred to them) would remain his final legacy.

Following his retirement from the University, Professor Lodge devoted the whole of his scholarly efforts to the study of Vidofsky's writings. Through careful analysis of the Russian folklorist's grammar and verbiage, the Professor believed he could reconstruct the original peasant stories in all of their many variations.

When Virgil's parents died, the Professor read of the tragedy in the papers and used his standing in society to secure the adoption of the "the miracle child." To Virgil he bestowed his surname and his vocation. He attended to Virgil's schooling personally, teaching the boy to read at age three. For thirty years they lived together in the house, working together, seeing almost no one. Then he died, leaving Virgil to continue with his work at the age of thirty-one.

In this, as in all things, Virgil has proved a dutiful son. Every night, he applies himself to the study of Vidofsky's language, cross referencing the Professor's notes and translations so as to identify potential points of variance within the purified texts. At dawn, he retires to bed and sleeps until noon, at which time he eats his daily meal, sustaining himself on deliveries of bread and milk. At half-past four, he enters the library to begin the day's work.

The dullness of this routine, exact in every particular, is relieved only by his first sight of Katherine at dawn and by his second glimpse of her at twilight when she returns from the factory with her hair down, her heeled shoes rapping on the pavement.

*

Saturday evening. Shortly after eight o'clock, the doorbell sounds. He listens, disbelieving, and is rewarded by a second chime.

He descends the stairs to the front door and cracks it open, peering outside over the chain. A woman lingers on the stoop, wreathed in the perfume of pressed flowers.

She turns to the crack in the door. Katherine: dark hair, eyes like gray moons. Terror seizes him, pinning him into place with the surety of nightmare.

"Mr. Lodge?" she says. Her voice is delicate and pretty, though her speech is unrefined. "It's all right. I'm Katherine Sutcliff? I live across the street with my mother—Rose Sutcliff? She knew your father years ago. When she was a girl. She isn't well, you see, and she'd like me to read to her. Only it's so late now, I doubted I'd find anything—"

He removes the chain and opens the door. He hopes she cannot see his shaking. "Rose Sutcliff," he says, pretending to recognize the name. "Of course. Please come in."

She smiles, flashing a mouth of perfect teeth, and steps into the hallway. The smell of her perfume is overwhelming. It fills the dome of his skull, the confines of the narrow corridor.

"I worried you meant to keep me out there all night."

"No," he says. "It's just—I need to be careful. The Professor's books…"

He gestures vaguely, miserably.

"Isn't that the truth?" she says. "Mother and I were robbed last fall. They made off with her savings. Every penny of it."

"Oh dear. That's terrible."

He is dizzied by their proximity to one another, by the whiteness of her teeth and the smell of her breath and skin: sweat, the sweetness of dried roses. Light-headed, he turns and proceeds to the staircase, glancing over his shoulder to ensure she follows.

"I gather you were hoping to borrow a book?"

"It's my mother," she says. "Her gout pains her terribly of late and she cannot get out of bed. I've been reading to her for weeks now but she's grown tired of His Word and it's all we have. Then I remembered her saying once how your father was always reading, standing at the window of his room, and I thought maybe we might be able to borrow something."

They reach the library with its towering shelves, its long tables heaped with books and manuscripts. The stench of dust, pervasive, serves to conceal the smell of her perfume, and he finds he breathes easier in its absence.

"What does your mother like to read?"

"Ghost stories. Books with murders in them. Detective stories."

"I believe the Professor may have owned a few novels. Let me see if I can find them." Virgil scales the library steps to the highest shelf and retrieves an early edition of *The Moonstone.* "Here we are," he says, descending, but she does not hear him.

She appears entirely absorbed in a copy of *Ex Tenebris Tenebrae,* which she must have plucked from one of the desks. It is Volume I of the Professor's English translation, published twenty years earlier in a limited run of fifty copies.

The book includes all of Vidofsky's original artwork, including the etched frontispiece at which Katherine now stares with obvious fascination. Her brow is furrowed, her lower lip folded into her mouth. The frontispiece depicts a woman posed with a writhing serpent—an obvious reference to Vidofsky No. 1, "Of Man's Fall and the Conqueror Eve." However, the Professor also believed the image doubled as an allusion to the gray woman of Vidofsky No. 27.

Vidofsky has placed his subject in a woodland clearing, pine trees visible behind her head. The woman, veiled, stands with legs akimbo, pinning the snake with one bare foot, long hair streaming behind her like river weeds. In addition to the veil, she wears a flowing skirt, but her chest is exposed, marked by a single breast.

"She is an androgyne," Virgil says. "A hermaphrodite."

Katherine raises her head. She regards him blankly.

"Vidofsky was fascinated by something he described in his writings as 'the lure of luminal,' which is to say, the indefinable attraction exerted on us by things or places that cannot be categorized by a single word, but which seem to exist, as it were, in the spaces *between* words — or, indeed, between worlds — where the signifier and the signified thin and merge together. The gray woman, by being both man and woman, embodies this state of essential flux. Even the color 'gray' suggests..."

He trails off. She is not listening.

"Are there ghosts?" she asks.

"Pardon?"

She taps the frontispiece. "In the book. My mother loves ghost stories." She lowers her voice and leans toward him, close enough for him to feel the warmth of her breath on his ear. "She's something of a *believer*, I'm afraid. Father Greenaway despairs of her."

Virgil swallows. He steps away from her, stammering. "Well, yes, there *are* ghosts, of a kind, but I'm not certain that — perhaps she might not prefer..."

"Can I borrow it? I'll bring it back to you."

Surprised, he can merely nod.

She thanks him profusely and wishes him good evening, preceding him down the stairs to the door. He watches her cross the street to her building. She turns and waves from the stoop and then she is gone. He closes the door and secures the chain.

The house is silent. He settles his weight against the wall and gazes up at the ceiling, invisible in the dimness. He breathes deeply, inhaling with every breath the certainty of solitude, the memory of her perfume.

*

He passes the remainder of the evening in restless frustration, unable to concentrate. The hours stretch, counted off by the clock downstairs, which rings first for eleven then twelve. He attempts to read from Vidofsky No. 1 in the original Cyrillic, but his eyes rove the page without comprehension and the characters rearrange themselves, forming the outline of a face—her face—and he tastes once more the sweetness of her scent in his lungs.

At one o'clock, he goes to the window.

From here, the city lies open before him, gas-flames flickering on shadowed streets and alleys. In the distance, a few lights glimmer, house-fires that wink like dying stars, flares that burst and streak and leave no trace upon the heavens. Even the street lamps crackle and fade with the dark, rendering all notions of space meaningless. He drifts off.

The dream begins, like his childhood nightmares, with the loss of the light. The moon is down. The stars are gone, blotted from the sky. Despite the darkness, he can discern the outline of a hooded figure standing on the stoop of the tenement building opposite.

It is the woman he saw on the previous night, though he can no longer be certain of her sex. She is exceedingly tall, surpassing Virgil's height by a foot or more. Her skirts are wide and shapeless, her veil spun from a queer black material, darker even than light's absence.

She waves at him, beckoning, and begins to run—wild and graceful, a shadow swung before a swaying lamp. Outside now, he chases after her. His slippers pound the pavement but fail to absorb the impact of each step. His ankles throb. His calves burn with the effort of pursuit.

Inevitably, he slows. He falls behind, sliding backward into the mouth of a city that feels increasingly drab and colorless, suffused with the monotony of routine. Ahead of him, the veiled woman rolls like a black wave over cracked earth and pavement, racing westward into the teeth of nightmare while the rest of the city recedes to placid normalcy.

She is making for the lake. The rotten wharves, the shuttered warehouses. The rails that bend and crisscross, encircling the city like spider's silk.

He stumbles. When he regains his feet, she is nowhere to be seen. From the west, a whistle sounds, a low susurrus like the notes of a flute in water — then suddenly closer, so loud and shrill it cuts him from the dream.

It is Sunday morning, the twilight soured, not yet spent. He collects himself from the floor of the library and retires to bed, intending to steal another few hours of rest. But he sleeps until two when he is woken by children playing stick-ball in the garden behind the house.

His head aches. He draws the curtains.

*

After supper, he walks down to the lake, retracing the woman's steps from the dream. Basswoods are flowering. Musk spills from their open blossoms, so that he thinks again of Katherine Sutcliff, the scent which lingers even now in the downstairs corridor of the house, in the stillness of the library. The thought of her has preoccupied him since he woke, driving him out-of-doors for the first time since the Professor's funeral.

In recent decades, the city's harbor has

shrunken in size and significance. A few warehouses show signs of recent activity, but many have closed their doors for good, and the lake-shore is deserted at this hour. Birds sing in the abandoned railway station. The tracks, used only for freight, swarm with weeds and wildflowers.

At dusk, he turns and heads for home. Behind him, in the space over the lake, constellations have arrayed themselves in interwoven patterns, changing with the changing seasons. Springtime. The air hums, charged with possibility: the retreat of the frost, the birds' mating songs, the life which swells and bursts from the basswoods.

*

She is waiting for him when he arrives home. Rising from the stoop, she greets him cheerfully, the borrowed book held to her breast. He can smell the spring on her, the tang of perfume in her hair. "I hope you haven't waited long," he says.

"Not long," she replies, smiling brightly. "Besides, it's a beautiful evening."

"It is."

"I wanted to return this to you," she says, proffering the Vidofsky. "I meant to bring it by this morning, before church, but Mother wanted to show it to Father Greenaway."

"Father Greenaway?"

"He's our priest—and very proper, too. He doesn't go in for spirits and so on, but Mother thought it might convince him, the book. That's why we had to bring it with us."

"Convince him of what, precisely?"

"Well, it was that last story, the one with the two friends and the gray woman, the crossroads where they left the body."

"'And in that place there was a nothingness,'" he murmurs.

"Right," she says. "That's the one. Mother said it was like one of Our Lord's parables, but instead of showing us how we should be kind to our neighbors, say, or give up all our possessions, it shows how Christ returned from the grave—and why. The man in the story, Silas? He was neither dead nor alive but it didn't matter either way. Because of the crossroads.

"Now Father Greenaway seemed willing to accept her argument that far, but then she said the same was true of Our Lord. His very life, she said, was a place halfway—not halfway between man and woman like in that picture but between Man and God. For him, there could be no lasting death—and so there could be no resurrection either."

Katherine pauses dramatically, expecting some manner of reaction from him. Shock? Revulsion? Virgil says, "Your mother sounds like a remarkable woman."

She laughs. "Oh, she is that, and no mistake! But Father Greenaway said the book was the vilest blasphemy and told her she must have nothing more to do with it. Not that she listened. She wanted me to read to her again tonight, but I said I couldn't—not after what Father Greenaway told us. Then she said she'd read it herself, but I couldn't possibly let her do that. The good of her soul, you understand. Besides, it gave her bad dreams. So I hid it away in the pantry until she went to sleep. Then I brought it here."

He takes the book from her. The leather cover is gritty, dusted with bread flour. "I'm sorry it has caused you such trouble."

"It isn't your fault. I know you meant us no harm. Will you be at home tomorrow night? I'd like to bring you some supper. To thank you, I mean."

He nods. His tongue, flaccid, fills his mouth, choking off his breath.

"Well, then," she says, grinning. Her crimson lips curl back, baring bone-white teeth. Her gray eyes shimmer with starlight. "Until tomorrow."

*

He carries the book upstairs to the library and lays it down on the desk. With a damp cloth, he wipes the flour from the cover and lights a second candle for closer inspection. He is surprised by the care with which the book has been handled. The binding appears undamaged, the pages intact. He sighs, relieved, and fans the leaves with his thumb.

The book falls open to Vidofsky No. 11: "Of Other Worlds and the Passageways Thereof." The accompanying etching depicts a cobble road, a horizon crowded with unfamiliar constellations. A minotaur. A spider. A serpent with forked tongue.

A massive hole has been torn into the sky. This "passageway" yawns at the center, its edges ragged and spreading. Two figures stand before it, discernible only in silhouette, black strokes on the faded page.

"Do you see it?" the Professor asked him.

This was last February, and the end was drawing near. It pained the old man to speak but he coughed until his throat was clear. His eyes hungered. "These two figures, Virgil. They are you and me and all the others. You and me and the dark that awaits us."

Two days later, he was dead.

In the etching, the Professor had imagined his future, the oblivion of the grave, but to Virgil, the passageway is an opening into the past, the emptiness for which he has always yearned, which swallowed his parents long ago. He should have joined them there. Instead, he was spared, baptized by chance or fate into the no-space of the present.

He has always believed this, but tonight, something is different. Tonight, the prospect of death is merely terrifying. All longing he reserves for his memories of Katherine Sutcliff — her painted smile, the basswood odors on her hair and skin — and he marvels at the road that stretches before him. Perhaps, he reflects, Vidofsky's silhouettes are looking *away* from the void, rather than toward it, their faces turned to the world beyond the page.

It is the first time he has even considered the possibility.

*

Six o'clock. He dresses himself in his finest suit, unlaundered in the weeks since the Professor's funeral. He fastens his ascot tie and polishes his shoes to a high shine. A dry boutonniere — a white lily — completes the ensemble. He descends the stairs to the corridor, where he positions his chair against the wainscoting ten feet from the doorway.

He waits. At six-thirty, the bell rings and he opens the door to her. She wears a dress of beaded black linen. Like him, she has dressed up for their meeting, changing out of her customary work clothes. With both hands she holds a piece of heavy white crockery.

"It isn't much," she explains, joining him

in the corridor. "Merely some things we had lying about the house. But I thought of you here without a housekeeper to look after you — and you'd been so kind in lending us that book..."

He shakes his head. "Please," he says. "It was nothing."

"Maybe to you it was, but not to Mother. She wanted to come with me, to thank you herself, but the stairs were too much."

"What a shame," he says.

She indicates the crock in her hands. "I made this for you this morning. Before work. It should still be good, but it needs warming up. Where's your kitchen? If you like, I can put it in the oven for you."

"I — I think I would like that, yes."

A moment passes. She regards him pointedly. Her dark hair cascades down her back and shoulders, neatly framing her oval face. Her eyes are gray and lustrous, nearly opalescent.

She prompts him. "The kitchen?"

"Ah, yes," he says, flushing. His pulse catches in his throat, rising like a gorge. "How foolish of me. Come this way."

He opens the door to the dining room and leads her through to the kitchen. The counters are bare. The basin is crowded with empty milk bottles left to soak.

Katherine bends over to open the oven and light the gas. Her movements are rapid, precise but efficient, and he wonders at the reasons for her haste.

"Your mother," he says, fumbling for a suitable topic of conversation. "You said that she knew the Professor?"

"A long time ago," she says, sliding the crock into the oven. "I believe he was her tutor? She would have been just a girl at the time. I gather something happened, and they parted ways, but that was nearly fifty years ago. Her memory isn't all it used to be."

She turns around. "But I expect you must know all about that, living here alone with the old Professor — and you a young man yourself. I'm ashamed to say it, but it's like living with a child sometimes. She sneaks outside. Late at night. After I've fallen sleep. She goes out in her veil because she thinks she's late for her wedding. That's sad, isn't it?"

He murmurs his agreement. "It is sad," he says, distracted.

He recalls the woman he had glimpsed from his window — the same figure of whom he later dreamt — and realizes what he had, in fact, seen.

"Anyway, it's nearly seven," Katherine says. "I should be getting back to her."

"No," he blurts. "Wait."

She tilts her head. She regards him passively.

"I thought — which, is to say, I wonder

if — that is, assuming you are available — you might consent to dine with me?"

Her mouth opens, but she does not speak. Her expression flickers so rapidly he cannot gauge her reaction with any degree of accuracy. Then she exhales.

"Now *really*, Mr. Lodge," she says. "I'm flattered, of course, but I don't think that would be proper. Do you?"

She smiles, gently, tongue darting behind white teeth.

He cannot meet her gaze. "No," he manages as he retreats toward the dining room. "I suppose not. But, perhaps, if your mother were to — "

"I'm sorry," she says. She steps toward the doorway, turning sideways to pass him where he stands. "But as I said, I really must be getting home."

His fists shake, useless. He thinks of the paint on her lips, the perfume she wears — not for him but for another — and the blackness yawns beneath him.

Despair seizes him, coupled with an acute stab of terror. He grabs at her desperately, a drowning man scrabbling after flotsam. His fingers close around her right arm.

She flinches. "Please," she says, "let go — "

"Katherine," he says, urgently.

She struggles against his grip but cannot free herself.

His nails dig into her elbow.

There is fear in her eyes, the horror of a trapped animal. Panicked, she flails wildly at him with her free hand, but he catches her wrist and presses it to his chest. He will not let her go.

"Katherine," he repeats.

She kicks him. Her shoe-tip catches his shin, impacting the bone so that he loses his balance. Falling, he attempts to maintain his grip, but she escapes his grasp and flees through the dining room, panting, her heels clattering on the hallway floor.

The door flies open, and she is lost to him forever.

He goes to the window, shin throbbing, and looks out at the street.

A younger man has come to Katherine's aid. He holds her in his arms as she shakes and sobs and points toward Virgil's house. Her rescuer nods, solemnly, and walks her to the door of the tenement before tearing away down the street, shouting for the constables.

*

The time is short.

Virgil slips out the backdoor and flees through the garden, splashing through puddles of muck, ruining his best clothes. At the back of the garden, he vaults over the low fence and lands in the adjoining alleyway.

He starts to run. He makes his way westward, following side-roads and alleys until he reaches Depot Street. The smell of sex is on the air, breathed from bud and blossom — more pungent now for the falling dark, the dusk which pours from the east, plunging the city into night. The moon rises over the lake, swathed in black and violet.

He descends the hill to the waterfront. His coat tails fly out behind him, the wind filling his jacket like a sail and driving him onward. Shouts follow him, cries of startlement or alarm, but he is not listening. From somewhere far off comes the shriek of a constable's whistle, the clangor of a bell. He urges himself to greater haste. The wind howls in his ears.

Past the warehouses, he crosses the railroad tracks and leaps onto the disused platform. The station roof has caved in. The windows are broken. He dashes to the platform edge, where he pauses with his hands on his knees, lungs heaving. He does not dare to look behind him.

The whistle sounds again. He leaps from the platform and pelts down the tracks, gasping as he runs, unable to breathe for the force of the blood surging through him.

Half-a-mile from the station, the lake chill settles over him, freezing in his lungs. Weariness engulfs him. His legs buckle, pitching him forward into the weeds.

His head strikes the ground. Bright specks dance into his vision, blinding him. The stars, invisible, bore into him like eyes.

The world returns gradually, re-casting itself from shades of twilight, pieces of dusk. Twenty yards ahead of him, the tracks enter a tunnel, a place halfway. The interior is unlit. The opening seethes and pulses, exuding the blankness of nightmare, the no-life for which he has always been fated. He may have escaped it once, but it will come for him in the end — as it did for the Professor, as it does for all men on this earth. He has to keep moving.

He lurches to his feet.

Night withdraws from the tunnel mouth, opening to admit him, so that he thinks of a woman's lips, poised in the moment before speaking, before she spreads her arms in embrace. Damp air surrounds him, seeping into him like breath — her breath — gathering him into her skirts as he staggers forward, with arms thrust out, because he cannot see.

Inside, the walls hum with refracted sound. The clatter of footsteps. The screech of vibrating metal. Ahead of him, the blackness churns and judders. The earth rumbles underfoot. The walls quake and shed plumes of dust.

And then — from out of the darkness — a paralyzing light —

LOUISA

The ball was over, the night far spent. The bells
of Trinity Church tolled three times, rupturing
the calm of early April. The final bell circled the
rim of my empty wineglass, producing a faint
vibration that ceased at the touch of my finger.
Three o'clock: the hour known as the wolf's
hour, the time at which most children are born
and at which most men die.

I was tired. I remember that clearly. In
those days, I was not a regular ball-goer, being
somewhat reserved and predisposed to
melancholy. Since the death of my parents two
years before, I had lived alone in the family
house with only my manservant for company. I
would never have thought to attend a society
ball had my friends not suggested it. By three
o'clock, however, my companions had left. I had
remained not for the dancing, but because I
simply could not bear to return to the cold and
dusty townhouse I once thought of as home.

Quite by chance my gaze settled on a
young woman across the room. She must have
arrived late as I had not seen her before. The
dress she wore was high-necked but flattering
and clung to her body in a manner that accented
her slim figure.

But it was the color of the dress, rather
than its cut, that so arrested me. In color, it was
green, but there was something indefinably

sickly about the shade, something putrid, and I thought of red cedar, which I have seen planted in many cemeteries, and the smudged, slightly dirty quality of its needles. But even this comparison is not entirely accurate.

The woman stood by the bar, wineglass in hand, while the other ball-goers passed to either side of her. I watched her for some time, my weariness forgotten. She half-turned, sensing my gaze upon her, and caught my eye. She smiled. Taking one sip from her drink, she placed it, nearly full, onto the table behind her and began to walk toward me, making a direct line for me through the dispersing throng.

She shimmered. There is no other word for it. Candlelight moved across her dress in the same way that sunlight glimmers on a wave, and more than a few heads turned as she passed. Her complexion was pale and exceedingly delicate, while her hair was curly, honey-blonde. Her eyes appeared to be of the same indescribable color as her dress.

Two yards away, she halted and faced me without speaking. I was nervous. Sweat dribbled down the inside of my jacket.

"Good evening," I said.

She presented me with her ungloved hand, the gesture of a lady expecting her due. I stooped and planted a kiss upon the knuckle. Her hand was unexpectedly warm, as though hot with fever. A damp, musky smell—strong but not unpleasant—clung to her skin.

I introduced myself. "Andrew Todd," I said. Unsure of how to continue, I fell back upon convention. "At your service."

"My service?" she murmured, teasingly. Her voice was soft, girlish, but her speech was refined. "In that case, I could do with another drink."

Her forwardness took me by surprise, the more so since I had watched her leave her glass behind. "Wine?" I stammered.

"Gin."

I went to the bar counter and returned with a pair of tumblers. I took my gin straight, but to hers I added a splash of soda. We clinked our glasses together.

"A toast," she said, speaking with the same soft, impossibly alluring voice. "I drink to you, Andrew. And to new friends."

She raised the glass to her lips.

"But I don't even know your name."

"Louisa."

She drained her glass in a single swallow. The color came into her cheeks, further emphasizing her preternatural pallor, and for a moment—only a moment—her features appeared haggard and sunken, her eyes red and horribly bloodshot.

By now the ballroom was nearly empty. The floor was clear and only a few stragglers haunted the shadowed margins of the room. It was the darkest hour of the morning, a time of loneliness and reflection, but that night I was conscious of nothing but the woman who stood before me. In her presence I heard no foreboding in the door which banged hollowly against the wall, nor did I see anything of sadness in the nightly duties of the old attendant, who ascended a ladder beneath the chandelier and proceeded to snuff the lights.

"It is late," she said.

"It is."

"Much too late for a woman to be out on her own. It isn't decent."

"No?"

"Nor is it safe," she added playfully.

"I quite agree."

"But I trust you," she said. "Will you take me home?"

She peered up at me.

I faltered, unsure of myself. I was taken aback by her earnestness, if only because it seemed so unnecessary. She must have known — how could she not? — that I would not deny her anything.

"I would consider it an honor," I replied. "Where is home?"

"Anywhere you would like it to be."

After that, we did not speak. I offered her my arm, which she took. Her fingers settled into the crook of my elbow, and I became conscious again of her incredible warmth. Even through the fabric of my jacket I could feel the heat of her body, which seemed to pulse and flare from her fingertips as with the beating of a heart.

Together we crossed the dance floor, passing the attendant, who sat on the lowest rung of the ladder, the doubter across his knee. Of the chandelier's two dozen candles, only a single wick remained ablaze. It was the last light of any kind in the room, and the servant polished the silver snuffer by its faint illumination. Somewhere nearby a woman cried out, as though in pain, only to be shushed into silence by a man—and I saw the two of them moving together in the shadows.

We stepped outside.

Snowflakes whirled on the northern wind, spinning down from a cloud-black sky, visible to us only where they billowed about the streetlamps. It was a beautiful sight—perhaps the most beautiful I have seen—but it was a spring snow, the last of the season, and I knew it could not last. Behind us, the doors to the ballroom groaned shut. The noise caused me to turn round. Through the diminishing crack between door and frame, I watched as the attendant ascended the ladder, extended his doubter, and snuffed the final light.

*

We began to walk. Arm in arm, we proceeded

down the boulevard under naked trees that swayed and rattled. Points of snow rained down around us, glittering in the void of space like the stars they hid from view. The road led us to the river and across the bridge.

From there we made our way to my house — or to my father's house, as I still thought of it then. Stevens was abed, and I escorted Louisa up the creaking staircase to the upper hall, where the curtains admitted a coppery light from the courtyard outside.

I remember: I halted on the top stair to look back at her, straining my eyes to discern her shape in the darkness. In that gas-lit twilight, she appeared half-present, a ghost in amber. Shadows writhed on the wall behind her, sweeping down across her face with the gusting wind.

When we reached the bedroom, she preceded me through the doorway.

Snow light poured into the room through the open curtains. She walked to the window and there turned to face me, the falling snow mirrored on her features in a procession of flickering shadows. Her gaze betrayed a bottomless longing, a suffering beyond the ability of a man — any man — to understand.

"Please," she said, and then nothing more, as if to say: *think not of me, think not at all. I am yours or I am nothing.*

I went to her and surprised myself by

taking her in my arms. She shivered once and then grew supple. She did not protest when I removed her dress. The fabric slid from her shoulders with a serpentine ease and she wore no corset underneath.

An enormous scar ran the length of her left side. From breast to hip, the skin had knitted itself into an uneven ridge that sloped to a bone-white troth. A few black hairs were visible where they pushed like grass from the colorless flesh. I leaned in to kiss her. Our lips met and my eyes strayed to the window at her back, where a frosted web had formed on the glass: a delicate tracery, numinous and insubstantial like the lives of the unnumbered dead.

*

I woke up alone. The bed beside me was empty. The clothes were flat and un-rumpled, as though they had not been slept in at all. I leapt to my feet, taking time only to don my nightgown before dashing into the hall. I met my manservant on the stair. Stevens carried a tray with my breakfast. The odor of boiled eggs turned my stomach.

"The young master was out late."

"Never mind that. Did you see anyone go out?"

"Go out, sir?"

"Just now. Did you see anyone?"

"No, sir. Assuredly not."

I sat down at the top of the steps.

"Would the master like his breakfast?"

"No," I said. "Leave me in peace."

"Very well, sir."

I rubbed at my eyes. My temples pounded from the after-effects of the alcohol. My thoughts formed themselves slowly and only with great effort.

Louisa must have slipped out as soon as I had fallen asleep. Departing in the dark, she had left me dreaming, even as the snow came down in glowing waves and the river subsided to froth and melt-water. She had left me nothing of herself, not even a card with her full name. *Louisa.* That was all I knew of her. How would I find her again?

During the following months, I gave myself over completely to the vices of this sleepless city, attending every banquet, ball, and function for miles. I stayed late, often through to dawn, sometimes engaging in conversation with the other ball-goers. More commonly, I simply lingered by the bar, a gin and soda in hand, and waited for her to pick me out again, to gather me up in her arms and take me home — wherever home might have been.

My lust for her was like a fever of the brain, a spell under which I sleepwalked the midnight streets of this city in spring, and then in summer.

Night after night I crossed and re-crossed the fog-wreathed river, unwilling to go home, unable to sleep. For months, I slept no more than a couple of hours each night. To sustain myself, I drank black coffee by the pitcher—an affectation at which Stevens sniffed in disapproval—and my health began to suffer. Those few activities that had once brought me joy now gave me no pleasure but served only to affirm an essential numbness, which I came to envision as a black and silent sea on which I floated facedown, a dead man.

My friends, observing these changes in me, begged me to leave off my mad quest, to forget about Louisa altogether and return to a respectable lifestyle. One evening in September, they confronted me in my bedroom and pleaded with me to see a doctor. Only then did I realize that they thought me insane. No one had seen me with Louisa at the ball, and they were solidly convinced I had imagined her. Perhaps I had. I confess the notion had occurred to me before, but I had quickly quashed it for fear of admitting to myself the same madness my friends saw in me. At the time, their suggestions enraged me. I snatched a platter from the table and chased them from the room, wielding the dish like a cutlass. When they were gone, I slammed the door so loudly that even the imperturbable Stevens jumped, juggled a teacup, and cursed under his breath when it shattered on the floor.

Later that night, after my anger had cooled, I reconsidered my situation from my friends' perspective and saw they were right to be concerned. Viewed in the light of reason, my self-destructive behavior during the previous summer appeared, at best, irrational, and at worst, entirely mad. I resolved to take my friends' advice.

That night, I stayed in and did not attend the ball being held across the river. Instead I retired early and slept deeply for the first time in months. In the morning I called on each of my friends in turn and apologized for my abominable behavior. Fortunately, I am a man blessed with the best of companions, and they welcomed me back into their lives without resentment, and indeed, with real joy. I still thought of Louisa, it's true, but I quickly returned to my old habits with the same single-minded determination with which I had once left them behind.

*

By October, I believed my madness to be over. I felt once more myself and did not hesitate when my friend Nathan suggested we attend a séance at the table of one Miss Volkov.

The young medium had moved to the city in the spring of that year and caused no small sensation once tales of her abilities began to circulate. One man, a widower, claimed to have glimpsed the ghost of his wife at Miss Volkov's table, while another woman, who had suffered many miscarriages, felt the touch of tiny hands in the dark.

"But they weren't cold like I expected," she told a gathered crowd. "I don't understand it, but their flesh — it was as warm somehow. Soft and fragrant like the air they never breathed."

All guests at Miss Volkov's table reported on the music they had heard during the course of each circle. Whenever the medium entered her trance — and was thus oblivious to the world around her — the guitars and zithers that sat on the table behind her picked themselves up and began to play, first one instrument and then another, until three or four were being plucked together in an eerie cadence.

The resulting music proved utterly alien to the ears of its audience: slow and soothing in one moment, painfully dissonant in the next. "It was like the sound of your heart," one man told me. "Late at night. If you lie awake and listen."

These stories had circulated since the spring and I had heard many such tales during my months of ball-going. Naturally, I was curious.

Nathan and I arrived at the Volkov house shortly after nine in the evening. The medium's residence proved to be an attractive house in the style of the Georgian Revival. We waited several minutes on the ornate stoop before being admitted by a servant in suit and tails.

The man appeared to be mute. He took our coats from us without speaking. From his hand gestures, we understood that we were to follow him into the parlor. There an assemblage of six women in widow's black crowded about a circular table at which were three empty seats: one each for Nathan and myself and one (I gathered) for Miss Volkov. The manservant showed us to our seats, bowed slightly, and vanished into the hall.

The parlor was square and high-ceilinged, steeped in shadow. The windows were dimmed with black shawls, so that the only light came from a solitary lamp at the center of the table. Placed against the far wall was a rectangular bench that held an assortment of musical instruments. There were guitars and lutes, even a saw.

Nathan and I introduced ourselves to the gathered women. It quickly became apparent that they were spiritualists all, the intensity of their passion for theosophy and Christian Science matched only by the agony of their bereavement.

Almost immediately, I regretted our coming. Whereas I had expected the strange, the exotic, I had found instead the merely tragic. "Is this your first time at the table?" one women inquired of me. Her tone was eager, her eyes sorrowful, and the faces of the other women also bore the same curious mixture of grief and hope. Noticing this, I shifted uncomfortably in my seat and allowed Nathan to answer for the both of us.

After a quarter of an hour, we heard footsteps in the hall outside. The women fell silent, rapt with anticipation. The footsteps ended outside the parlor doors.

"Extinguish the light," a voice commanded from the hall. "So that I may enter."

There ensued a flurry of activity as three of the women tried to snuff the lamp simultaneously. Nathan looked at me and rolled his eyes.

The lamp went out, plunging the room into darkness. The double doors creaked open, and I shortly perceived the patter of bare feet on the floorboards.

This new visitor sat down in the chair opposite me. She wasted no time in joining hands with the mourning women, and I soon found myself a part of her circle, with Nathan's hand clasped in my left and a widow's hand in my right.

"Come to me," Miss Volkov intoned. "O Empty Cup. O Face of the Nameless Dark. You who were with me at my birth. Who will be with me at my death. Speak to me of the forgotten path. Tell me of the un-trodden ways."

The ensuing stillness magnified all sound

so that my heartbeat came muffled through the veil of its echo, and the rapping of a hand beneath the table (for what else could it have been?) resounded with the sonic force of a rock-fall in a cavern. The rap came once, twice.

Miss Volkov spoke again. "We are not alone," she said.

The fine hairs lifted from the nape of my neck. A tremor climbed my spine and lingered near the base of the skull.

"My spirit guide is present," the medium continued, her words flowing together. "She says there is one here who has borne a great loss. One who has known too much of suffering and too little of joy. Listen. Do you hear? It is the voice of your sweet Rufus."

With that, Miss Volkov's intonation altered, taking on the tinny brittleness of a young child's voice.

"Mama?" the voice said. "Are you there?"

"Rufus!" one of the sitters cried. "Oh, God, child. I'm here. I'm listening."

"Mama. You must—"

"What, baby? What must I do?"

"He says you must learn to live without me."

"Who does, Rufus? Who says that?"

"The Lord, Mama. He says you have grieved too long."

"Rufus, I—Rufus, don't go!"

"Goodbye, Mama," the child said. By

some trick of ventriloquism, the voice seemed to fade from the very air. "We'll meet again. The Lord promises it."

Another rap came from beneath the table, the blow striking the wood so violently that the table leapt into the air. Nathan's hand went clammy in my own.

The medium's booming voice returned. "O Sainted Oblivion," she chanted. "O Blackened Heart and Harbor. Do you see me, here, in the mouth of your nothingness? My soul's music plays on your unending sea."

From out of the darkness came the faint plucking of a guitar, repeating the same three dissonant notes that existed in no key. They were like music's mirror inversion: utterly strange and unfamiliar. To the atonal plucking of the guitar was added another, which joined the first in a madman's approximation of harmony. The two instruments played together for a time before being joined by the unearthly piping of a saw. The melody it played belonged to no school of music I could name, but its essential pathos could not be denied.

The music struck me at my soul's center, and the resulting wound opened my mind to vistas of paralyzing emptiness, eclipsing all hope with wave upon wave of dizzying black. Inevitably, I thought of Louisa, and the sadness I had glimpsed in her: the consuming melancholy of one who has never been happy.

The music was beautiful, yes, but it was also corrupt, as her dress had first appeared to me, and I felt myself adrift on an ocean of alien sound that might drag me to its bottom as easily as it might bear me up, and carry me onward, and carry me home.

I did not hear the music stop.

All I knew was that the room was suddenly silent.

Minutes passed before Miss Volkov spoke.

"Bring up the light," she said. "Our circle is ended."

I sighed with relief. Nathan laughed nervously and wrenched his hand free of my grip. His palms were slick. Someone struck a match and the lamp flickered to life.

Opposite me sat the mysterious Miss Volkov, and at my first sight of her, I lost all composure. Here was the woman for whom I had searched so long in vain, the woman with whom I had spent a single night and whom I had known as Louisa.

With a strangled cry, I pushed back my chair and jumped to my feet with such clumsy violence that I nearly knocked the table on its side.

Miss Volkov—Louisa—regarded me with confusion. In her eyes I saw no sign of recognition. "Are you ill?" she asked kindly. "I will call for the doctor."

"Don't — don't you know me?"

My heart was beating wildly. All eyes in the room were upon me and then upon Miss Volkov as she shook her head. Her denial cut deep, and I took a hesitant step toward her. She shrunk away, ill at ease, and Nathan caught my arm before I could approach any nearer.

"Louisa!" I cried. "It's me. It's Andrew."

For the first time, the medium's composure wavered.

"What name did you call me?" she whispered.

I did not have the chance to respond, for Nathan took me firmly by the elbow and spirited me through the double doors into the hallway. The mute manservant presented us with our coats and shooed us outside, slamming the door behind us.

It was raining, a chilling downpour. The northern wind sliced through our coats and turned the rain to hail. Nathan called us a hansom and helped me into the seat.

I wrapped my coat around me and listened to the rattle of ice on the canvas roof. Nathan sat beside me, saying nothing. I could tell my actions had embarrassed him profoundly, but he was a true friend, and I sensed his concern.

Half an hour later, the carriage deposited me outside my house. "I shall call tomorrow," Nathan said as he helped me dismount. The driver rapped his whip against the horse's flank, and the carriage drove off into the night, leaving me alone to cross the empty courtyard. Brown leaves whispered over the flagstones, forming tornadoes where the wind trapped itself against the brick walls. Cold rain plashed upon my head and snaked down through my hair.

Short of the doorway, I looked up into the sky, low and heavy with rain. In the mouth of the cosmos I saw the same darkness I had encountered at Miss Volkov's circle, the half-seen shadow that gathered about me, even now, that threatened to strangle the life from me.

I forced myself to keep walking. Inside, I mounted alone the steps I had once climbed with her and collapsed onto the bed in my room. Shivering and cold, I waited up until dawn, listening to my heart as rain tapped at the window.

*

The days grew shorter, the nights frigid. My despair grew, as did my obsession, and in time, my darkest impulses turned violent. I was as a man drowning. Wildly I kicked from the depths I had glimpsed at her table, willing myself to surface, though the waves held me under.

On most nights, I watched her house from the shelter of a nearby overhang, hoping for a glimpse of her through the parlor windows. But the shawls remained in place — they were never removed — and the parlor remained as closed to me as the doors of my own happiness.

During the following weeks, I came to understand that Louisa's routine was firmly established. Every night, at nine, the front door opened to admit the sitters. At midnight the door opened again to let them out. Following each séance, the mute manservant remained behind and typically did not depart until well after two. Not once did Louisa set foot from the house.

At eight o'clock on the evening of November 14th, I took up my nightly vigil at the Volkov house. Shortly after nine, the last of the sitters arrived and were ushered inside by the mute manservant. The doors were shut, the lamp extinguished, and the faint strains of music could subsequently be heard through the covered windows of the parlor.

Shortly after midnight, the séance concluded. The sitters began to slip out, and I retreated into the shadows for fear of being seen. As usual, the manservant was last to leave, departing well after two o'clock. He tugged the flaps of his coat to his breast and hurried to the end of the lane, vanishing into the gloom beyond the farthest streetlight.

Once he had gone, I emerged from my place in the darkness and rapped with my knuckles on the oaken door — timidly at first, but then with some assurance. I received no response. The house lay silent, the windows unlit. Suddenly desperate, I balled my hands into fists and pounded on the door. After a minute, I spied the glow of the gas lamps in the foyer and heard the muffled approach of rapid footsteps.

I swallowed. I let my hands drop to my sides. The door groaned inward, and there stood my Louisa, the woman known to the world as Miss Volkov. She was wrapped in a gray shawl, which she wore over a white nightshirt.

For a long time we did not speak. Now that she stood before me, I found I could not bring myself to utter the first word.

"It's Andrew, isn't it? Andrew Todd."

"At your service," I said, weakly.

"You've been watching me."

I nodded.

"Earlier tonight, when I spotted you from the window, I nearly sent for the police. Surely it would have been the least that you deserve."

She was right, of course. Standing on her stoop in the dead of night, I was thoroughly ashamed of my behavior during the preceding days.

"But something stopped me," she continued. "Something you said."

"What—"

She cut me off. "Why have you come here? Tell me the truth."

"I—I needed to see you," I said. "That night—the night we spent together. I've tried—Lord knows I have—but I cannot forget it."

My words produced no change in her expression. The gas lamps flickered behind her head. "You needed to see me."

"Yes."

She sighed. Something slackened in her face, as though she had bowed to some unavoidable end. "Then you'd better come in," she said and motioned for me to enter.

I did not know what to say and so said nothing. I stepped over the threshold and made two tentative steps in the direction of the parlor. I had assumed she would receive me there, but she caught my wrist.

"No," she hissed. "I don't go in there."

"But the séance—"

"Only then," she said, releasing her grip. She mounted the steps and looked back at me pointedly. "Come," she said. "We can talk upstairs."

We ascended the two flights together. She led with me following close behind, as though in reverse reenactment of the night we met. The upstairs was entirely unlit and she carried no candle. Evidently I had roused her from bed. Probably the manservant waited for her to retire each evening before going home himself.

"In here," she whispered, and ushered me down the hall to the master bedroom. A large four-poster lounged in one corner, its oaken frame hung with violet drapery. The coals of a dying fire languished in the grate. An ivory-faced clock sat on the mantle, its wooden frame carved into the shape of an elephant. The hands read ten to three.

"We can talk in here," she said. "We're safe here." Her choice of words struck me as singularly odd. I realized then that she was distinctly uneasy, afraid. Her eyes darted from side to side, occasionally settling on the clock.

She sat on the edge of the bed. "Please," she invited me, patting the clothes beside her. "Sit." I sat. No sooner had I done so then she stood and began to pace the length of the bedroom, walking from bed to hearth and back again.

"Louisa," she said. "That's what you called me. That night you came to the circle."

"Is that so strange?"

"It isn't my name."

I blinked. "But—"

"It's Wilhelmina. Mina to my friends."

"You said—"

"What did I say?"

"You told me your name was Louisa."

Her eyes narrowed. "I did no such thing."

"We were at the ball. It was late, just gone three o'clock, but you—"

"No!" she shouted with surprising vehemence. "It's impossible. You've mistaken me for someone else. I'm not who you think I am."

I rose from the bed.

"You are," I said and placed my hands around her waist. Her nightgown was pitifully thin, and I felt the ridgeline of her scar beneath my left hand—but surely it should have been under my right? Her expression was neutral, her eyes rendered bottomless by firelight.

"You *are*," I insisted and leaned in close. "You are all I've ever wanted."

Our lips touched. She went completely rigid.

She slapped me across the face. Blood rushed to my cheek, filling the imprint of her palm. "Why would you do that?" she managed in a terrified whisper. Her lower lip trembled, wet with my saliva. "What kind of woman do you take me for?"

My head spun.

"Get out!" she screamed. "Go!"

I wanted to run but found that I could not. I was too exhausted to move, too miserable and lonely to do anything but remember the night we had spent together, even as she continued to shout at me, to label me a bastard and a pig.

Her anger seemed boundless, insatiable. But then she spotted the clock, its hands poised a hair's breadth from three, and all of her attempts at rage evaporated.

"Oh God," she whimpered. "The clock."

"The clock?"

"Don't you see? Don't you know she's jealous of me? All that I have. All that she could never possess. The séance — didn't you wonder how I did it? The music — that awful music."

"It was your servant," I said. "The room was dark. He came in while we were distracted. We were listening to that boy, Rufus, or whatever —"

"No," she said. "There was no such trickery."

"Then what —?"

"There was only her."

With a click, the clock's mechanism engaged. The elephant's trunk and tail — actually hammers — drew back and struck a concealed bell. After the third chime, the medium reached above the mantle and stilled the bell beneath her fingertips.

"Only who?" I asked. "What are you so afraid of?"

She took more than a minute to respond. Her voice was hoarse, so dry it seemed to crackle, but her answer made no sense.

"Louisa."

Downstairs, the parlor doors slammed open. The medium — Louisa or Wilhelmina, I no longer knew what to call her — froze. For one wild instant, she looked at me, or rather, through me, her eyes like those of a fallen fox who knows the riders are near. To this day I have never seen such terror in a human face.

We heard footsteps below us, passing through the foyer and onto the staircase. Each step possessed a cavernous quality, as had the raps beneath the medium's table, and I recalled the manner in which they had been amplified by the hush of the parlor. A similar principle must have been at work here, for it did not seem possible that a single individual could produce such a dreadful, heart-stopping clamor.

And yet the footsteps grew even louder as they ascended the stair until they were so thunderous that the entire house rumbled and pitched like a ship in a gale. Wilhelmina sobbed. I drew her close against my chest and rocked her as she shook. The strength drained from her legs, and I had to hold her fast to prevent her falling.

The footsteps reached the second floor and proceeded down the hall. The house quaked. Ash swirled in a cloud out of the fireplace. Coals bounced from the grate like stones on a river's skin. The clock wobbled dangerously, nearly crashing to the floor.

Wilhelmina wept.

I held her tightly, my heart racing for all of my attempts at reason. I had always viewed myself as a man of learning, a devotee of the natural sciences, but when the footsteps halted mere feet from the room, I watched the open doorway with the bated breath of a true believer.

I waited, but no ghost or monster appeared there. Outside, a carriage passed and clattered into the night. Inside, all was calm. The blood drained from my ears as the room grew noticeably warmer. Wilhelmina trembled against me. I brushed the hair from her ear and watched the clock for a full minute before I spoke.

"Look to the doorway," I said. "We're quite alone."

Her breathing steadied. The terror passed from her lithe frame, replaced in short order by something like resignation. She stepped away from me, but did not look to the door. Instead, she merely gazed at me, her face no more than a yard from my own. She closed her eyes.

In the next moment, she was seized from behind and lifted from the floor. She hurtled backward into the fireplace, striking the mantel with such violence that her eyes rolled white inside her skull.

I dashed across the room and dropped to my knees before her fallen body. I listened for a heartbeat: she was breathing but unconscious. I took hold of one arm and hefted her weight onto my back. There was no one else in the room — I was sure of it — but there was undeniably some*thing*, some other entity that was invisible to me. I felt it drawing closer: a nearly indiscernible darkening at the edges of my vision, like the shadow that precedes a megrim.

It took hold of Wilhelmina. It ripped her from my arms and pitched her through the air, knocking me off-balance. I tumbled forward into the hearth, spilling headlong with my arms extended, crying out in pain as the flesh burned from my hands.

I stumbled to my feet and looked to the bed where the medium had landed. By now she had regained consciousness. Her eyes were open, but she did not cry out, not even when the bedclothes were ripped out from under her, leaving her sprawled atop a naked mattress.

Impossibly, the duvet began to rise into the air of its own accord. Suspended two yards above the bed, it twisted itself into a fibrous cord, the stuffing spilling out as the fabric shredded. White down filled the air, feathered and fine like spring snow.

I lunged for the duvet but missed. On my second attempt, I managed to grasp hold of it, only to have it torn from my grasp. The air moved before me, taking on a rippled translucence, as of a fist submerged in a frothing river. Too late I attempted to dodge the coming blow: it took me hard in the stomach, and I collapsed to the ground.

The invisible entity then returned its attention to the knotted duvet and to the medium who lay prostrate on the bed. Blood dribbled from Wilhelmina's right ear where she had struck the mantelpiece. Recovering my breath, I attempted to rise, but was slammed back into place by a blast of pure heat. The room went white. Sweat dripped from my brow.

When my vision had cleared, I saw to my horror that the remains of the duvet were cinched firmly about the medium's neck. The ends had been twisted into a kind of coil, which tightened slowly, slowly. Helpless, I watched as Wilhelmina's face turned red, then purple. Blood filled the whites of her eyes, and I knew that she was dead. But still the rope continued to strangle her, the cord pulled tight as a wire, loosing a spray of arterial blood.

Finding my strength, I leapt to my feet and sprinted for the door, barreling down the stairs into the foyer. I crashed through the front door, letting it shut slam behind me, and ran until I had reached the glare of the nearest street lamp. There I paused to regain my breath, panting in the cool air until the panic had departed. I glanced behind me, but the street was quiet.

I could not go to the police, of course. No one would believe my story, and there were no other witnesses to her death. If the sitters were questioned, it would surely emerge that I had been observed outside her house on more than one occasion, and it would be clear that I had waited until her servant had gone before entering.

Reporting her death would gain me

nothing but the noose — and I doubted that even death could deliver me from the memory of Louisa. Even then, as I steadied myself against the street lamp, I imagined she was somewhere close by, which was impossible, for I had seen her killed before my eyes, strangled for reasons I could not possibly understand.

I heard footsteps from the end of the lane — an officer completing his rounds. I had no choice. I could not let myself be found near the house. I lit for the shadows and scuttled home through a city that seemed increasingly more corpse-like than somnolent. Houses folded into headstones as I passed. Naked trees blackened and slouched toward an inevitable, all-consuming rot. From somewhere far off, I heard the peal of a church bell.

It was four o'clock.

*

You might recall the sensation that attended the death of Miss Volkov. That was not her real name, of course. She was in actuality one Wilhelmina Davenport, formerly of Falmouth in Vermont. She had changed her surname and relocated to southern New England in order to capitalize on the success of Mme. Blavatsky.

According to the papers, which I followed with obsessive interest, her manservant returned home on the morning following my visit to find that she had been murdered. Her mangled corpse was discovered in the master bedroom beneath a dusting of white down.

During the coming weeks, the police posted regular notices in the papers, but no one came forward with information. Eventually, public interest waned and the investigation was discontinued — much to my relief, as I had lived for weeks in constant fear that I had been spotted near her house. Following the investigation, the medium's remains were sent home to Vermont and buried in the family plot.

Six months after Wilhelmina's death, I had reason to travel to Falmouth. While there I visited the cemetery in which she was buried. It was a miserable day, pelting down with rain, and I spent the better part of two hours pacing amid the graves. When the downpour intensified, I sought shelter beneath a red cedar and was reminded once more of her green eyes.

The day had dimmed into twilight by the time I located the Davenport plot and found the stone beneath which she lay. Above me, the sky sprawled, gray and dead. By its faint light, I kneeled before her grave and squinted to make out the names inscribed there.

WILHELMINA DAVENPORT
1867-1894

LOUISA DAVENPORT
1867

It was well after midnight when the
minister found me. I was babbling to myself as I
wandered between the stones, soaked to the skin
and feverish with pneumonia. The minister took
me by the arm. He attempted to lead me from
the graveyard but I refused. Later, he returned
with the sheriff, who bound me in cord like a
hog and dragged me from the cemetery. "No!" I
screamed. "Take me back! We must wait 'til
three! We must wait 'til she comes!"

Or so I am told.

In a year's time, I made a tentative
recovery and stepped from the shadow of the
long loneliness in which I had dwelt since my
parents' death: that black sea receded, and I
staggered toward shore. My friends welcomed
me back into their circle, and I took up a career
as a dealer in fine art. This choice of livelihood
further served to drag me into the light, and
eventually, I shook myself free of my old fears
altogether. I sold my father's house and
purchased new lodgings in a more fashionable
quarter.

My newfound position took me to many
society functions, where drink flowed freely and
dancing lasted into the early hours. It was at one
such ball that I found myself earlier this year. I
had just introduced a potential sponsor to a

young artist whom I had taken under my wing. While they spoke, I stood to one side, drink in hand, and guided the conversation toward the subject of patronage. The clock in the room struck three — it must have, though I admit I did not hear it — for someone touched my elbow, and I heard a familiar voice in my ear.

"We'll meet again," she said.

I turned round, but she was gone.

THE TEMPEST GLASS
Or, How Love Deserted the Reverend Danforth

I am not a religious man. All my life, I have
avoided the church as studiously as the more
devout might seek to avoid the lure of the bottle,
say, or the pleasures of the flesh. Though I have
summered in Westminster since the age of
thirty, I have never attended services at the local
meetinghouse. Thus it was only by chance that I
met the Reverend Abel Danforth.

I had heard rumors, of course. He was
reputed to be a Calvinist of the meanest sort,
said to rhapsodize each Sunday on the horrors of
Perdition. He was tender in one moment,
unforgiving in the next, and delivered his
sermons with a certain urgent terror, as though
he too feared the descent of fire from heaven.

The Reverend Danforth had driven some
to despair and many to convert, while
motivating many others, like myself, to keep as
good a distance from the man as propriety
allowed. Having heard the stories, I felt certain I
knew him through and through. My father was
likewise a religious man, unfailingly harsh in his
convictions. Through him I learned not only to
fear God, but to fear those like my father who
would claim to understand His Will. And yet the
Reverend, when I finally met him, proved not at
all like I had imagined.

It was a Saturday in July, getting on

toward noon. The morning's storms had departed, leaving behind some faint clouds and a lingering humidity. I took my coffee on the lawn, as was my custom in those days. The grass sparkled before me, making diamonds out of the sunlight, and damp steamed out of the flowerbeds, whirling in the soft glow that filtered through the beeches. I concerned myself with the morning mail, a task I had long delayed. Thoroughly absorbed, I did not even notice the man until he was midway across the lawn.

He must have come from the woods, though he now appeared oblivious to his surroundings. His speed was ponderous, that of a man in a reverie. A pair of spectacles dangled from a chain round his neck, while his suit was black and shabby. His white collar, though sweat-stained, glimmered faintly.

I realized at once whom he must be and was surprised foremost by his youth (he was no older than thirty, and quite handsome as well) and also by his manner. For this fearsome firebrand, heir to Edwards and his kind, appeared to me much closer in disposition to Goethe's Werther: bookish, thoughtful, and decidedly troubled.

He carried himself with an aura of near-implosive introspection, as though he struggled to resolve some as yet ill-defined question. The best part of a minute passed, during which his plodding course brought him within ten yards of where I sat, watching, at once perplexed and (admittedly) a little amused. However, my enjoyment of this queer scene died the moment the Reverend strayed from the gravel path, and I could only look on in horror as he trampled through a bed of my nasturtiums, leaving a trail of shattered blossoms behind.

This was one offense I could not stand. "You there!" I shouted. "What on earth do you think you're doing?"

The minister spun around. In truth, he appeared every bit as surprised to find himself in my presence as I was to have him there. He knew me, I was sure, if only by reputation.

By that time, I had achieved the status of Westminster's most infamous summer resident: an unreformed drinker, connoisseur of fine tobaccos, and a dedicated man of leisure. Any of these facts would have been enough in itself to render me anathema in the eyes of the pious townsfolk, never mind my professed agnosticism and oft-repeated criticisms of the church.

To Danforth's credit, he did not take this opportunity to lecture me on the dangers of my lifestyle or the necessity of personal salvation. Instead, he stepped gingerly over my nasturtiums and approached me where I sat with the mail.

He offered his hand.

"I am terribly sorry," he said, speaking stiffly. "About your flowers"

"No apology needed." I took the offered hand and squeezed, though I did not go so far as to offer him a seat beside me.

"Thank you. It's good of you."

"Yes, well, what I may lack in Grace, I make up for in graciousness—or so I like to believe, at anyrate."

Danforth showed no sign of having heard. Evidently he was a man with little time for wit.

"I forget myself sometimes," he said. "When I walk. My thoughts turn toward matters of the Fall and human depravity, the Flood and the old covenant. It is easy to become lost in such things. Maggie tells me I could do with a little more worldliness."

"Is that so?"

"She's joking, of course."

"Of course," I said, though I wasn't so sure. "Whereas I have altogether too much of it. Worldliness, I mean."

He looked at me carefully, saying nothing.

"Perhaps you and I might try a hand of bridge sometime? Between the two of us, we might effect the perfect partnership. Your sanctity, my depravity. What do you say?"

His brow furrowed. He sucked his lower lip, and I could see that he was considering the best way in which to refuse my offer while leaving his well-tended sense of Christian charity intact. It appeared that irony, too, was a concept with which he was unfamiliar.

I threw him down a lifeline. "But perhaps Mrs. Danforth would not approve?"

"There is no such person."

"Oh. And Maggie?"

"We are to wed this winter."

I congratulated him and said the usual kinds of things. He smiled awkwardly, looked at his feet, and said (again) the usual kinds of things, though I sensed the topic of marriage made him distinctly uncomfortable. With all of his talk of depravity, I shouldn't wonder.

As we spoke, the sky clouded over again, throwing us into the shadow of the now-hidden sun. It became clear that Danforth was anxious to move on and resume his meditations elsewhere, presumably someplace well-clear of idle wit.

I wished him good day, and he apologized once more before stalking off. This time, he stepped carefully over the flowerbeds and followed the downhill slope of the lawn to Morse Brook, which fed into the Connecticut half-a-mile away.

He was nearly out of sight when he halted. He remained stationary for a time, standing with his hands at his sides, looking up. I followed his gaze into the west, where the faintest trace of a rainbow was visible — but not for long.

The day was turning. In the distance, the cloud-cover thinned and dissolved, punctured by a profusion of visible rays. When the sun emerged, wiping the last traces of color from the sky, the minister lowered his head and continued on his way.

*

At the time, I thought nothing of it. It was a curious encounter, yes, but I felt reasonably confident I would have no more interaction with the Reverend Danforth. I had no intention of visiting his church and was likewise certain I would not find him on my lawn again. As it happened, though, I was to encounter the Reverend once more before that summer was out — and in nearly the last place I expected.

By this time, it was mid-August. The days were long and sunny, characterized by damp heat and an ever-present drowsiness. It was, as I recall, a summer of exquisite contrasts: sunlit days, rain-filled nights. On the morning after a particularly violent storm (which had done no more to further the cause of my nasturtiums than had the minister's visit), I received a letter from my friend Franklin Talbot.

Franklin and I had met twenty years earlier when we were students at Yale. Since then, we had remained close, frequently seeking each other's counsel on matters both practical and aesthetic. Some time before, I had recommended Westminster as a suitable spot in which to escape the Boston summer, and Franklin had accordingly rented a house in nearby Putney, no more than ten miles from my own summer retreat. His house was a grand Georgian pile, easily a hundred years old, and named, somewhat mysteriously, Willow Wood—mysterious, I mean, given the total absence of willow trees on the property.

On that particular morning (glorious, as I remember it, but so, too, were all mornings that summer) Franklin invited me to a dinner party that was to be held at Willow Wood in one week's time. Several months had passed since I had last seen my friend, and I looked forward to this opportunity to catch up properly.

He wrote: "You may expect an intimate affair—and no, Julius, not that kind of affair—with no more than seven or eight attending (your esteemed self, included). Do write back to tell me you can make it. There will be one or two new guests, including my cousin Ann Margaret, up from New York. I'm hoping I might show off the Tempest Glass."

Ah, yes. The Tempest Glass.

Franklin had discovered this curious object in the attic of Willow Wood some five years before. It was a thing of real beauty, a cut glass mirror measuring some three-feet-by-one and inset within an exquisite design of sheaves and laurels. Evidently, the previous owners had not approved, finding it gaudy. But Franklin was besotted. He blew the dust from the glass and decided then and there that he would display it in the house. After careful consideration, he chose the parlor and selected a position of prominence over the hearth.

For a month, all was quiet. And then, one morning, the maid noticed something queer. It was not yet dawn, unseasonably cold, and she had risen early to light the fires. Having banked the parlor fire, she stood and collected her bucket. But something stopped her.

The mirror had changed. Where it should have reflected the opposite wall (dominated by a portrait of Talbot himself), it had gone completely blank: cold and gray, the color of slate. What's more, the surface of the mirror was in motion. The glass itself rippled, teeming with waves that traversed it horizontally, dark and foaming, as though whipped up by a storm.

Understandably, she turned and took flight. Later, she described her ordeal to Sanders, the butler, who in turn presented the matter to Franklin.

My friend laughed. "My God," he said. "I've never heard such nonsense. Isn't it a little early in the year for her to be reading ghost stories?"

The butler said nothing. His bearing was grim.

Normally, this would not have given Franklin much pause (grimness was, after all, rather the man's usual state of being), but there was something else there too: a tremble of the lip, an aversion of the eyes. Sanders was frightened.

Franklin decided to tackle the matter head on. "Is something the matter?" he asked.

"It isn't 'nonsense,'" the butler replied. "And you mustn't take the Lord's name in vain." (Did I mention that Mr. Sanders was a member of Danforth's congregation?)

"But surely you don't believe her story?"

The butler nodded. Grimly. "I do," he said. "I have seen it myself."

He would say no more about the matter. Franklin consulted the maid, who told him the tale much as I have related it here. At this, my friend's curiosity was well and truly kindled and could not be extinguished by mere second-hand experience.

For the better part of a week, he took to studying the mirror, watching it for hours at a time, though the waves never appeared. One night, I even joined him in keeping vigil in the parlor. Again the glass remained defiantly mirror-like, revealing nothing save the reflection of Franklin's portrait, which appeared to us with startling suddenness when I lit a candle, giving us both a fright. Nerves aside, the night proved uneventful. All the same, we agreed there was something distinctly odd about the thing and swore an oath to each other on our friendship that we would not spend a night alone in its presence.

Meanwhile, rumors were spread among the servants, followed by the usual superstitious whispers one encounters in such places. Matters devolved to the point where none of the house staff would enter the parlor as long as the mirror remained. It was, they said, a thing of ill omen. The previous owners had done right by locking it in the attic.

Franklin had little choice but to remove the mirror from the parlor and relocate it upstairs to one of the guest rooms on the third floor. After a time, he took to treating the whole thing as a joke. The mirror became nothing more than an object of curiosity, something to be shown off to relatives and guests at dinner parties.

Five years later, the majority of Franklin's acquaintances were all too familiar with "The Tempest Glass," as he had fancifully dubbed it. However, my friend's enthusiasm for the thing had not yet waned, and I fully anticipated an evening of spiritual talk and general good cheer. I accepted his invitation.

*

And so it was that one week later I found myself in Willow Wood's parlor (now distinctly mirror-less) engaged in conversation with the beautiful Ann Margaret Smythe, my friend's young cousin. She was eighteen years of age and as enchanting a creature as any I've encountered: possessed of a naiveté that seemed half-affected, as though she knew far more of the world than she was willing to let on.

Despite the difference in our ages, I found myself much taken with her, and it was with some sadness that I noticed the ring on her finger. She was, I thought, altogether too lovely to belong to one man alone. She had been in Westminster for no more than a month, and in that time had managed to get herself engaged to one of the locals. I counted this as society's loss and expressed a hope that I might meet her husband-to-be.

"And so you shall," she said. "He will join us tonight for dinner."

Shortly afterward, the bell sounded, and she allowed me to escort her into the dining room. I showed her to her seat beside her cousin — the seat to her right was left open, awaiting her fiancé — before sitting down opposite Franklin, sandwiched between two older women by the names of Rose Montgomery and Ethel Ford. Though they resided together in New York, it was clear to me that their relationship was Bostonian in nature.

At the far end of the table sat Mr. Lattice, a local man and owner of a dry goods shop in Brattleboro. Among our happy company, he had achieved near-legendary status, noted chiefly for his singular dullness.

Soup was served and cleared away, followed by the fish course. We consumed the meal in near-silence, punctuated by bursts of conversation that sparked and faded away. An atmosphere of expectation had fallen over us as we awaited the arrival of our final guest: an empty chair at table often produces such an effect.

Midway through the second course, we heard the bell. The tinkle of chimes was followed by low voices and the din of footsteps in the hall. Then the door swung open — Ann Margaret's face exploded into a smile — and the Reverend Danforth entered the room.

Franklin stood. "Welcome, Reverend!" he exclaimed and gestured to the empty seat beside Ann Margaret.

"Thank you, Franklin," said he. "It is, as always, a pleasure."

He spoke stiffly, and even on this happy occasion, appeared singularly detached. He greeted his fiancée with the vaguest of nods — which only caused her smile to widen — and sat down between her and the housekeeper Mrs. Carr, who had been pressed into service at the last minute to ensure an even number round the table.

Franklin made the usual introductions. Danforth in turn acknowledged each guest in a perfunctory manner: "A pleasure, I'm sure," or "Pleased to make your acquaintance" and so on.

When it was my turn to be introduced, our eyes met across the table. He must have recognized me, but if he did, he showed no sign of it. "A great pleasure," he said, and then it was on to Miss Ford.

Sanders arrived with the meat course and proceeded to lay our plates before us. All was quiet for a spell, save for the rattle of plates and cutlery, and then we became aware of something else: the Reverend Danforth sitting with head bowed, lips moving in a murmured prayer.

My ears caught only one or two words here and there, but it was the usual sort of thing you might expect, replete with references to "Grace" and "faithfulness," etc. I don't mind saying that it made us distinctly uncomfortable — well, most of us anyway. Ann Margaret sat beside her fiancé with head lowered, eyes closed. After an interminable two or three minutes, the Reverend muttered a sulky "Amen" that was echoed by the beautiful creature beside him.

Heads were raised, eyes opened, and the rest of us, taking our cue, immediately fell upon our rapidly cooling food with the hunger of

Tantalus. Perhaps it was the august presence of this man of God, but the topic of our conversation soon shifted to unearthly matters — and inevitably — to the mystery of the Tempest Glass.

Most of us had heard the maid's story many times before — though, to Franklin's credit, it really did change very little with the telling. However, the tale was clearly unfamiliar to Ann Margaret. She pressed her cousin for details, inquired into past owners of the house, and even hazarded a theory (ingenious but flawed) on the illusion-producing properties of mirror-glass.

By contrast, her fiancé remained silent, his face a mask of cold composure. Clearly the man was not enjoying the story, for all of my friend's efforts. Franklin even went so far as to mimic the maid's piping voice, making a rather creditable attempt at the Yankee burr. Nevertheless, Danforth remained unmoved.

Franklin addressed him directly. "Tell me, Reverend. You are a man of the church. Do you not share my maid's belief in the supernatural?"

Danforth exhaled heavily. His spectacles had slipped to the end of his nose, where they threw back the candlelight. I noted my reflection in both lenses. "It's true," he said, "that I am a man of God. And yes, my faith is a simple one. But I am no simpleton."

"I assure you," said Franklin, "I meant to

imply no such thing."

"I know — and no offense was taken. The fault lies not with you but with the question itself. Whatever you may think, all beliefs in the supernatural are not in themselves equivalent — and this so called 'spiritualism' is the exclusive territory of fools and charlatans."

Ann Margaret protested. "Surely, Abel, you are too harsh — "

Franklin lifted his hand. "No, my dear cousin, he is correct. And I do not profess any active belief in spiritualism. But I do think there are matters that cannot be so easily explained away — either by science or by theology."

Here I added my assent. "The Bard put it best, I think. 'More things in Heaven and Earth' and so on."

The minister shook his head vehemently. "Utter nonsense," he said. "True faith in the Word allows for no mysteries but one."

I could not let such a remark slip past me unchallenged. The hook was well and truly baited: what choice had I but to bite?

"What, then, of Mr. Darwin's theories? Or those of William James?"

"What of them?"

"You must concede that the world is changing — more rapidly now than ever before. Things once thought impossible have proven all too easy. The phonograph. Electric light. Islands are emerging from the seas of ignorance that have hitherto surrounded us. Soon a new continent will be revealed, more wondrous and dangerous than unexplored Africa."

"And the Scripture?"

"It will have to change, adapt itself. Much as it has always done. We no longer believe in the geocentric model—as did Martin Luther, or your Calvin. And the science of geology casts significant doubts on the reality of the Flood account. I wonder if you are familiar with the recent work of the German theologians? Wellhausen writes that…"

As I continued, Danforth's face darkened to the color of cooked beets. Up to this point, our debate had been spirited but good-natured. But now I trailed off, sensing that my hapless barque may have passed (once more) into dangerous waters.

The minister's brow hardened. An edge like steel came into his voice. "First you profess some openness to the tenets of spiritualism—which would be laughable were it not outright blasphemous—and now you dare to openly question the authority of Scripture. I fear, *sir*, that I cannot abide such talk."

He stood up from the table in what struck me as a rather theatrical fashion. Ann Margaret looked at me, her blue eyes showing surprise and hurt, her pretty face warped with anguish. In that instant, I repented of all my sins and blasphemies and resolved, from here on out, to be kinder to the minister, whatever the madness of his convictions.

Ever the gracious host, Franklin caught hold of Danforth's arm and begged him to remain. "You must forgive Julius. He is fond of friendly debate." He cast a purposeful glance in my direction. "Overly fond, I sometimes think."

Here then was my opportunity to redeem myself in the eyes of Ann Margaret. "Alas," I said. "My friend is correct. I apologize if I crossed a line."

Duly mollified, the minister resumed his seat at the table. His fiancée's face registered relief, then joy. She grinned openly at the entire table, even sparing a glance for myself, who had come so perilously close to ruining her evening.

And then—before my eyes—this charming smile transformed itself into something more subtle and curious and even a little wicked.

"If you will allow me to speak," she said. "I believe I see a means by which we might settle the question."

Instantly, she received our full attention. She turned to her cousin. "Franklin, you and Julius have expressed a fascination with spiritualism. While you may criticize the Christian religion, you are open to the idea of the supernatural as a force distinct from the miracles described by the scripture. Is that more or less accurate?"

We had to concede that it was. Next she cast her gaze upon the minister. "Whereas you, dear Abel, profess a belief in the Word of God and a disdain for the vagaries of spiritualism— whether they may manifest themselves at a séance or, indeed, by way of a haunted mirror."

Two chairs down, Franklin grinned. "Yes, yes," he said. "I believe I can see where this is headed—and I wholeheartedly approve."

On the other hand, I was still in the dark. "And for those of us who do not share my good friend's apparent aptitude for mental transference…?"

"Well," Ann Margaret said. "It's simple, really. Franklin related how the two of you once stayed up all night in the presence of the mirror and saw nothing. Nevertheless the experience left you sufficiently unnerved that you would not dare to pass a night alone with it."

"Quite right," I said. Whatever my other faults, I have never shied away from admitting my essential cowardice.

She went on: "As Franklin knows, Abel has already elected to stay here tonight as a guest. We have given him a room on the first floor, but perhaps we might allow him to stay on the third? The room with the mirror. What do you think, Abel?"

Danforth pushed the spectacles up his nose, his eyes leaping into focus behind them. "Very well," he said. "If it will help to lay these idiot rumors to rest, then I consider it my duty as a Christian minister."

I will confess that I felt a twinge of nervousness then, though Franklin was all mirth. He clapped his hands with delight and declared the discussion at an end. "The matter is settled. By tomorrow morning, we shall finally have an answer to the riddle of the Tempest Glass."

*

After dessert, our party adjourned to the parlor where a lively game of charades ensued (the Reverend Danforth abstaining on what I could only assume were moral grounds), followed by Franklin's demonstration of the gramophone — an event that caused the minister no little distress. He seemed genuinely terrified of the voice that issued from it, even though it was sweetly singing *Claire de Lune*, and I found myself worried on his account for his upcoming stay in the third floor guest room.

By this time, it was growing late, so I made my farewells to Lattice and the Bostonians and surprised myself by shaking the minister's hand. "My apologies, Reverend, for any offense I may have given. I look forward to hearing about your experiences tonight."

"I accept your apology," he replied, "and offer my own in return. I can see now that I overreacted. As for tonight, there will be little enough to discuss."

"Yes, well, be that as it may... some caution might be warranted, eh?"

Next, I said goodnight to my host, saving the enchanting Ann Margaret for last. When I came to her, I bowed and kissed her outstretched hand. She regarded me placidly, the hints of a smile on her lips, her skin like warm honey in that light.

"Farewell, dear child. You mustn't worry yourself too much on account of your husband-to-be."

Her eyes glittered, sharp with firelight. "Oh," she said. "I'm not worried."

"No?"

"On the contrary, I think tonight will prove most interesting."

*

The first indication I received that something was amiss came in the form of a scrawled note delivered to my door shortly after eleven the next morning.

Crisis. AM much distraught. Come at once. FGT.

Fearing the worst, I rang for the valet and called downstairs for a carriage to be readied. My mouth had gone dry and mealy. While I dressed, my imagination — overly vigorous even at the best of times — presented me with scene after scene of fantastical horror. Here was the minister sprawled on the floor, stone-dead, his mouth stretched thin in agony. There he was, trapped inside the mirror, eyes wide and staring, while Ann Margaret screamed and pounded her fists on the unyielding glass.

I arrived at Willow Wood not long after noon. To my relief, there were no circling constables, no parasitic journalists — only the reliable Sanders, who nodded in greeting and showed me into the parlor. Inside, I found my friend seated before the French windows with a tumbler of sherry cupped in both hands, his face downcast, as though it bore within its likeness all the sorrows of the world.

"What is it?" I asked. "What has happened?"

"It is," he began, "the Reverend Danforth."

My stomach lurched.

"He has broken off the engagement."

"Ah," I said.

With that, my ghoulish fantasies faded to nothing, and I thought of the way a midnight apparition is revealed by dawn to be a limp and tattered curtain.

My relief must have shown, for Franklin became angry with me. "Have you no feelings at all? No kindness? No pity? My dear cousin is upstairs weeping, utterly inconsolable, and all you have to say is 'Ah?'"

"You must forgive me. I was in shock. It is a beastly thing."

"The brute!" He drained the rest of his glass. "And to think I gave him my blessing to marry Ann Margaret, that I sheltered him under my own roof… It sickens me, Julius. Sickens me."

He poured himself another sherry. By now, the decanter was half-empty.

"And the mirror?" I asked.

His eyes widened. "The mirror? Confound the damned thing. I intend to have it melted down at the earliest opportunity."

"But Danforth — did he…?"

"He did. He came down this morning in something of a state. When I asked him what was the matter, he fed me some tripe about the Flood and made some excuse to be on his way. It was only later that I learned from my cousin what had actually transpired."

"Which is?"

"This morning, after spending the night with the mirror, he came into her room on the third floor and informed her that their engagement was at an end."

"He gave no reason?"

"None. He simply turned and left the room. It was shortly after this that I spoke to him, but he said nothing of it."

He sipped from his sherry, sloshing the

liquid around in his mouth before swallowing it down. He sighed. The anger drained out of his face, leaving behind a genuine sadness.

"Ah well," he mused. "I suppose it really is for the best. Better to be rid of him now when he has no claim to Ann Margaret's money."

I echoed this conclusion and poured myself a drink, opening the French windows to admit the balmy air. Sanders brought in lunch and we spent the next hour or more engaged in conversation on matters as trivial as they were irrelevant.

All of this had the effect of brightening Franklin's mood considerably so that I dared to bring the discussion back to the subject of the Tempest Glass.

"Danforth mentioned something about a flood?"

"Not *a* flood. *The* Flood. Noah's Ark and all that."

"Oh?"

"Apparently, he lay himself down to sleep shortly after retiring. He fell asleep almost immediately and slept soundly—for a time, that is. Then, in the dark of the night, he was awoken by a noise like rushing waves. Recalling the maid's story, he lighted the lamp and approached the mirror where it sat in its usual place on the chair in the corner.

"There he saw the same thing as the maid and the butler. Gray waves rippled across the glass, their peaks white and tufted as in the midst of a storm. But he continued to watch, longer than the maid had dared, and soon the waves darkened, becoming more brown than gray—and frothing. Spray boiled off in great clouds as the waves crashed together, and he distinctly felt the cold kiss of moisture on his cheek."

I chuckled. "I didn't realize the Reverend was given to such fanciful description."

"Well," Franklin admitted, "I may have embroidered the language somewhat, but you see what I'm driving at. The water splashed out of the mirror, wetting his face and shirt. But still he could not look away. Eventually, the waves passed, leaving the waters brown and dirty and rapidly receding. What he saw next terrified him. As the floodwaters sloughed away, shapes surfaced out of the murk."

"Shapes?"

"Farmhouses. Carriages. Horses bloated with rot. Bodies floating facedown, the corpses of mothers and children. A telegraph pole with wires trailing out behind it. He—"

I had to interrupt. "I thought you said he had seen the Flood? The man's shortcomings are considerable, I grant you, but surely he can't believe they had the *telegraph* in the days of Noah."

Franklin shrugged. "They were his words, not mine. 'The Flood.' He was very clear about that. Now if I may continue?"

"By all means."

"Nonsense or not, I could see the whole thing had left him quite distressed. I hadn't taken him for the Millerite type, but I rather fancy he imagined that he had witnessed — in that mirror — the end of the world. 'The broken covenant,' he said. He kept repeating that phrase. 'The broken covenant.' As though it were all his fault. Just punishment for sins he had committed. I have to admit that I found it all rather strange."

"Not so strange, perhaps. He is, I believe, a practitioner of Total Depravity."

Franklin laughed. I was glad of it: it was the first time that day I had heard that familiar laugh. "Indeed. Well, as I said, he was obviously upset, so I asked him to mention nothing of the matter to Ann Margaret. But when he heard her name, a change came over him."

"A change?"

"I can't be any more precise than that. If anything, I would say he became even more serious — though that scarcely seems possible. 'Oh,' he said. 'There is little chance of that.'"

Franklin stared into his empty glass with an air of mournful contemplation. "I suppose that should have been my first warning."

"You mustn't blame yourself. How were you to know?"

I patted his hand reassuringly.

"Thank you, Julius. I am glad you are here."

"And Ann Margaret?" I asked.

"She returns to New York tomorrow."

"Tomorrow? That is sudden."

"Yes. She is most adamant about it."

"Ah," I said, with a touch of regret.

Franklin appeared lost in thought. With the sherry glass in one hand, he watched the shadows shrink from the lawn. He brought the glass to his lips and ran his tongue round the rim.

"The broken covenant," he muttered. "God. What a madman."

*

Naturally, there are postscripts.

The next morning, her engagement broken, Ann Margaret returned to New York. I assumed that was an end to the matter, but in the months that followed, I heard gossip of the most shocking kind. Franklin would say nothing about it, neither to confirm or deny, and I knew better than to press him. Whatever the truth of these rumors might have been, I never heard talk of a child, so perhaps there was nothing to them after all.

As for Franklin, my friend took ill in the fall of '09. He died abroad, stricken with fever while staying in a rented Tuscan villa. He is buried over there. His grand-nephew informs me that his tomb is carved from a warm red marble unique to that region of Italy. It is, he avers, a truly remarkable stone, one that seems to catch the light itself, retaining its glow in a way a mirror never could.

On this point, I should also add that Franklin ceased to show off the Tempest Glass immediately after the incident. Later that summer, he sent it to be melted down — much to the collective relief of his household staff. "A thing of ill omen," indeed.

Which brings me to Danforth himself. As I understand it, he never recovered from his night at Willow Wood. His sermons became listless and uninspired, delivered by rote in a halting monotone that terrified his parishioners far more than any promise of hellfire. In time, he took to tramping the hills as his full time vocation, absenting himself from his church duties for days or weeks at a time, so that the congregation had no recourse but to remove him from his post.

Danforth took this development in stride, or seemed to. For years afterward, he continued to live on in Westminster, working odd jobs to support himself. He never married. One summer, I arrived in town only to learn that he had sold his cottage and taken the early train north — heading for Canada, the locals reckoned, though he never made it that far.

Two decades passed, during which I heard nothing of the man, and I confess I had nearly forgotten him altogether when I received the news from Waterbury.

This was during the summer of last year, my first season in Vermont following the floods of '27. In the days after the storm, one of the local boys — the grandson of my gardener, from whom I heard the tale — traveled north to assist in the ongoing recovery.

In Waterbury, the lad was posted to a team that was dispatched to search the surrounding landscape for a local hermit, an older man known to the folk of nearby Ricker Basin as "The Reverend." Perhaps you can guess the rest.

They never found him, but they did find his house — what remained of it, anyway. The former minister had chosen to spend his final years in a one-room cabin in the basin of a rocky cleft. When the waters came roaring down the Winooski, they bore down on his retreat with all of the force of an avalanche, blasting the cabin to pieces.

The gardener described the scene in great detail: a wasteland of displaced boulders, fallen trees, and uprooted stumps. Oddly enough, the only object standing proved to be a telephone pole, which had been deposited there by the flood, its severed wires twitching like vines in the frigid autumn gale. Overhead, the sky was gray and patchy, threatening more rain.

The searchers picked through the wreckage of the cabin. They uncovered little of interest save for a waterlogged bible, some old clerical garments, and a pocket watch inscribed on the back with the words *To A from AM*. The watch may have once had value but the mechanism was long broken, the face rusted shut. They left it behind in the wreckage and departed that melancholy scene under a persistent drizzle.

The gardener's story ended there, but my imagination—overactive, I fear, even in my old age—has supplied these final details.

The rain continued, filling open graves and exposed cellar holes, the empty eyes of Abel Danforth. He lay with his face to the sky in some forgotten hollow, never to be discovered. Mid-November. Winter was near at hand. The wind gusted and howled, stripping the last leaves from the trees, even as the sun emerged to streak the sky with color. A rainbow.

What was it Franklin said?
God: What a madman.

HOUSE OF THE CARYATIDS

My father told me this story on his deathbed. He was young, not yet thirty, but the War had marked him when he was little more than a boy himself, and besides, he was ill.

More than once, I found him seated on the floor of the bedroom, wearing his tattered uniform with his legs crossed beneath him. His eyes were open, but he looked at nothing, his face turned away, as though to a past I could not see.

Nerves, the doctor said, but I wonder if the poison ran deeper than that somehow, pulsing in his failing organs, beating in his blood and brain. I was just a child, but even then he seemed a vacant shell, bird's egg-thin, cracked by the horrors he had witnessed.

And yet for all that, he was a cruel man, often violent, and I have not forgotten his anger: the roar of his voice in the house at night and the bruises my mother carried with her. This rage sustained him for most of my childhood, burning him up body and mind until at last his illness worsened and he no longer had the breath to shout.

For days he lay incoherent, sweat-soaked and babbling from the grip of nightmare. Clarity dawned only in his final hours, whereupon he summoned me to the bedside and sent my mother from the room. He thrust out his hand.

He grabbed me about the collar.

"Look at me, boy," he said. His blackened teeth were visible. The hot breath streamed across my face, rank with the odors of medicine and decay. "Look at me," he repeated, speaking with such urgency and terror that I recalled the words of the angel from Revelation.

Come and see.

*

You cannot imagine what it was like [he said], that hell they called Shiloh. The rebels yelling as they swarmed from the trees, screeching like banshees as the grapeshot burst among us. And so much blood. Bodies stacked like cordwood up and down the lines, and still the guns were sounding. I was sixteen. I threw myself down among the bodies and hid there all that day, quivering with the stench of death in my nostrils, so sickly and strong I could scarcely breathe, and always the blossoms raining down from the peach trees, settling over me like snow.

As I've said, you cannot imagine it. The fear. The shame of it.

But maybe you can understand what came later. Why we marched through Georgia with Sherman. Why we did the things we did. Or maybe not. It hardly matters now, but by God, we made that country howl. We set their fields alight and left them smoldering behind us, laughing and singing with our heads full of hate and bootlegged liquor.

This was in December of '64. We were inseparable in those days, the three of us: myself, the Irishman Barry, and William Nichols, an artist turned to soldiering.

Nichols was only a corporal but was born of wealthy parents and plainly accustomed to having things his way. What's more, he was an educated man, a graduate of Yale, and I wondered at first what caused him to enlist. I knew better than to ask him, of course, but Barry once mentioned an incident involving a woman in New York, a shop-girl who had turned up dead, but it was more than his own life was worth, Barry averred, to speak of it further, and anyway, I'm not sure I believed him, not then.

That morning was particularly hot, as I remember, sunlight blurring the dogwood with the magnolia and all of it shimmering with damp. The three of us had left the camp at dawn on a foraging party but later sneaked away from the others so as to prowl alone that empty country, searching out whiskey or ale or a woman's company.

At noon, we came to an old wagon road and this we followed uphill 'til we reached a kind of promontory. From there we spied a large plantation below, a square house ringed with columns. It looked to have been abandoned during the previous summer, and in some hurry, for the crops lay un-harvested, the pastures brown and sickly.

We descended the far side of the ridgeline, catching ourselves when the sodden earth crumbled and gave way underfoot. The sun beat down on us, hotter than before, and the world itself seemed to shrink from its glare until the rest of our regiment came to seem immeasurably far away, the road back masked by rising heat.

We came to a crossroads marked by a splintered signpost. "The Pillars," it read, "1 mile," the sign angled in such a way as to point down a narrow road.

The earth was muddy, the track well-faded, but we took it gladly, dreaming already of that big house and whatever we might find inside. And though the distance may have been a mile by the crow's flight, the route proved torturous in the extreme, dipping and weaving all the time, circling round swamp and sinkhole alike, so that it was the best part of an hour before we emerged at the edge of the plantation itself.

The fields were flooded, half-submerged. Tufts of old cotton mingled with overgrown weeds and grass. The winter rains had washed away most of the old wagon track, but its former course could be discerned where it cut through the fields and made a loop before the big house. The mansion faced south, its columns flaming like beacons with the sun shining on them.

Barry pointed. "You see them?" he asked me. "The women."

"Women?"

"The pillars, boy. You see how they're shaped?"

I shaded my eyes and looked again and sure enough I saw them, the women. Every one of those pillars had been carved in the shape of a standing woman. A few had their hands at their sides while others seemed to be holding flowers, open books, sheaves of grain.

"Caryatids," Nichols said. "That's what they're called."

We continued across the fields at a good clip, preceded by our shadows where they stretched over the cotton. Soon we reached the entrance, where two columns flanked the high doors. These pillars were taller than the others, reaching the height of the roof, and they were a different color too. Whereas the other columns were white, or mostly so, these were made from a darker stone shot through with rusty veins.

The first of these pillars wore a shapeless, robe-like garment that covered her from head to foot. She had no face but for those folds of sculpted cloth, and her hands were clasped before her, as though in prayer. The second pillar couldn't have been more different. This woman was naked but for the armor on her forearms and shins. In one hand she carried a bow. With the other she lifted a sword high over her head, its tip forming part of the cornice overhead.

She snarled at us, her mouth open.

Barry tried the doors, but they were locked fast, barred from the inside. So we circled round to the far side of the mansion, skirting the boundary of a small burial plot marked with a dozen wooden crosses. A shiver went through me at the sight of it, but then the wind was kicking up as well, and I caught a whiff of something like flowering weeds or cotton gone to mold.

We found a back door. This, too, was locked, but Nichols kicked it in with ease and we followed him inside. The hallway was dim, un-windowed, with closed doors stretching to either side of us. Nichols opened one. He ducked inside, shrugged, and moved onto the next, battering down one door then another, using the butt of his rifle, smashing bolts and hinges.

All of the rooms were empty. In one doorway I lingered long enough to take in the straw-covered cot, a pair of cheap candlesticks crusted with wax. A bedroom of some sort, I thought. Slave quarters, maybe. The curtains were drawn, but a wan light seeped through, casting a checkered glow on the floor, and I saw that the boards were clean and largely free of dust.

By now Nichols and Barry were far ahead

of me. They had reached the end of the hall, where a heavy door blocked our way, sealing us inside that narrow corridor. Nichols struck out with his rifle-butt. This caused the door to shudder, though it didn't yield, not even after a second blow and a third. Barry simply grinned and tried the handle. It was unlocked.

He stepped through, and I followed, emerging behind him into the largest room I had ever seen. The ceilings were high, the space beneath unfurnished save for scattered piles of silk cushions, which were grouped about an assortment of braziers and candelabra.

It seemed we were inside an entry hall of some sort, though the high doors were nailed shut. To our left, a wide staircase swept down from the upper floor, while a marble pedestal sat at the center of the room, opposite the stair, upon which perched the statue of a naked man.

He was four feet tall, nearly life-sized, his eyes round and piercing but also distant, as though he were straining to see across an unbridgeable chasm. Only when I looked closer did I notice the horns nestled within the loops of his hair and the hooves he had in place of feet.

Nichols was drawn to it immediately. He approached the statue with short, shuffling steps and came to a halt directly beneath it. He sighed and smiled queerly, his face darkening with a memory of other days. "Exquisite," he said.

I looked at Barry, but the Irishman looked

at least as surprised as I felt, and then I recalled that Nichols had once been an artist. Maybe he had been a sculptor.

For a while, we were quiet, and I walked toward the doors, drawing up short when I noticed the picture at my feet, lying half-concealed beneath a silk pillow. It was a daguerreotype image of a man in a ladder-back chair: tall and gaunt, his hands long and thin. The glass casing had cracked, allowing in the damp, so that the man's face had been blotted out, though the doctor's bag on his knee bespoke his profession. A statue could be seen in the background, a naked man with hooves, and I realized the photograph had been taken in that very room.

I thought about picking it up but decided against it. The picture made me distinctly uneasy, though I couldn't say why. Just a feeling, I suppose. So I went to the window and peeled back the drapery to look outside. Shadows moved on the statue of the covered woman, and beyond her, the flooded fields rippled and frothed.

Barry broke the silence.

"This Goddamned heat," he said, mopping his brow. "I'm thirsty."

"You're always thirsty," Nichols said, who appeared to have shaken off whatever spell had come over him. "Comes with being Irish, I expect."

"Maybe so," Barry replied, gamely. "But the kitchen can't be far from here."

I rejoined the others where they lingered round the statue, and Nichols led us down a second corridor, one running parallel to the first. We passed closets stuffed with stained linens, bedding ragged with age or overuse. The kitchen lay at the end of this hallway, a cramped space floored in stone with small windows opening onto the rear of the house.

We laid our rifles by the door. Inside, the great hearth was unlit, mounded with old ashes, and a flight of stairs led down to the cellars. To the right I spotted a small door inset within the wall. It caught my eye straightaway, being no more than a yard on a side and situated some three feet off the ground.

"A dumbwaiter," Barry said. "You find them in houses like this."

Nichols threw wide the pantry doors and began to rummage, looking for whiskey, I guessed, or wine. Finding nothing, he cursed and dashed a shelf of canning jars onto the floor.

"I'm going down the cellar," he said, and swept from the pantry, trailed by Barry, who paused just long enough to pluck a pickled onion from the floor and sink in his teeth.

I didn't go with them. I suppose I was still nervous, still unsettled. Or maybe I was just tired. I don't know. In any case I set myself down upon the counter and fanned myself with my cap, listening to the wind through the columns outside, bringing in the storm.

After a time, rain broke from the clouds and clattered against the windows, and a few whoops of laughter drifted up from the cellar. Nichols had found the spirits, evidently, and I lowered myself to the ground, thinking I might go and join them.

Then I heard something, and froze. I listened hard 'til I heard it again.

The sound of someone breathing. Coming from inside the dumbwaiter.

The blood surged inside me. Shaking now, breathing fast, I stalked noiselessly to the doors and retrieved my rifle. It wasn't loaded, but I slid the bayonet down over the barrel and thrust it out before me as I approached the dumbwaiter. The breathing grew louder, or so I thought, and then choked off altogether, as though he or she were holding the breath inside them.

A bottle shattered downstairs. Nichols roared with laughter, and I knew they couldn't hear me even if I were to cry out. I was alone in that moment, as I would always be alone. There was nothing else for it: I slid the bayonet under the latch and lifted it free.

The door creaked open. Inside was a negress, a slave. She looked young, younger than I was, and I was just nineteen. She might have been a pretty thing once, but her masters had been awfully cruel to her. Her front teeth were missing, and there were white lines etched about her lips, scars where her mouth had been forcibly widened, the tongue sliced away.

She made no sound, but it was plain enough that she was frightened, and I lowered the bayonet. This caused her to breathe easier — at least for a time, anyway — at least until we heard footfalls on the cellar stairs and Nichols entered the room.

*

My father paused. He hesitated, as though unsure of how much he wished to impart, and the silence stretched between us. In that shared emptiness, a sparrow alighted upon the windowsill. It twitched its head from left to right and then back again, turning one eye on me and then the other, and it was several minutes more before my father resumed his story.

*

We saw to her, the girl we found. Afterward, she scuttled away into the dusk. The wind was still blowing and the downpour showed no signs of ceasing. Four o'clock. We were running out of daylight, but those southern storms never lasted long.

"We'll wait it out," Nichols said.

He refilled his flask from the bottle he had

found and handed it round. Barry helped himself to a swallow then offered it to me. I drank greedily, tipping back the flask 'til my throat ached and the floor seemed to tilt beneath me, sliding away into the cellar's mouth.

"Now, now," said Barry, easing the bottle from my grip. He loosened my fingers one at a time, saying nothing all the while, and Nichols, too, was quiet as he listened to the storm and watched the raindrops slither down the windows.

Barry asked me if I wanted to go upstairs. I nodded. Nichols offered no reply, so we left him where he sat, gazing off into the distance with his pants around one ankle, looking in that moment like the statue he had so admired.

We climbed the staircase to the upper floor, walking without purpose or direction, passing bedrooms and a gentleman's study, and Barry beside me all the while, speaking softly, trying to give comfort. "You did nothing wrong," he said. "You *did* nothing."

But I wasn't listening, and when we came to the doctor's library, I left Barry standing in the doorway and made my way over to the window. The upper half of the frame was domed by a fan of colored glass. Through this I saw the back of the woman-warrior's head, her hair red and streaming against the storm. Her neck was thickly muscled, the tendons showing like knotted ropes, and her sword was visible where it soared to the cornice, splitting the rain as it winged toward the glass.

I stood there for a while—I don't know how long—but the next thing I remember, Barry was calling to me across the library. The ground at his feet was scattered with scraps of loose paper, and he held a drill in his hands.

He motioned me closer, and I crossed the room to where he stood, my steps muted beneath me so that I seemed to be half-floating, moving slow and silent as a somnambulist.

"Look at this," he said, grasping the hand-crank and turning. The bit revolved slowly, the toothed end flecked with black stains. "It's a barber-surgeon's drill. For taking out teeth."

He opened his mouth. "Like these," he said, grinning, showing off rows of rotten stumps—and I thought of the negro girl, the gaps in her otherwise perfect teeth.

I didn't say anything.

"I found it in there," he said, nodding toward the nearest bookcase. "It was on top of those ledgers." One such volume had fallen on the ground. I noted the name upon the cover. Thaddeus H. Field, M.D., Esq. The doctor's accounts were listed inside, with columns showing payments received and so forth, his patients given numbers rather than names.

Thunder rumbled in the distance. Barry rifled through the papers at our feet, reading from notes or letters, pages what appeared torn from an anatomy textbook. He showed me one leaf of paper that bore the imprint of a woman's foot from toe to heel. The stain was brown and dark with age, the outlines blurring where some of the ink had leached through.

"Excellent news," he read aloud. *"Client 107 reported a dramatic increase in pleasure & duration of experience following this latest surgery to the pelvic regions, &c, a fact which I have this evening verified to my own satisfaction. Nonetheless I believe that further surgical intervention may yet prove desirable, given the girl's youth as well as —"*

Footsteps from downstairs. A crash like falling stone.

Barry cut himself off.

"Your rifle," he hissed. "Where is it?"

"The kitchen. I didn't..."

"Stay here," he said. He pressed the drill into my hands. "It isn't much," he said, "but it's sharp enough."

"No," I said. "Don't go."

He unsheathed the knife at his belt. The light was nearly gone, but the blade glittered, reflecting his face in all its anguish and resolve.

"I'll come back for you," he said, and disappeared down the corridor.

I was alone. Rain slapped the window, rattling the frame, and I fought to master my panic, worse now than at Shiloh, and the awful quiet pressing down on me.

Brown stains on the floor. A woman's footprint traced in blood.

Sweat poured down my back, driving shivers out to the tips of my fingers, causing the blood to beat in my veins. It throbbed in my ears, rising steadily in pitch, whistling like irons in the forge or the cry of the warrior-woman as she raised her sword aloft.

Her scream, heard or imagined, slashed through my eardrums, boring into my brain, and I thought of the tongue-less girl, the scars about her mouth, those last words from the Doctor's diary. *Nonetheless I believe that further surgical intervention may yet prove desirable...*

The drill twitched in my hands, a living thing. It slipped free, striking the floor with a heavy thump, and the wind roared again, whipping the rain through the statue's hair and spattering the glass like the spray from a severed artery.

I fled.

The upper hallway ran the length of the house and came to an end before a tall, multi-paned window. The sun was visible through the glass, setting now, bursting from layers of storm-clouds to drive the reddish light before it. I hastened forward, halting when I reached what appeared to be the master bedroom.

I looked inside. The bed was unmade, the clothes caked in black stains.

Behind me, the hallway dimmed. The

light had been blocked, and turning round, I saw her. A woman had appeared at the end of the corridor, robed and hooded like the statue outside. I could not say where she had come from, but she stood there perfectly still, a living statue, as motionless as marble, with her hands clasped before her and the window blazing at her back, setting her edges alight.

Then she stepped forward. It was the slightest of motions, noticeable only because the red light flickered about her, and she moved with a strange, irrational slowness, as though she were a long way off despite the mere yards that separated us.

I couldn't breathe. My lungs heaved, contracting uselessly, and she advanced on me with all the certainty of hellfire, preceded by the stench of rotting cotton, the odors of musk and mold.

Her long garment swished along the floor, but it wasn't a robe like I had thought but a single sheet of white muslin, a burial shroud wound about so many times it concealed the shape of her body completely.

Sounds: breaking glass, an upturned table.

The boom of a rifle downstairs.

The noise stirred me into motion. I wrested my gaze from the figure and started to run, sprinting headlong down the hallway, heedless of the din I made, conscious only of my need to escape from that faceless woman. But her footsteps clanged behind me, louder by far than my own, sounding in that moment like two steel bars rapped together, beating a forced march.

I lost my footing. I crashed into the wall and gashed my scalp. Warm fluid ran down into my eyes and I blinked rapidly to clear them. The woman was now two yards away, creeping toward me at the same unreal pace as before but getting closer, closer.

Heat radiated from her body as from an ash-black coal, and the muslin twitched over her concealed mouth, moving outward then deflating, clinging to her parted lips, as though she were trying to speak, though I heard nothing.

Then she was upon me. She leaned across me where I lay, her lips moving without sound. Her warm breath issued from the shroud, damp with the perfume of decay. I gagged, nauseated, and the hallway spun around me, blurring with the onset of vertigo, and I forced myself to focus on that open mouth lest I black out altogether.

The mouth stopped moving. The message, whatever its nature, had been delivered. For a moment the woman remained perfectly still, as though once more a statue — and then, with painstaking slowness, she brought her hands to her face and peeled back the shroud.

The house vanished, the hall with it. Her hair bound me like ropes, holding me fast, scalding my flesh and penetrating me inside and out. I tumbled backward, falling within myself, descending to a hell like Shiloh or the burning fields east of Atlanta: depths from which I could not surface, though I raged and howled and made of myself a living death.

This sensation lasted ages, an eternity, and yet no more than a few minutes could have elapsed before Barry found me and shook me awake.

The woman was gone. The hallway was empty, awash in a cool blue light. The rain, too, had ceased, and the stillness was general. Barry knelt beside me, his hands about my shoulders.

"You're alright," he whispered. "You're alright."

I coughed, tasting blood and shit and moldering cotton.

"They're downstairs," he said, "the other women. That girl, she must have run to fetch them. I heard them, their voices, but there were too many, and I did not dare show myself."

"And—Nichols?"

Barry shook his head. "That statue he'd taken to—I found it lying broken on the floor. That was queer enough, and I thought maybe he was responsible, but then I found him in the kitchen. He'd been stabbed, the blade driven clean through. They must have used your bayonet."

"Or a sword."

A shadow flickered across Barry's face.

There was something he hadn't told me, something he had seen downstairs. He couldn't speak of it, of course, just as I would never relate to him what had happened in the hallway.

"We have to go," he whispered. "They're downstairs searching but it's only a matter of time before they find us. Can you walk?"

I nodded. We heard voices, footsteps from below.

Barry helped me to my feet. We ran.

*

Here my father's voice faltered and cracked toward inaudibility. Spittle dribbled from his lips, collecting at the corner of his mouth, forming a yellow crust.

"We fled that place," he said, "and ran away cross those flooded fields. We sheltered in the trunk of a hollow tree and waited there 'til morning. When we made it back to camp, we were arrested and held under charges of desertion. Barry argued that we had simply gotten lost, which was true enough in a way, and eventually, they let us go.

"We never let on what had happened to Nichols. The army declared him missing, but they didn't waste much time in looking. Barry and I kept the secret between us, all throughout that winter, though we never discussed it, not even with each other.

"Then Bentonville came and Barry fell to a rebel bullet. The shot struck him through the gut so that it took many hours for his life to drain away. Near the end, he called for a priest and offered up his confession. What passed between them, I'll never know, but the priest looked shaken when he emerged from the tent.

"As for the Pillars—it's still there, I'm sure of it, though I've never found it on any map. Maybe it's better that way. By chance we had found it and by chance alone we escaped. We may have left that place behind us, at least for a time, but I'll return there—and soon."

He fixed his runny eyes on me. "But you must know that," he said. "I can see it in your eyes. I can see *her*. You've done nothing wrong, I know. You've only listened. You may be innocent, but so was I, and still we must be punished. Do you hear her? Her footsteps? She's coming for you, my boy, sure as she's coming for me."

He exhaled. "Won't be long now."

He turned his face to the window. The sparrow had not stirred from the sill. It gazed in at us through the glass like the dispassionate eye of the Ultimate Observer.

Several minutes elapsed. Sunlight drained from the horizon, and a shadow crept into the room. We sat together without speaking, each of us equally alone in that half-light. Then the sparrow took wing, bursting forth with a flurry of movement, and I was afraid.

My father's last words came as a strangled whisper.

"I'm tired," he said. "Let me sleep."

WHISPERERS

He steps onto the platform at Brattleboro. The
air is crisp, the blackness dappled by the lamps
along Main Street. Late November. Vapors
whirl at his lips only to be scattered by a blast of
cold air, the wind that shrieks from the nearby
Connecticut, blowing the rain into flurries.

The aging porter brings round his bag. He
deposits it on the platform at Carter's feet and
stands to one side, shuffling his feet, expecting a
tip. Carter gives him what he can. The old man
doesn't hide his disappointment but merely
stares down at the few coins in his palm, his
mouth twitching along one side, the opposite
corner hanging down.

Carter cannot face him. His eyes find his
feet, and after a time, the porter withdraws. The
old man drifts away toward the station, his long
scarf blowing out behind him, snapping at the
air like a ragged pennant. Carter thinks again of
his wife, recalling the scarf she wore that night
in Magnolia, when they were first courting,
when they walked together along the esplanade.

He remembers. The wind came roaring
from the sea, skimming the spray from the
waves, flinging the damp into their faces as they
followed the curve of the shoreline. The moon
surfaced from a crumbling bank of clouds even
as a strange cry rang out from somewhere far
off: a queer, keening moan like the bellow of a

beast in lust.

At first, Carter thought he had imagined it, but when she grabbed at his arm, rigid with fright, he realized that she had heard it too. She folded her hand into his, weaving their fingers together. His heart raced, but the sound did not come again. Another wind: her long scarf blew out toward him, the end crossing his chest, circling round his neck.

The porter disappears into the station. The doors slam shut, leaving Carter alone on the platform. He glances uphill toward the brick buildings and store-fronts of Main Street, scarcely visible through the blowing snow, and recalls, dimly, the ecstasies they once inspired in him — was it only a year ago? Tonight, they appear stained and dirty, a jumble of cracked facades broken by wind and endless winter.

He collects his bags from the platform. He makes his way outside.

A Ford truck roars to life, its headlights blinding. George. The other man has come to collect Carter from the station as promised. The truck's engine coughs and sputters, finding a rhythm as its breath unspools against the night.

Carter walks toward the glow of the headlights, passing through a cascade of flurries that whirl and hover in the air around him. They toss and glitter, shimmering like the sea in summertime, spinning away with a breath from the river.

*

"George."

"It's good of you to come. It's Henry. He's not well."

"What, exactly, is the matter?"

"The doctor can't say. Three times now he's been to see him, but left each time shaking his head. It's outside his area of expertise. Says Henry needs to see a specialist."

"It must be serious, then. I'm sorry, George."

"It's in his head, the sickness. Apparently, he's healthy as a horse, though he's wasting away for lack of food. Sarah brings him breakfast each morning, but he won't touch it."

"He is trying to starve himself?"

"We don't know. He won't talk to us. Not Sarah. Not even me. Only you, Randolph. I know you didn't spend more than half-an-hour with him this summer, but whatever you said — well, it made some impression on him."

"I see. You would like me to speak to him?"

"If you could. I feel just awful about it, calling you up here on a night like this. It's a long journey, I know, but I didn't know what else to do. Henry scribbled your name on a scrap of paper. Asked me to send for you, though I could tell by his bearing that he doubted you'd come. I told him — well, I told him that he didn't know you."

"Your telegram mentioned there was some urgency?"

"A new doctor's coming to the farm tomorrow. An alienist from the Retreat. It's got Sarah terribly worried. She's afraid they'll want to take him from her. If you could just talk to him. If you could just… Well, it'd mean the world to me. Sarah too."

*

Carter's first and only meeting with Henry Ackley took place during the previous summer near the end of his second trip to Brattleboro. He had come up from Providence for a meeting with a group of local writers. Afterward, he rode back with George, who remembered, halfway to the station, that he had need to call on his friend and neighbor Henry Ackley.

Their visit to the Ackley farmhouse lasted less than an hour, the other men drinking round the table while Carter sipped a glass of milk. At one point George suggested that Henry show Carter his watercolors. Carter assented, and the two men went together to the barn.

One corner of the squat structure had been converted into a makeshift display space that housed Ackley's paintings. Only a few could be displayed at any given time and the remaining images — of which there were several dozen — were stored in a work cabinet.

Ackley painted landscapes, mostly: unmistakably crude but nevertheless affecting. Some were painted on loose pieces of canvas, while others had been added to the reverse sides of postcards mailed years before from places like Burlington or Montreal. The barn was dark and cramped and reeked of mold and hay.

Carter's companion was taciturn by nature. He spoke but rarely and with the restrained humility characteristic of such rural Novanglians — as though, even in pride, he were always half-ashamed. Carter found himself oddly at ease in his presence and spoke for some time about his own work. The other man expressed an interest — polite rather than eager — and Carter offered to mail him a copy of his latest tale, a somewhat fantastical tale of dark gods and degenerate cults that had appeared in print that winter.

Returning to the farmhouse, they met up with George and made their goodbyes. Ackley walked the two of them to the door, waving from the threshold as they descended the hill. As George swung the truck round, Carter glanced back at the house in time to see Henry disappear inside, the door slamming shut behind him, while Sarah Ackley looked out from an upstairs window, one hand raised in farewell.

Upon his return to Providence, Carter

sealed two of his stories into an envelope and dispatched them to southern Vermont. Months went by — months of personal upheaval, of increasingly desperate letters from his wife in New York — until this morning, when George's telegram arrived. *Ackley ill*, it read. *Asking for you. Come quick. Urgent.*

The note found Carter seated at his writing desk, where her latest letter lay open before him, scarcely a page in length where his had run to twenty. He had read it once already and made it less than halfway through a second read before lowering it to the desk, unable to continue. It was shorter than her previous letters but otherwise no different: in twenty lines of cursive, it asked of him the one thing he knew he could not give her.

As soon as he read George's telegram, he knew that he would go. He packed his traveling bag and left the house, leaving her letter lying open on the desk. The ends of the paper curled upward, sloping toward the folds, causing her neat script to circle back upon itself: slouching and coiled, a bathing viper.

*

George guides the truck to a stop and kills the engine. The headlights fade from the hill. The Ackley farmhouse, fifteen yards distant, fades to a silhouette, its outline discernible only by the steep plunge of the roof-line. No lights are visible inside.

The men dismount from the cabin and proceed uphill toward the house, moving in and out of the whirling darkness. The yard is snowy and moon-latticed, silver in the glow that comes through the oak trees: jagged and thorny, stripped by the raking winds.

"The house is dark," Carter remarks. "Surely they haven't retired?"

George shakes his head. "It's Henry's doing. He insists on it, the darkness. Says he can't stand to look at her. Sarah, I mean. The poor woman. It's got her half-crazed with fright, the more so because he won't talk to her, because he won't give any reason why."

They keep walking. Their steps carry them up the terraced lawn, where the bedrock breaks through in bone-like ridges, showing like rooftops in a flood, the brown waters that roared down the Connecticut little more than a year ago.

They step onto the porch and approach the front door. A wintry gust sweeps uphill from the road, slashing through the wool of Carter's overcoat. George knocks. On the third rap, he is answered by the din of footsteps from the other side.

Sarah Ackley opens the door. She holds a candle in one hand, using no holder so that the wax drips and hardens on her nails and fingers.

Its dim illumination gutters on her face, separating itself into a series of web-like lines that crack and dissolve into wordless relief at the sight of Carter. She steps aside and ushers them into the mudroom.

The roof is leaking. A bucket has been set out to catch the falling drops. Snow-melt ripples within, shimmering where it catches the candlelight. Sarah beckons. They follow her through the kitchen to the closed door that leads (Carter assumes) into the larger bedroom. Here she stops. She offers George the candle, but he waves it away. She shrugs, the slightest of gestures, and disappears through an adjoining doorway, her long skirts trailing on the floorboards.

A draft creeps into the kitchen. The stench of mold is unmistakable, tinged with the odor of wood rot. From the mudroom: the splash of a drop in a bucket.

Carter looks at George. The other man nods and reaches for the handle, the bedroom door creaking open on its hinges. The room beyond is dark. Even the window is but a silvered line, the shade drawn to. They go inside.

Carter's eyes adjust slowly, fixing themselves first upon the outline of a bed in the corner and then upon the shelves that line the near wall, laden with books and candles. A high Windsor-style chair is positioned before the covered window. Henry Ackley sits within.

Draped in a blanket, he is recognizable only by his silhouette, his features hidden save for the line of moonlight that spans his throat, its edges merging into shadow. He faces them, or appears to, but is completely motionless, incontrovertibly silent.

George speaks first, acknowledging his friend with the stern greeting so common to New England farmers: "Henry."

No response.

"I brought Randolph with me. I thought—"

"Get out, George." The change in Ackley's voice is startling. Once strong and resonant, it is now little more than a harsh whisper: snake-like and sibilant, sharp with the suggestion of bile. "It's Mr. Carter I need to speak to."

George's mouth drops open.

Carter silences him with a hand on his elbow. "If you would be so good as to leave us, George, I believe that Mr. Ackley has something he would like to discuss."

George swallows, his Adam's Apple bulging. "I'll be in the kitchen," he mutters. "If you need me." He wheels round and stalks into the other room, drawing the door shut behind him.

The two men are alone in the darkened bedroom.

"I'm glad you could come," Ackley

whispers. "It's a long way from Providence."

"Yes," Carter agrees. "It is." He looks about the room, his gaze settling on a second comb-backed chair. "May I sit?"

Ackley grunts and nods, his head falling forward, the silver line moving up to illuminate his lips: black and crusted, caked with spittle.

Carter settles into the second chair. He places his hands together at the level of his chest, bridging his fingers to peer above the tips. He says nothing but merely waits, knowing, somehow, that the other man will speak.

"You must think I'm mad," he says. "They all do. Even George."

"Perhaps he does," Carter says. "But I am not George."

"It was your stories, you see. The ones you sent me."

"Oh?"

"You mailed them to me months ago, I know, but it was only recently, after the *incident*, that I had time to read them. When I did... well, they gave me a kind of hope. They made me think that maybe—just maybe—you might understand."

"Go on."

Ackley coughs and covers his mouth, his hands like white marble in that sliver of moonlight. He clears his throat.

"It started three weeks ago," he says. "When I found the body."

*

I left early that morning, Ackley says, before Sarah was up. I kissed her on the forehead and slipped out of the house, taking the truck as far as East Dummerston before going ahead on foot. I brought my gun with me, thinking I might shoot a bird for dinner.

I took my usual path through the woods along the hills south of the Hadley farm. The woods were quiet—I remember that clear enough. I saw no one, and the stillness seemed heavy somehow, if you catch my meaning, though there was one point where my ears caught the bark of some roaming animal—a coyote, I reckoned, baying to raise heaven, as though in the midst of some sickness.

I walked as far as the stream that runs round the northern edge of the Hadley property. My plan was to ford the stream and cross to the woods on the other side. The stream's slow-moving and shallow and no more than a couple of feet at its deepest—most of the time, anyway. Not that day. Rain had fallen hard during the previous weeks, and the water was brown and frothing.

It was too dangerous to cross there. I decided to follow the stream downhill for another mile. I knew it got wider at the mouth: shallower too, where it meets the West River.

The trip took me half-an-hour or so — a pleasant enough walk, though I heard that strange barking again: closer this time but still far away. Again it put me in mind of a coyote — possibly rabid — and a part of me hoped it might cross my path so I could put a bullet in it. The meat would be worthless, but surely death would be the most merciful thing for it.

Anyway. Like I said, it wasn't more than half-an-hour before I reached the stream's mouth. The water was running faster than usual, but not so deep that I'd get swept away. I lifted my gun over my head and set one foot down in the stream, the water changing the way it does, reforming round my ankle, closing about it like a fist. I pulled out my foot and set it down again, the stream remaking itself all round me as I waded out toward the center.

That was when it happened. Halfway across, I happened to look upstream. Twenty yards away, the stream-bed cracked and thrust upward, making a kind of shelf. The stream rushed over this, forming white bubbles at the lip that tumbled over each other, fanning out to all sides as they slowed with the current.

But there was something else too. At first I thought it was a man swimming. Then I thought maybe it was a woman. She wasn't swimming, though.

The corpse drifted over the shelf and plunged forward with arms extended, the current turning her over and over. She landed in the shallows and went under. A few seconds later, she surfaced again, flopping over on her back as the current weakened, floating her toward me like she was no heavier than a leaf.

She was fifteen yards away. Then ten.

When she got within five yards, I could see that she was wearing a linen dress. For a moment, she looked oddly at peace — her arms at her sides, her face turned up, hair streaming with the current — and my heart went out to her, whoever she was.

I reached out with the butt of my gun and managed to catch hold of her shoulder so that she spun round fearful quick. I scarcely had time to transfer the rifle to my right hand and reach for her with my left. It was blind luck alone that allowed me to get hold of her wrist. The water frothed all around us, brown and filthy, but I held her fast within that churning current, her dark hair flowing down her chest, half-hiding her face.

Her face — God, how can I describe it? Her eyes were missing, fish-eaten. Her flesh was pale, dreadfully pale, but the worst thing about it was the way it *moved*. There was water beneath her skin, forming waves that raced across her forehead and across her shattered face so that for a moment she seemed more wax than flesh.

It was a terrible thing: so motionless, yet

so alive. Believe me, I was scared, more scared than ever before in my life, but even the fear I felt then was nothing to what came next. For that corpse — pearly and white, gorged with gases and rippling like a bed sheet — I recognized it, Mr. Carter. I don't expect you to believe me, but that dead thing —

It was my wife.

*

For a time, Carter is silent. He sits perfectly still, his eyes closed. A waxen face floats in the air before him, adrift in darkness, but its features are not those of Sarah Ackley. When he speaks at last, he finds he cannot raise his voice above a whisper.

"The corpse that you described… surely it had been in the water some time?"

"It had. You could tell that just by looking at it."

"But you yourself said that you had kissed your wife that morning."

"That's right. At least I thought so at the time."

"And now?"

"When I saw her face — her dead face — I panicked. The blood drained from my head, and I fell to my knees in the midst of that filth. The current wrestled her from my grip and carried her downstream while I looked on, helpless. A minute later, she was gone."

"What did you do?"

Ackley shrugs. "I ran. Wouldn't you have done the same? Soon as my senses returned, I waded back across the stream and scrabbled up the bank. Cold and shivering, soaked through, I bolted through the woods like a frightened hare, running until I reached my truck. I jumped in and stomped on the gas, screeching toward home."

"Your wife was there?"

He nods. "I found her—it—in the yard. Raking the leaves out of the flowerbeds, the same as my dear wife used to do: the girl I'd once courted, the woman I married who I now knew to be dead. Drowned. Left to rot in that muddy stream.

"But what was this *thing* that had taken her place? So alike in every detail and yet so different. The skin it wore was but a kind of mask, pale and waxy like the flesh of my drowned wife. At times this mask slipped loose, giving me a glimpse of what lay beneath, something dead and squirming. Something foreign. Something alien.

"These lapses were few and seldom, never lasting more than a moment. Eventually, they stopped altogether, as though this creature, whatever its nature, had finally mastered the trick of being human. So I took to watching her. All day long sometimes. I scrutinized her every action and expression until her daily habits came to seem more and more strange to me: the way she did up her hair in the mirror, taking hours over it in the morning before church, or the way she embroidered pillowcases for George's children, sewing little hearts into the margins.

"It was all so artificial, so inhuman. It was only then that I realized — like your Mr. Thurston — the full horror of my predicament. I took to my room and then to my bed. I insisted on it, the darkness. That way I wouldn't have to see her face."

"I'm afraid I don't follow you," Carter says. "Of what were you so afraid?"

"Don't you see? I'd already gotten a glimpse of what lay beneath that mask. I saw the horror it concealed: the tar-black darkness of the sky at night, the empty places that lie beyond the stars. But what if it were to slip free altogether? What then?"

"I don't know," Carter replies. His voice is hoarse.

"I hear them whispering in the kitchen at night. George and that — creature. My other friends too. But they know nothing. They understand nothing. Not like you, Mr. Carter.

"Because the mask never slips. Not once. After a while, you stop expecting people to believe you, which is just as well, because you never can tell, can you, who might be one of them: who among us is flesh and who has already been replaced, switched with a double made from wax. A brain that you can never know. A body you can never touch."

Ackley lowers his face into his hands. Moonlight shows in a faint band across his fingers, emphasizing their pallor.

A strong wind rocks the house, the window rattling in its frame. As it subsides, Carter's ears catch the creak of a floorboard from the kitchen. George is pacing, treading the same loose board again and again as he waits for him to emerge.

Carter shifts his gaze from the window, allowing it to settle on the man who sits across from him, invisible but for the line of his white hands. He sighs. It is some time before he can bring himself to speak, breaking the silence with a ragged whisper.

"There is—something I can tell you," he says. "Something that happened to me once, long ago, beside the sea in Magnolia."

*

An hour later, Carter steps from the bedroom. He clicks the door shut as an electric light blazes to life behind him. Its illumination creeps from beneath the closed door, driving winged shadows into the kitchen.

George's eyes widen. "My God," he says, taken aback. "What did you say to him? That light hasn't been on in more than a week."

Carter shakes his head. "It was—nothing," he says. "He needed company, someone to whom he felt he could speak frankly. That was all. He was right in thinking I might understand, though it was not for the reasons he imagined."

A moment passes, but Carter does not elaborate. George's expression wavers. His features register confusion, then excitement. "I have to tell Sarah," he says, and disappears from the room.

In the dusky kitchen, Carter's shadow looms impossibly large on the window behind him. The glass is cracked along its length, starred with autumn snow. He looks up, notes the light fixture overhead. He finds the cord. The light winks on, chasing his shadow from the window.

Sarah appears. In this light, Carter can see her clearly for the first time. She, too, has changed since the summer. Her features are haggard and gaunt while her eyes are darker than he remembers: flat, lifeless. He cannot bear to look at her.

Brushing off her gratitude, he makes his goodbyes and heads for the door, followed by George, who doffs his cap to Sarah and walks with Carter to the truck.

*

Brattleboro Union Station.

The building is dark but for the light that seeps from a back office. Branch-shadows flitter across the windows, swaying with the winds that gust and bring in the snowfall.

"You're sure you won't stay the night?" George asks. "I hate leaving you off in the cold like this—especially when there's a warm bed waiting for you down the road."

Carter shakes his head. "Thank you," he says. "But I fear I must decline your kind offer. There is—business—waiting for me at home."

The other man nods. "I'm grateful to you, Randolph, coming all this way. And on such short notice. It's—" He pauses, searching after the right words. "It's damned good of you."

Carter offers his hand. They shake.

"Goodbye, George," he says. "I'll write soon."

He dismounts from the cabin and crosses the street to the station. Three times he nearly slips, his feet sinking in the slush that fills the road: glazing store fronts, burying parked cars.

He enters the waiting room. The fire is out, the room unlit. From the porter's office comes the rasp of soft snoring. Carter takes one look at the long benches, slouched in deep shadow, before continuing through the far doors that lead out to the platform.

Outside. Again the river lies before him,

striped by the lights of Main Street. Again a faint cry sounds from somewhere far-off, echoing with the storm-winds off the Connecticut, howling into nothingness. Alone on the platform, he thinks of a letter left at home — face-up on the desk, the signature half-visible — and knows what he will write in response.

Time passes. An hour or a minute, it makes no difference. Silence closes in: black and supple, fragrant with snowfall. *Ad Oblivionem*. The cry comes again. Closer now. Clearer. Soon it emerges fully-formed from the diminishing distance.

The blast of a train whistle.

He steps to the edge of the platform.

THE NAKED GODDESS

This is a true story, though none here may
believe it. The events I will relate happened to
me when I was a young man of twenty-four. I
have carried the memory with me these five
decades, never once confiding in another soul.
When men told their tales round the fireside at
Christmas, I bit my lip and said nothing,
unwilling to face their sad mutterings, their brief
but pitying glances. Long have I kept my silence,
but now, at the end of my life, I find there is little
left to me but this story. In the quiet of the night,
when the house is cold, and the beating of my
heart scatters all sleep, I close my eyes and see
their faces, her face: her skin like porcelain, her
hair as deep and black as were her sightless eyes.
Fifty years ago, she was but a dream, and in the
intervening years she has become even more so,
such that I sometimes question whether or not
she was ever real, or if she were merely a
fragment of my youthful imagination, a vision
brought on by exhaustion or the storm. I am an
old man now and no longer believe that it
matters. Nevertheless, I will tell my story. Each
man may decide the truth of it for himself.

*

In my youth I studied classics at Brown and
graduated to the life of a gentleman scholar, a

lonely but not unrewarding existence for those who are well suited to it. My father was no classicist, nor could he claim any real education, but in purchasing our rambling country estate, he had also acquired a magnificent library. For years, I spent my every waking hour there, cloistered among the books and dust and crumbling manuscripts.

Cicero, Augustine, Boethius: these men were as real to me as the musty library in which I labored. Indeed, there were times, late at night, when I fancied that the muses themselves had gathered about me, hidden within the web-like shadows that formed beyond the light of a single candle—and when I fell asleep over my books as I inevitably did, I dreamed of the Roman forum and of the clouds above Helicon.

It was a languorous and carefree existence. In truth I did not know a day's labor until the year I turned twenty-two and my father's untimely stroke brought the true state of our family's finances to light. Unbeknownst to me and my sisters, he had engaged in speculation some years before only to see his investment dry up to nothing. He fell into debt and kept off his creditors by borrowing more—a cycle that repeated itself year after year until the morning he dropped dead at the breakfast table.

We were ruined. I spent three days boxing up my beloved library to be sold at auction, retaining only one volume—a seventeenth century edition of *The Consolation of Philosophy*—for myself. It seemed an appropriate choice, as I too, like Boethius, had fallen from glory, but philosophy was to provide scant solace during the days that followed. The bank took the house, and to support my sisters, I found work as a clerk for a Boston railroad.

It was there that Mr. Sexton Whistler took me under his wing. He was a kindly man who had known my father when they were children. He was saddened to hear of the ignominy that attended my father's passing and of the circumstances that had subsequently befallen my family. Out of sympathy, he arranged to have me transferred to his department, which oversaw the expansion of the railroad into central Vermont. I served him for two years as a clerk before he took me on as his private secretary.

By that time, the railroad lines had reached as far as Rutland with the eventual goal of connecting with Burlington and from there on to Canada. However, before the railroad could expand, they first had to secure the necessary acreage—an unenviable task that had fallen to Mr. Whistler. He spent his days haggling with truculent farmers, who possessed neither wit nor breeding but believed themselves gentry merely because they owned their twenty acres of sod and stone. After many months of exhaustive effort, Mr. Whistler had finally negotiated the purchase of a corridor south of Vergennes. He needed only the signature upon the deed of sale.

To this end he arranged for me to travel to Vermont in order to procure the necessary signature. "It will not be easy," he warned me as he handed me the file. He peered at me over the desk, his pince-nez gleaming in the candlelight. "You are aware, of course, that the railroad has made only the most tenuous inroads into the state. Much of your traveling will be by horse and the roads there are difficult — often dangerous. Yours is a thankless task — I admit that — but there is no one I trust more."

Disarmed by such praise, I stammered my thanks and took the folder from him.

He nodded his farewell. "Good luck," he said. "And Godspeed you."

*

Later that evening, I boarded a train in Boston and traveled through Worcester and Springfield en route to Vermont, crossing the state line just as dawn was breaking. The train stopped in Brattleboro to take on coal and water, and by the time the engine lurched forward again, morning had broken in earnest, and the cabin swam in the soft gold light of early August.

Overgrazing during the last few decades had caused the state's agricultural backbone to collapse, and the train bore me north past abandoned hill farms, countless in number, where walled-in fields went untended and filled with the beginnings of forest. I tried to read, but the sun shone brightly upon my face, and the shadows of birches flickered soothingly on the opposite wall of the cabin. A breeze entered through the open window, redolent with the scents of pine and cedar, and I drifted off with my book in my lap.

When I woke, the train had halted.

"End of the line," the conductor called into the empty cabin. I wiped the sleep from my eyes and stepped outside onto the platform at Rutland.

The town center consisted of little more than an assemblage of low brick structures: dirty, ramshackle, and ultimately indistinguishable from one another. The road from the station proved to be an unpaved track, winding and deeply rutted, and I sank in mud to my ankles as soon as I stepped down off the platform.

I purchased bread and meat at a dry goods shop and procured a horse from the local stable. He was a truly miserable beast: fly-covered and emaciated, his spine showing like a coil through stands of fibrous muscle. "The best I've got," the stable master assured me.

He called his boy who brought the horse round and strapped a saddle across his back. The pony whinnied loudly, his mane tossing, and would not take the bit. The boy advanced, proffered the bridle, and then retreated once more when the pony gnashed his teeth. This went on for some minutes and the lad soon grew apologetic.

"I'm sorry, mister," he managed. "I'm sorry."

I waved off his apology and begged him not to trouble himself. Once the horse was bridled, I tipped the lad as generously as I could manage and took the reins from him, leading the ill-tempered beast north at a steady clomp.

It was a fine day. The sun lingered near the meridian and the wind came soft and constant out of the west, fanning away the day's heat. As I rode, I ate a meager luncheon, keeping the horse to a leisurely stroll, and in time, the road began to climb.

Soon we were among the mountains, where the pastures of southern Vermont were replaced by rank upon rank of maple and pine. Here the trees grew in thick profusion, swallowing wind and sun alike.

Ten miles from Rutland, I came to an ill-defined crossroads, where the road forked to north and west. The map I had purchased was of little use: no such intersection was noted and the surrounding landscape was entirely devoid of landmarks. Overhead, the sky was dark with the approach of stratus clouds from the east. Under that forbidding sky, one fork appeared as good as the other. I chose the north.

For many miles the road continued to climb, winding through forgotten towns, villages left empty when "merino fever" subsided and there was no longer enough food. I rode for hours and met no one. A quiet desolation lay upon that deserted landscape, gathering over the abandoned farms and cemeteries that climbed the slopes of every forested hill. There was something of beauty there—in the push of a sapling through a fallen roof or the growth of moss on a weathered gravestone—but it was a grim beauty, founded in suffering and failure: both beautiful and terrible, and indeed, more terrible for being beautiful.

Lost in reflections like these, I grew heavy-hearted and preoccupied—so much so that I scarcely noticed the storm as it winged in from the east, turning the sky to cinders. Only when the first crack of thunder rent the air did I become truly conscious of my danger. I put my heels to the horse and rode hard for shelter, kicking the pony's flanks until he whinnied and strained against the reins. Still I kept on, urging the horse to a faster pace, even as the rain swept down and soaked me to the skin.

I did not know what lay ahead of me. The map had been sparsely notated and I was well and truly lost. At best I hoped for a night in an abandoned farmhouse, a place with its roof intact that might keep off the rain. And so I was quite unprepared for the sudden appearance of a mountain village, which surfaced from the driving rain with the unexpected clarity of a storm-following rainbow. I tugged hard on the reins and managed to wrestle the pony to a stop.

The village with which I was confronted displayed all of the characteristics of abandonment. Darkness had nearly fallen and yet no lights showed in any window. The houses themselves were strained to collapse, sagging inward beneath the weight of a hundred mountain winters. The walls may have once been whitewashed, but they had gone so long without a fresh coat that they now appeared uniformly gray: the color of old bones. The church steeple possessed only the smallest fraction of its former metals and those plates that remained bore a deep patina.

The church was no more than twenty yards away, but I could see no name indicated above the double doors, and its windows were naked frames. A placard stood near the doorway, a standard notice board where announcements should have been inscribed. It was completely empty, eroded into obscurity, and a nearby pile of weeds and rubbish threatened to bury it altogether.

As I have said, every sign pointed to abandonment. At the same time I could plainly discern the sounds of chickens at their feed as well as the distant play of human voices. I grew uneasy. A part of me wanted to ride on and seek shelter elsewhere, but the downpour continued without ceasing and the hollow sang with the sounds of rain. After a long pause, I sighed and dismounted.

Taking the pony by the lead, I walked to the door of the nearest house and pounded twice upon the splintered wood—loudly so as to be heard above the rain. Hearing no reply, I knocked again. This time I was rewarded by an answering shout from within.

"I'm comin'," a creaking voice called. "Have ye no patience?" The voice in question was that of an old man. I could hear his footsteps from inside the house. They approached at such an exceedingly slow pace that I took him to be a cripple.

The door swung open.

There were no lights inside the house—all shutters drawn against the storm—and the old man stood in the darkness of the doorway, his face downturned. He was dressed in rags, strips of clothing that clung to him like leaves to a dying tree. His hair was similarly unkempt, and a gnarled beard fell past his navel.

"Well?" he demanded angrily. "What do ye want?" He did not lift his head when he spoke, and his nostrils flared, as though he were seeking me by scent. Only then did I guess what should have been obvious: he was blind.

I proffered my apologies. "I beg your pardon, sir. I was riding north when the storm broke upon me. I—"

"Foolish of ye," he interrupted. "Bein' about in weather like this."

I could not deny it. "The rain came quickly," I said. "I could not have anticipated it."

"Couldn't ye now?" he snorted. "I've felt it comin' for days I have—and me bein' a humble farmer and not a gentleman like yer self."

His remark took me by surprise—surely he could not see me in my coat and riding boots. Probably he had taken my cultivated speech as proof of breeding. Ignoring his obvious dislike of me, I put my dignity to one side and proceeded to ask for shelter.

"It'll be but one night," I added hastily. "And I'd pay you, of course. My horse and I will be gone by the time you wake."

"Will ye?" he sneered. "Listen to your beast a-breathin'—a sadder sack o' bones I ne'er heard. Ye may wake, 'tis true, but not afore me, and ye surely won't be goin' much farther on *that*." He burst out laughing, slapping his thighs.

As for me, I had endured as much as I meant to suffer.

"Very well," I said. "I shall seek help elsewhere. Good day."

As I turned away, his attitude changed

abruptly. I had gone no more than five paces when he hurried out from the house, hobbling after me with the aid of a cane. When he reached me, he offered profuse apologies and grabbed at my arm with all of the strength that remained in his claw-like fingers. "Pay me no heed," he said, "Please, sir, I beg of ye. I've forgotten m' manners—I'm an old man, and visitors are few."

He made a pitiful sight: his lips upturned in entreaty while the eyes remained lifeless. For the first time I could see them clearly. They may have once been blue, or perhaps gray, but now appeared black, as though they had been burned out with a hot iron. A milky film covered the dead pupils and white flecks floated across the blackened irises. I looked away, feeling sickened and aghast; more charitable emotions were beyond me. Thankfully he could not see my disgust and instead squeezed my arm and asked again for forgiveness.

"You're forgiven," I assured him. "But please—let me go!"

"Ah!" he cried and dropped my arm as though scorched. This sparked another round of profuse apologies, the man seemingly near tears, and I turned away from him, convinced he was not only blind but mad. Again I pressed forward, sinking shin-deep in the foul mud, but this time the old man did not pursue me.

"Ye'll want to see Mary," he shouted after me. "'bout a room."

I turned to see him hunched over his cane. Rainwater streamed down his face, twisting in channels past his dead eyes.

"Mary?"

"That's right. And she's got a stable too. For the horse."

"Where does she live?"

He lifted his hand to point but quickly let it drop again. It was an unconscious gesture, I realized, one left over from an earlier life, before he had been blinded. "Up the road a-ways," he said. "Hers is the third house past the church. She's got chickens, she does, and she likes to sing. Ye're sure to hear them, one or the other."

I shouted my thanks and began to walk again. I led the pony up the road past the church, the beast huffing beside me like a bellows, sounding as exhausted as I felt. Our route took us past the church, which existed in an even sorrier state of disrepair than I had first thought: the roof looked as if it might cave in at any moment, and the bell had fallen from the belfry.

As we passed the church, my gaze lit on the heap of rubbish I had spotted earlier. At this distance, I could see that the pile consisted primarily of weeds and soil but with the bones of many small animals—chickens or rabbits—scattered throughout. Some bore the marks of fire as from a roasting pit.

Past the ruined church, my ears picked up

the faint strains of music — the sound of someone singing at their work — and I remembered what the old man had said. The voice was undeniably a woman's, and though it was not a pretty voice, it possessed a certain feminine charm that was magnified twice over by contrast with the squalor that surrounded me.

I drew up in front of the nearest house. The tiny cottage appeared as ramshackle and deserted as the rest of the houses in the village. But the voice came again, and this time, I recognized the tune as something from my churchgoing days. Encouraged by this sign of life, I rapped at the door and was answered by a cheerful reply from within.

Moments later, the door opened inward and I found myself face to face with a woman of uncommon beauty. Her skin was exceptionally pallid, as smooth and white as unblemished alabaster, and her statuesque form called to mind the caryatids of Athens. Perhaps most remarkably, she wore a pair of gold-rimmed spectacles inset with black lenses. They made an odd juxtaposition with her physical beauty, and I realized then that she too was blind.

"Yes?" she asked, her voice unusually rich and husky for a woman's. "What is it?" She could not see me, but still she smiled — a smile so warm and welcoming that I could not help but feel at ease. I explained to her that I was traveling north when the storm fell upon me.

"Where were you going?"

"Vergennes."

She repeated the name with no hint of recognition. "I fear you may be lost," she said. "There's nothing to the north of us but mountains. Another village or two. Nothing more."

"And Vergennes?"

She shrugged. "You must have taken the wrong path."

"Oh," I said, recalling the mountain crossroads I had encountered earlier that day.

"But do come in." She stepped out of the doorway. The house beyond was as black as night, but I felt no disquiet in her presence. "You must shelter here tonight."

"And my horse?"

"There's a shed out back. It isn't a proper stable, but the roof's intact. Give me the lead. I'll take him there."

Naturally I protested. "But you —"

I cut myself off.

"Yes," she said graciously. "You're quite right — I am blind. But you'll find I manage well enough."

Embarrassed, I handed her the lead. She took it from me and led the pony round the corner of the house. "Go inside," she called over shoulder. "And take your rest. The wood box is well-stacked. Build up a fire to warm yourself."

"I am in your debt," I said.

But she had already gone.

I left my boots in the entryway and entered the house in my stocking feet. Once my eyes had adjusted to the gloom, I found myself in the common room. A rectangular dining table occupied the center of the room while the walls were lined with bookcases. I approached the nearest of these and squinted to browse the titles. It was a strange assortment, encompassing old encyclopedia volumes, several books on astronomy and the movement of planets, and at least one scholarly work on optics and the properties of glass.

Like the other houses in the village, hers occupied a single floor. Doorways placed along the near wall led (presumably) to the kitchen and to the bedrooms. The hearth was situated along the opposite wall and the wood-box sat nearby, filled with fresh logs and kindling. I stacked some of both inside the fireplace, added a fistful of tinder, and struck a long match.

As the fire flared into life, the room took on color and dimension. To my surprise, I observed that the parlor was virtually spotless. Every surface had been carefully dusted and the floorboards gleamed, freshly polished. Even the books were in immaculate condition. The gold spines of reference volumes shone faintly in the dim light. Only her bible, a lectern-sized King James, appeared somewhat battered, as from lengthy and repeated consultation, but where the spine had snapped, so too had it been mended—and rather recently by the appearance of the glue. I found this last observation particularly poignant as I knew she could no longer read.

I took a seat at the table and turned the chair to the fire, allowing myself to grow warm and dozy even as I wondered to where my hostess had disappeared. As if in response to my unspoken question, a door banged shut beyond the parlor—the back door, I assumed—and Mary soon entered the room, her darkened spectacles glinting in the firelight. I made to rise from my chair, but she waved me back into my seat.

"You've made a fire," she remarked. "Good. A house is nothing without a fire."

She approached the hearth and ran a hand through her wet hair. One or two drops gathered at her fingertips and fell away, gleaming as they caught the light so that I thought of precious stones. It was a lovely sight, and I was suddenly sad that she could not see it.

The storm had not let up. Rain drummed without abatement on the wooden roof, and the lightning came frequently with thunder following hard behind.

"Your horse is stabled out back," she said. "He's out of the rain now and has plenty of food—for the first time in months, I'd wager, given the state of him." She waved off my gratitude and proceeded to raise the subject of supper. "Will stew be alright?" she inquired. "It's rabbit," she added. "I don't need my sight to empty a trap."

I thanked her and again she smiled. As she retreated through the doorway, I was struck—though not for the last time—by the confidence with which she walked and the grace this imparted to her every step. In any town or city she would have been beautiful, but here she seemed singularly unearthly, simultaneously real and unreal in the manner of a dream: the muses that had come to me in the stillness of my father's library. She vanished through the doorway, the damp hem of her dress leaving a trail of raindrops, and I disappeared into my thoughts.

After a time she returned from the kitchen bearing a tray on which was set a wooden bowl and a mug of cold water. She placed these before me on the table, and my stomach lurched at the aroma that wafted from the bowl. I was ravenous. The stew was plain , unseasoned, but on that night it seemed to me the most exquisite meal that I had ever eaten. I finished my bowl with the speed and manners of a man long starved.

All the while, she sat across the table with her spectacles fixed on me, and though it was quite impossible, I felt as though she were watching me, calling to me from the depths of all that darkness. Trapped in this mountain village, she was isolated many times over, alone in a truer sense of the word than I had ever thought possible, for all my youthful loneliness. I felt pity for her, of course, and something more, something I cannot describe. When I was young, I did not have the proper words. Now that I am old, I find I cannot utter them.

She waited until I had finished eating before attempting conversation. "I take it Obadiah must have sent you?" She went on to describe the filthy old man in some detail, omitting only the horror of his damaged eyes.

"Yes," I said. "That's him. Bit of an odd sort, isn't he?"

"The poor man," she said. A sadness fell across her features and she sighed heavily, as a mother might when discussing a wayward son. "He doesn't look after himself."

"No," I agreed. "I thought him mad."

"He is," she said. "A little."

She did not elaborate.

Firelight streamed over her glasses, a rippling sheet that warped and shifted as the fire flared. Their black depths swallowed my reflection.

I changed the subject. "I couldn't help but notice your library," I remarked. "It really is impressive."

"It is," she agreed. "But it isn't mine—not in truth."

"No?"

"The books belonged to a traveling preacher. A German. These spectacles were his. This house too. Here he taught me all he knew about science, philosophy: the will of God and the path to sanctity. From the beginning, I believe he saw me as a kind of student — even more so when I consented to marry him."

"He was your husband?"

She shook her head. "We never married."

"Oh." Her lack of emotion surprised me. Awkwardly I shifted my gaze to my lap. "I'm — sorry I raised the subject."

"There's no need," she said neutrally, her voice unclouded by anger or regret. She tapped the bridge of her nose, indicating her spectacles, the blindness they hid.

"He did this to me," she said. "To all of us."

"But — how —"

"Not deliberately," she added quickly. "You mustn't misunderstand me. You saw his books on astronomy? He believed he had determined the date of the world's rebirth and the coming of the Christ. Of course he could have done no such thing — isn't it written that none shall know the hour?"

Confused, I murmured my agreement.

She went on: "As the appointed day drew near, he bade us dress in robes of white to meet Our Savior. My own robe was meant as my wedding dress. I was to be his bride that day—my purity a sacrifice offered up to Heaven—and in the stillness of this house, in the dark of the long night, he showed me the path to sanctity.

"On the next morning we ascended the mountain. There he promised us that we would see the Risen Lord and greet our loved ones as they stepped from their graves. But the Bridegroom never came—at least not in the form that we had hoped.

"A marvelous thing happened—a miracle, some might say—but we were struck blind. Abandoned by God, we sought comfort with our pastor, but the German had gone. For a time we even believed that he'd been taken up bodily, just as he had promised us. Now I know that he simply fled.

"When we returned to the village, we discovered that we had been robbed, our houses emptied of all valuables—everything but these spectacles, which I found on the table, and the books you see around us. He left them behind for us—for me. This alone was a blessing for it allowed us to understand."

"To understand? But surely you cannot—"

"To never forget," she said. "Our sacrifice was inadequate. Our sanctity, for all of his assurances, was flawed. The Lord was swift and unsparing in His punishment."

"And the preacher?"

She shook her head. "We have no pastor now, nor do we need one. The German taught me all he knew. It is only a matter of time now before we are forgiven. Like Paul, we have reached Damascus. But our sight has not returned."

She fell silent. Plainly her story was at an end.

Did I believe her? I did not. I was too young, I think. Certainly I was too beguiled. A wiser man might have fled the table then and there and run off into the night. Had I done so, my life might have proved a happy one. Death might be far off yet instead of drawing near, as it is, in the quiet of this dead season. But I chose to stay: to smile at her from across the table although she could not see me—to change the subject once more—to continue in idle conversation when what I wanted most of all was to touch her hand and confess I found her beautiful.

It was a foolish decision, yes, but even knowing all that I know today, I believe that I would make the same choice again. In fact I am certain of it.

"Is that why you keep them?" I inquired, shifting the topic of conversation as casually as I could manage. "His books."

She nodded. "Of course. I may need use of them. One day."

"And the bible?"

"That too was his. He left it to me."

I nodded. "It's a marvelous volume."

"Isn't it? I've done my best to mend it."

"You've succeeded beautifully."

Her forehead wrinkled. "Despite my lack of sight, you mean."

"Beautiful by any standard."

"You flatter me."

"I do no such thing, I assure you."

"Thank you," she said quietly. "You're very kind."

She blushed and averted her face. The crimson rose and followed the curve of her neck, darkening her features in the firelight. Where she had appeared beautiful before she was now truly radiant: bathed in the light of other days and utterly transfigured. In that moment, my dreams invaded the waking world, my youthful muses clad like the Word in flesh, and I ached with the pain of an unacknowledged emptiness, a sea of desires too long unfulfilled.

"Come," she said. "I have made up your bed." Rather unexpectedly, she extended her hand. She bade me take it. "The hall is dark," she said. "And I have no candle. Let me guide you. Otherwise you'll surely fall."

What choice did I have? I took her hand and followed her into the darkened hallway, where there was no light save the fitful flash of distant lightning—already more gray than silver—and though the roar of the storm shook the house to its foundations, I walked beside her without fear or hesitation and allowed her to lead me into an unlit bedroom.

The lone window was shut, permitting neither light nor draft, and the air inside was suffocating: as black and stifling as the deepest bowels of the earth. Still I held fast to her hand, cold and clammy in my own, and dared not let her go.

The heat was unbearable.

*

My sleep proved fitful and restless, my dreams blurred and tangled. The sky poured out in torrents on the roof, a ceaseless cacophony accented by occasional bursts of thunder, and I moved in and out of sleep with the passing of the storm.

Many hours after midnight — after the thunder had passed and a hush had descended from the mountains — I woke to an empty room and the murmur of soft voices from somewhere close by. In the hallway, a man and woman conferred in serious tones, whispering so as not to be overheard. The woman's voice was low and gravelly and uncommonly deep. Mary. The man's voice gave me no trouble either, for it was as shrill as hers was husky, as rough as hers was refined. Obadiah. Instinctively I wondered what had brought him to the house at that hour.

I did not rise or stir but lay abed with my thoughts and pretended to sleep, watching from the corner of my eye as moonlight streamed through the cracked window and crept along the floor. With my eyes closed, I listened hard but could not make out the thrust of their conversation. Some time passed—how long I cannot say—and then the two fell silent, a decision evidently having been made. I heard Mary enter the bedroom and the subsequent sound of her feet on the floorboards. She came to the end of the bed, where she halted, and I opened my eyes to see her standing there, revealed in a wash of moonlight.

She had taken off her spectacles. In the wan light of the moon, I saw her eyes for the first time and knew why she had hidden them from me. For her eyes were identical to the old man's in every detail: black and clotted and horribly damaged. She was naked, her dress lying cast off and discarded at the foot of the bed, and in her right hand she held a sickle above her head. In that moment she was fair as the moon, clear as the sun, more beautiful and terrible than armored Athena in all her glory. The blade caught the light again as it descended, brought down hard in an arc toward my leg. She meant to hobble me, to cripple me so that I could not flee, and I rolled away without thinking, crashing to the floor as the blow fell.

The blade bit through the bedclothes and

into the mattress itself, loosing a cloud of dust that shimmered in the gloom. Mary shouted in surprise and attempted to pry the blade from the bed. I crawled on hands and knees toward the doorway, only to meet Obadiah, who lifted his cane and dashed into the room at the sound of her cry. I leapt to my feet, wearing only my nightshirt, and threw myself hard to the right in order to escape the old man, who dropped his cane to lunge for me with both hands. From the hall I heard other voices, belonging to men and women alike, perhaps half-a-dozen in all.

Behind me, Mary freed the blade and came at me from behind.

"Hold him, Obadiah!" she shouted. "Hold him fast!"

"I got ye," the old man snarled and nearly succeeded in trapping me against the bureau. Somehow I managed to squirm free and fumbled on the floor for the nearest object. My fingers closed on the long shaft of Obadiah's cane and I brought it up hard, knocking the old man's knees out from under him. He crashed heavily to the floor, and I hurtled out into the hall, where I was confronted by a handful of men and women young and old, all of whom bore the marks of blindness: the dull and staring face, the black and burned-out eyes.

Terrified, I lifted the cane once more and swung it like a sword before me, striking indiscriminately at man and woman. They shouted, panicked, and parted before me, for I believe it was the very last thing they had expected. They had taken me to be an easy target, which in fact I was—being too weary and lonely to realize my danger, I had even dared to gaze upon the naked goddess, an offense for which Tiresias lost his sight.

I was not brave—you must think no such thing—as it was only desperation that gave me what some might call courage. I pushed through the assembled villagers and made in the direction of the backdoor whose location I had deduced before supper. My nightshirt tore as they grabbed at me, but I flailed wildly with fist and cane and soon broke from the crowd and sprinted toward the backdoor.

Wheezing, breathing hard, I fled outside into the light of the moon, which shone brightly amid the riotous stars. My heart raced, and I thought only of escape. I intended to find my horse and ride hard for Rutland. With a little luck, I could make it by daybreak.

I cast my eyes about me, hoping to discern the outline of the shed where my pony should have been stabled. There was no such structure, of course, and I was less than ten yards from the house when I tripped over what appeared to be a miniature hillock and went careening into the muck. Obadiah's cane broke my fall, snapping in two beneath my weight.

I stumbled to my feet. The villagers were

not far away. When I looked back to the house, I saw them coming for me, naked Mary leading the others through the back door, each man or woman running despite their blindness, hunting me by sound or scent.

I glanced down at my feet. The moonlight clearly illumined the object over which I had tripped. It was the corpse of my poor horse. His throat had been slashed with a jagged blade. His eyes were open and very round.

Sick with horror, I forced myself to keep running, turning right to cross over weedy lawns and ruined gardens, tracing a course roughly parallel to the road that led me, in time, to the ruined church. I pushed at the side door that opened onto the sanctuary and prayed it would give way. It did — for all of my sins that night, I was not yet abandoned — and I entered the moonlit building some fifty paces ahead of my pursuers.

Immediately I set about securing the door. I found some broken timbers lying nearby and wedged them into place beneath the knob. Knowing these would not hold the villagers for long, I ran to the back of the church in search of rubble and loose materials.

There I found that the stone pulpit had been pried from its place and laid horizontally across the floor to form a kind of altar. In the faint light, I noted that the stones were pitted and stained, charred by fire. I ran my fingertips

along the rough surface only to have them come
away black and sticky. With a chill I
remembered the pile of bones that abutted the
church building—all sacrificed on this altar—
and recalled Mary's cryptic remarks concerning
Paul and Damascus, the books she saved for the
day her sight was restored.

I understood everything: the mysterious
"path to sanctity" into which I too had been
initiated as well as the shocking duplicity of the
German, who had manipulated the town for no
better reason than that he could: because they
were weak and he was strong. I had fallen victim
to Mary, it was true, but she was herself a victim,
as were they all. Had the German caused their
blindness as well? I thought of his blackened
spectacles—his books on optics—and shivered.

The villagers were at the door. They
threw themselves against it, causing the timbers
to shudder. In a matter of seconds, they would
break through and fall upon me. Desperately,
my gaze veered from the door to the rafters and
then to the broken windows.

The base of the nearest window was
situated five feet above the floor. The empty
frame was just wide enough for me to slip
through. I could make it, I realized, but I needed
more time. I recalled the nightshirt I was
wearing, the way Obadiah's nostrils had flared
upon seeing me that afternoon. It was my only
chance. Stripping off the muddied garment, I left

it bunched up on the altar and sprinted in the direction of the broken window. I vaulted myself up and wriggled through the frame just as the door gave way and the villagers poured into the church.

"The altar!" Mary shouted. "Quick!"

Summoning what remained of my strength, I began to run. Naked and muddy, I dashed past Obadiah's house and from there down the mountain, the soggy earth pounding beneath my bare feet: running, running, never once looking back. My terror gave me strength, and I did not stop sprinting until well after daybreak when I collapsed in a heap on the Rutland road and a kindly farmer found me, clothed me, and brought me back to town.

*

For some days afterward I existed in a state of profound mental confusion. I lived solely on charity, and my nerves were such that I could not even speak to tell my story.

Eventually the stationmaster took pity on me and made arrangements with the railroad for me to travel back to Boston. And so it was that I arrived at Mr. Whistler's office without money or suit or the precious deed of sale with which I had been entrusted. All had been left behind in that desolate mountain village.

A lesser man would have been furious

with me—and justifiably so—but my employer was a better man than any I have known. He did not ask me what had transpired, nor did I feel that I could tell him. He even allowed me a period of convalescence with my sisters before I returned to work. When I did so, many months later, I was a changed man: my hair was gray and thinning, and I no longer yearned for the sunlit acropolis or the mountain of the muses.

The poet Callimachus writes that the great sage Tiresias went up onto Helicon and there saw Athena at her bath. He was struck blind by the sight, but gained in exchange the art of prophecy. When I descended from my own Helicon, I did so with my vision intact, but my loneliness redoubled and my hopes in ruin. And though I did not recognize it at the time, that night in the mountains signified the true end of my youth, for it marked the final consummation of my soul's longing: afterward, only dreams were left to me.

In time I came to replace Mr. Whistler as chief of the department. I invested my salary in the railroad and grew to be wealthy. I left Boston and retired to the country as had my father before me. However, I never replaced the books I sold at auction, nor have I returned to Vermont.

Five years ago, a friend of mine traveled there on business. He mentioned that he would be passing through Rutland and I asked him to make inquiries after the village in which I had spent that strange and terrible night in the summer of my twenty-fourth year.

I did not explain the reason for my interest. I did not confess to him, as I will to you now, that she has haunted my dreams throughout these many decades, and that these dreams were not all nightmares. I merely said that I had spent a night there long ago and wished to ascertain the fate of its inhabitants. I described the location to him as best I could and sent him on his way.

He had been gone but a single week when a package arrived from the Rutland post office. The package included a crudely printed pamphlet in addition to a letter detailing my friend's attempts to locate the village. Upon his arrival in Rutland, he had sought out the library and paid a visit to the map room, where he discovered that a newly created reservoir to the north of the city covered many of the old townships. If the village were located where I remembered, then it was surely now underwater and all of its horrors buried with it.

At the end of his letter, my friend directed my attention to the enclosed pamphlet, which was produced locally and included many local folktales and legends. "All hogwash, of course," he commented in his letter. "But knowing your fascination with the strange and ghoulish, I think you may find it of interest." I have the

pamphlet with me now and would like to read
to you from one passage in particular.

On the seventh of August in the year 18__
our region experienced a rare eclipse of the sun that
saw the state plunged into total darkness. This
fantastical event was preceded by signs and rumors of
the direst portent. In Hartford, a pack of wolves
descended on the town in broad daylight and killed a
dozen ewes before being driven away. Outside
Montpelier, cattle collapsed and could not stand. The
Winooski ran dry and the riverbed was found to be
black and slick with oily corruption. Fear and
trembling were general: never before had the
Kingdom felt so near at hand. From every pulpit, holy
men preached repentance. In one remote hamlet, men
and women donned white robes and scaled a
mountain to hear the trumpets sound. It is said they
went gaily, barefoot and singing, pilgrims to the
blackened star. No account survives of what
transpired there. To this day, the location of the
village remains unknown.

That is all, gentlemen. There is nothing
more to tell.

THE LORD CAME AT TWILIGHT

After Thomas Ligotti

From the Chronicle of Brother Johannes Kohl, O.S.B.

And so it was that the Appointed Day came to Muelenberg, arriving in our city like a thief in the night — and then, having robbed us of all hope and contentment, did not linger, and in departing left no sign of itself, so that I cannot now recall when it began.

I remember only a shout from the garden and the sensation of sudden wakefulness. Through the window of my cell, I glimpsed first the stars, glimmering in the east, and then the Cathedral spire like God's shadow on the sky. A light snow had fallen, and the cold wind howled through my room, slashing through the fabric of my robes.

The cry came again from the garden below. I recognized the voice of Brother Friedrich, our cantor, with whom I had been a novice and whom I counted as my dearest friend. He knelt weeping before Saint Martin's Oak with his face in his hands. The source of his distress was obvious. For that venerable tree — planted long before by the departed Abbott Martin, first of our Order to settle in Muelenberg — had been burned to a standing cinder. The stench of char was layered thickly on the air, and smoke stood in plumes at the end of each branch.

I donned my heavy cloak and dashed to the stair, passing cells from which the occasional head protruded—brothers roused, like myself, by Friedrich's cry. Downstairs, I emerged into the courtyard, where the oak swayed and crumbled, shedding ash in clouds. I dropped to the ground beside Friedrich and gathered him into my arms. The bell sounded from the Cathedral, tolling the hour, and I was surprised to learn that it was not yet Vespers.

Afterward, when he had recovered his faculties, Friedrich could say nothing of what had transpired. He thought that he had fallen asleep in his cell and that perhaps he had sleep-walked to the garden. The first thing he remembered of that evening was the rush of wind over his ears and the feeling of stiffness in his joints, as though he had knelt for hours with the smoking shell of the tree before him.

But Friedrich was not the only brother among us to have experienced this queer somnambulance. The Abbot himself was helpless to explain how he had come to be in the Scriptorium with a lit candle suspended mere inches above a pile of our oldest manuscripts.

Likewise the earth beneath the oak was found to be soaked in pitch and tar, even as the Prior discovered the complete absence of such flammables from the Abbey stores—a fact for which no one could account.

Confusion fell, mingled with suspicion. When word of his discovery reached the refectory, where the brothers had gathered, Friedrich loosed a strangled cry, so hoarse and ragged I feared he would never sing again. The Almoner bowed his head and prayed, feverishly, for understanding. The Abbott, upon whose strength and wisdom we relied, offered us no reassurance, but merely gazed down at his hands on the table.

Beyond the Abbey walls, Muelenberg had become a dream city. Townsfolk wandered the streets by day and night, proceeding slowly, cautiously—uncertain of the stones beneath their feet and yet unwilling to admit, even to each other, the terror they shared. Rumors spread of Saint Martin's Oak, causing no small wail to go up from the faithful, who saw in its destruction a sign of God's displeasure.

The city is cursed, said many. Their faith deserted them, and they sought instead distractions of the basest sort: drunkenness, avarice, and sins of the flesh. Even the Count, long reclusive in his leprous affliction, withdrew his patronage from the Church, so that the Cathedral was nearly empty on the Sabbath, excepting the Bishop and his priests.

With this gloom upon us, and winter drawing in, the Abbott fell into an impenetrable melancholy. Things appeared less real to him, he admitted, and he felt keenly the absence of the Paraclete. All was flesh, he said. He could give no reason for these doubts but believed they had their origin in that autumn evening when the oak had burned.

Soon discontent spread throughout the Abbey, manifesting itself in lazy illumination work and gossip at the refectory table. The Prior took to carrying a rusty ladle at mealtimes with which he might strike any offending rumormongers. Matins was sparsely attended of a morning, as many slept through the tolling bell, dreaming so deeply that even the threat of the Prior's wrath could not rouse them from slumber.

But most terrible of all was the change that came over Brother Friedrich. In the days after the fire, my friend retreated into silence and would not raise his voice to pray or sing. Removed from his position as cantor, he demonstrated little enthusiasm for his other duties, shirking them to wander the garden by twilight, returning to the oak tree again and again.

His discontent was plain to me, but he would not confide his troubles, save to admit that the tree often appeared to him at night in the moment before sleep. Indeed, he said, it seemed to him the embodiment of all that we could never know.

At the time, I pretended to confusion, but

in hindsight, I believe I understood his meaning, though I lacked the courage to utter such thoughts aloud. But Friedrich was always braver than I: the first to swear the Vows and the first of our Order to renounce them. He did so in silence, slipping from the cloister through the east gate, never to return to those hallowed corridors.

His departure wore hard upon me and was followed by the loss of many others. By November of that year, we were reduced to half our original number. My own life in Christ seemed more hesitant than before, less certain. Prayer times came to resemble a duty, a mere chore, bereft as they were of Friedrich's voice. My faith had been emptied of all beauty, all substance, like a wine-jug that has been overturned but from which one longs to drink.

And yet, for a time, this thirst was enough. Though empty, it sustained me through the chill of the subsequent winter, giving warmth by the desire it enkindled, the aching to be filled with something more: the substance of things half-glimpsed, or dreamt of.

In the spring, the Count initiated the construction of a wooden amphitheater outside the city walls. The builder, a Florentine of some renown, modeled its architecture on that of the Roman Colosseum, albeit wrought in timbers rather than in stone, so that we feared the Count intended a return to the barbarisms of the past.

The Bishop, too, was dearly aggrieved by the lavishness of the planned structure, as the Cathedral was in need of repairs and the church coffers nearly empty; but the Count would not hear his petition. Since autumn, the Count had abandoned all public appearances, to which he had once worn a silver mask, and it was rumored that his disfigurements had worsened in recent months, though these tales remained unconfirmed.

Work on the amphitheater continued without abatement through Lent and the Easter season. During that time, the townsfolk spoke of little else. It was said that the city's populace would fit within its walls, though to what purpose we knew not. The builders were from the south, and spoke a foreign tongue, while the two young boys who stole inside were returned in chains to the castle and never heard from again.

In April, the amphitheater was finished, and on the first of May, the doors were opened. Criers throughout the city announced the performance of a morality play to be held that very evening. The Prior forbade us from going — the Abbot being indisposed, and the Order dependent on the good will of the Bishop — but we later learned from the madwoman Anna, an almswoman who lived off the fruit of our gardens, of that first night's performance.

The amphitheater, she said, was a thing of

rare and marvelous beauty, with a flagstone stage ringed by half-a-dozen terraces supported by wooden joints and tresses. On that evening, the whole of the city crammed inside eagerly, laughing and whispering to each other in the hush of that new season.

The best view was reserved, naturally, for the Count, who possessed a box overlooking the stage, with a heavy curtain drawn round it on three sides. A tunnel was said to lead directly to the box from the building's exterior so that none might see him as he arrived.

Much time passed. The Cathedral bell tolled not once but twice before the actors emerged onto the stage from the undercroft below. At first, Anna assumed the subject of the play was to be the torments of hell, for it dwelt heavily on the sins of its three principal characters, depicting their transgressions in vivid, near-loving detail.

There were scenes of murder, theft, and rape; couplings with man and beast; and violence of the meanest sort directed toward a pair of maidens in white, much of it inflicted with a barbed whip. The actors—if actors they were—comported themselves with such zeal that many members of the audience crossed themselves and averted their faces, while others watched, enraptured, unable to look away.

Anna belonged to the latter group. She detailed the characters' exploits with obvious relish, giggling to herself as she described the violation of the maidens, which was followed in turn by the hearty consumption of communion wine and the spirited desecration of the Host.

The play ended shortly afterward, to the surprise of many, for there were no punishments dispensed to the sinners, nor blessings awarded the virgins. Nonetheless, the applause that greeted this non-ending was tumultuous, and the Count's satisfaction with the performance became widely known.

For a time, such entertainments were held daily, even on Sundays, when the whole of the city crowded itself into the amphitheater. All went to the theater, and all spoke of little else — all save for myself and my brothers in Christ, who were forbidden to attend. But from Anna we learned of its many excesses and depravities, the old crone dispensing gossip each morning as she waited for bread, and it was from Anna that we learned of the competition.

It was to be held on the Feast of Midsummer and could be expected to last through the day. Until then, all performances of morality plays were suspended on pain of death. Though modeled on the *agon* of old, we learned that the Count was desirous not of tragic drama but of ballads old and new. All singers and musicians, man and woman alike, were invited to participate, and some, we learned, made the journey from places like Florence and Vienna.

Excitement was general. As Midsummer approached, a strange fever came over the city, and an atmosphere of riotous jubilation prevailed. One evening, late in May, a crowd gathered in the cathedral square, several hundred strong, to demand access to the Bishop's store of wine. His Grace petitioned the Count, requesting the intervention of the City Watch, but to no avail. When the gates were breached, and the marauding crowd poured into the palace, the Bishop took flight before them, finding shelter in the sanctuary of his church into which they dared not enter.

Fires erupted from within the palace and gutted the building's interior. Later, when the smoke had cleared, hundreds were found dead inside, charred and melted together in attitudes of orgiastic frenzy. The Bishop, with typical gravity, declared it an act of Judgment from the Lord.

The riots continued throughout the early days of summer, incited by drunkenness and sustained by the Count's general insouciance. The Jewish quarter was demolished, the gypsies driven from the Square of Saint Mark. At no point did the Watch interfere.

Throughout this time the rhythms of life within our four walls continued to change and adapt, despite the Prior's attempts to maintain a comforting consistency with all that had come before. He tried first tolerance; but when our numbers continued to dwindle, he was moved to enforce a strict discipline, ruling over us with a rod of iron—or a rusted ladle, as was the case, with beatings administered to any found lacking in their devotions. This had no better effect, and it shortly became clear to us that something had changed, irretrievably so, and that neither faith nor kindness nor rigor could restore to us our lost brotherhood in Christ.

The first tragedy befell us in June, a fortnight before the Feast of Midsummer. The unrest was then at its peak, and sleep came not for fear of the chaos that lived—and bred—beyond the Abbey walls. Sometime after midnight, Brother Thomas ran screaming down the hall, so mad with fright that it took four of us to restrain him, and calm him, and coax from him the story.

The Abbott was dead. Thomas had found him in the Scriptorium amidst a mess of tattered vellum. His wrists had been opened by his own hand, his eyes reduced to black ash inside his skull. Nearby lay the bloodied knife and candle with which he had performed the deed.

We buried him in the garden, consigning him to the earth at the southeast corner in view of the skeletal oak. It was a lovely morning, as I remember, but I found no consolation in the clear skies overhead, nor in the temperate winds that sighed through the alder bushes.

With the Abbot dead, my dear friend

departed, and my own faith in ruins, I saw no reason to keep my Vows; and yet I was much too frightened to forsake the Abbey walls, to exchange one kind of emptiness for another as our Abbott had done—for he would know nothing but suffering in the darkness that had been prepared for him.

The Feast of Midsummer fell upon the Sabbath. On the evening before, while helping the Almoner, I received news of Friedrich. The story came from Anna, who had gone to the castle to beg scraps from the Count's kitchens. Anna, who confessed herself greatly excited for the next day's entertainment, sneaked from the kitchens to the great hall, where dozens of tables were set, with close to one hundred singers and musicians seated around, dining on meat and wine.

These were the *agon* competitors, all of whom were boarded in the castle at the Count's insistence. Among them, she recognized Brother Friedrich, though he had traded his monk's robes for a yellow traveler's cloak, such as might be worn by a minstrel, and his face, too, had changed. He looked older, she said, but could add nothing more.

That night, in the hour before Matins, I slipped through the east gate, as Friedrich had done half-a-year before, and wended my way across town as the sun began to rise. Long shadows crept over the blasted ruins left by the summer's riots, darkening the flagstones over which I stepped, silent as a ghost in that dim and purple twilight.

In time, I arrived at the castle, where I cried out for entry, only to learn from the guard that the balladeers had left an hour before so as to reach the amphitheater at dawn. With much thanks, I took my leave of him and ran to the city gates, surprised to find them open at this early hour. The watchman waved me along with a shrug and I passed through, joining the winding procession that stretched from the gates to the amphitheater half-a-mile away.

Although well-acquainted with Anna's stories, I had not myself lain eyes upon the structure before. Even at this distance, I could see it was an object of gargantuan proportion, as tall as the Bishop's cathedral and yet far grander in scale, with six terraced arcades fashioned from white timber. And though I feared what I might find inside, I understood that I could no longer turn back, having come so far.

The line moved with painful slowness. I attempted to cut ahead, apologizing to those I passed, assuring them my intentions in doing so were Godly and honorable. I thought my robes might afford me some protection, but I had gone no more than ten yards before a man seized me round the neck and cast me to the ground. There he proceeded to rain blows upon me until the line lurched forward once more and he tired of his sport.

It was half-an-hour before I managed to stand, by which time the line had moved well past me, so that I had no choice but to seek out the end once more, and to shuffle forward, blood-blind in one eye, while the sun poured down its heat and the ever-present stink of sweat and piss thickened with the resulting humidity, so pungent it brought me near to tears, until at last, with much relief, I passed into the long shadow of the amphitheater.

Inside, the *agon* was well underway. Even in the atrium, the noise was deafening, compounded of the cries and jeers of ten thousand persons in proximity, so that I could not even hear the singer upon whom they heaped their scorn. Once I was certain that I was not observed, I ducked to one side and made my way along the outer arcade until I came to a flight of wooden steps leading down to the undercroft.

At the base of the stair, I came to a heavy door secured with iron bands. The wooden slide shot back, and a voice inquired of me what I wanted. I told him I was a musician; that I had been accosted and robbed and such was the reason for my lateness.

He asked me to sing from the piece I had prepared. When I demurred, he slammed shut the slide and would not consent to open it again, no matter how much vigor I applied to my knocking. Eventually, I turned round in defeat and joined the crowd in the amphitheater.

All seats were occupied, but I found room to stand on the second terrace, some fifteen yards from the theater floor and located just above the Count's curtained box. No one remarked on my battered condition. No one paid me any mind at all, held rapt as they were by the performers on stage.

First came a dwarf who played the hurdy-gurdy and sang with breathtaking earnestness of the woman who had abandoned him. This drew from the crowd a chorus of taunts, culminating in a thrown stone that cut the dwarf's performance short and sent him running below with the broken instrument tucked beneath his arm. The stones lay in plentiful supply around us, provided by the Count, I assumed, so as to better measure the popularity of each singer.

Next came a lad of ten or eleven in urchin's rags. He sang of the Teutonic defeat at Grumwald with the melancholy of a man much older. Vividly could I imagine the doomed knights with crosses on their breasts, and the Poles on horseback, advancing with swords and lances gleaming. He was not yet halfway finished when the first shouts resounded, and the lad fled in terror of his life as the stones fell around him.

Throughout these performances, we had no glimpse of the Count, though word soon reached us that he was much displeased with the competitors thus far.

Only the harlot Iliana was awarded with applause. She was a woman of uncommon beauty, who appeared in red silks and sang of her many talents, choosing a melody like none I had heard before—so strange and haunting that I cannot now forget it.

Friedrich appeared on stage shortly before dusk. He wore a yellow cloak frayed from long travel, and his face appeared similarly careworn, scarred and creased, so that I would not have recognized him, save that his eyes were the same shade of gray. I shouted to him, but he did not hear. The noise of the crowd was overwhelming, many of whom desired the return of Iliana—at least until Friedrich opened his mouth, and a restless quiet descended.

The piece he chose was a song of praise, familiar to me from the hours we had spent in shared prayer. He sang in Latin, a language I doubted any one of the audience members understood, but they did not throw stones, nor jeer him offstage, nor even dare to speak: shocked into silence by the beauty of his song and the heartrending pathos with which it was performed.

Friedrich sang of the Lord's majesty and wisdom, of His unerring faithfulness and devotion to His people. He offered up this praise not to heaven, but to the curtained box before him, wherein sat the Count and from which Friedrich's eyes never strayed, not even when he had uttered the final note and the stillness lingered.

It was a thing of pure and bracing emptiness, so much like the darkness into which we had awoken, all of us, on the night the oak had burned. For the Lord had come at twilight, and left us again, so that we knew not in which way to turn for succor, and could only continue, sustained by the memory of a song which faded more each day and would soon be inaudible.

Friedrich produced a dagger from his cloak. He unsheathed the blade and held it aloft so all could see. And then, with one rapid motion, he jerked the dagger across his throat, the noise of rending flesh blotted out, mercifully, by the roar of applause that followed.

He collapsed and lay twitching, the life-blood pooling beneath him. Still the cheers continued. His corpse was dragged away, but the din did not cease, the crowd rousing itself to new heights of adulation when word reached us, slowly, that the Count was greatly pleased by this last performance. The competition was over; Friedrich was the winner.

At this, anger stole over me, and I could not quell the rage within my breast. I snatched a stone from the ground and leapt to the terrace below. The Count's box was unguarded, the Watchmen having joined the others in raucous cheering and applause. I threw back the curtain and readied the stone, steeling myself to do violence to the merciless leper inside, who had, I was sure, brought this madness down upon us.

But the box was empty. It did not hold the Count, nor could it ever have done so. The heavy curtain hung from three sides of the square box, while the fourth and final wall consisted of nothing more than unpainted timber. I dropped the stone and fled the roaring crowd.

The sun had set by the time I reached the Abbey. I slipped into the garden through the east gate, grateful to find myself alone, if only for a moment. I collapsed to my knees before the oak and looked up past the empty branches. Dusk lay over the world, heady with the fragrance of roses and wood-ash, the odor unfaded since the autumn.

The Prior found me there. He did not scold or shout but merely took me by the arm and helped me inside. I reminded him, he later said, of Saint John, my namesake, as he knelt before the cross and waited, breathlessly, for night to fall.

PUBLICATION CREDITS

"The Hollow" originally appeared in *Phantasmagorium 4*, ed. Joseph S. Pulver, Sr. (Gorgon Press, 2012).

"MS Found in a Chicago Hotel Room" originally appeared in *A Season in Carcosa*, ed. Joseph S. Pulver, Sr. (Miskatonic River Press, 2012).

"Dust from a Dark Flower" originally appeared in *Fungi*, eds. Orrin Grey and Silvia Moreno-Garcia (Innsmouth Free Press, 2012).

"The Photographer's Tale" originally appeared in *Theaker's Quarterly Fiction *36*, eds. John Greenwood and Stephen Theaker (2011). Reprinted in *The Mammoth Book of Best New Horror 23*, ed. Stephen Jones (Robinson, 2012).

"Whistler's Gore" originally appeared in *Mighty in Sorrow*, ed. Jordan Krall (Dunhams Manor Press, 2014).

"The Wayside Voices" originally appeared in *Black Static 30*, ed. Andy Cox (The Third Alternative, 2012).

"John Blake" is original to this volume.

"The Falling Dark" originally appeared in

Shadows Edge, ed. Simon Strantzas (Gray Friar Press, 2013).

"Louisa" originally appeared under the title "Wolf Hour" in *Supernatural Tales 20*, ed. David Longhorn (2011).

"The Tempest Glass" originally appeared in *Supernatural Tales 23*, ed. David Longhorn (2013).

"House of the Caryatids" is original to this volume.

"Whisperers" originally appeared in *Aklonomicon*, eds. Joseph S. Pulver, Sr and Ivan McCann (Aklo Press, 2012).

"The Naked Goddess" originally appeared in *Delicate Toxins*, ed. John H. Smith (Side Real Press, 2011).

"The Lord Came at Twilight" originally appeared in *The Grimscribe's Puppets*, ed. Joseph S. Pulver, Sr. (Miskatonic River Press, 2013).

Printed in Great Britain
by Amazon

44552342R00189